Praise for Lorelei James' *Long Hard Ride*

5 Lips and a Recommended Read! "...highly erotic love scenes as well as a poignant, pulse-pounding, intricately woven storyline."

~ *Kerin, Two Lips Reviews*

Recommended Read! "...raunchy escapades were provided with a backdrop of a wildly emotional love story."

~ *Indy, Joyfully Reviewed*

4.5 Blue Ribbons. "Sinfully erotic, poignant at times, and basically just plain wonderful, LONG HARD RIDE is simply delightful. Hang on to your cowboy hats because this book is scorching hot!"

~ *Natasha Smith, Romance Junkies*

4 Stars "...the story was hedonistic...the clever cast of characters kept the pages moving...I cannot wait to read it again."

~ *Suni Farrar, Just Erotic Romance Reviews*

4 Hearts "...this not a story of sex only for the sake of sex, hearts do become involved... Colby and Channing have an electrifying chemistry...emotionally stirring... a fast paced story filled with wild sex and plenty of passion..."

~ *Anita, The Romance Studio*

"This is a book full of good old boy charm from marble-sculpted cowboys that would make any woman whimper...It's full of friendship, kinship, and family, all from sources you'd never expect. It's full of fun and humor, roarin' good times at the rodeo, and it's definitely full of lip-smackin', toe curlin', sweaty, everything-goes sex."

~ *Sandy M., The Good, The Bad, The Unread*

Long Hard Ride

Lorelei James

A Samhain Publishing, Ltd. publication.

Samhain Publishing, Ltd.
577 Mulberry Street, Suite 1520
Macon, GA 31201
www.samhainpublishing.com

Long Hard Ride

Print ISBN: 1-59998-743-0
Digital ISBN: 1-59998-468-7

Editing by Angela James
Cover by Scott Carpenter

First Samhain Publishing, Ltd. electronic publication: May 2007
First Samhain Publishing, Ltd. print publication: March 2008

Dedication

To all those wannabe cowgirls like me...

Chapter One

On a drunken dare after too many kamikazes, Channing Kinkaid found herself standing on a shellacked bartop while a bartender named Moose sprayed her chest with ice-cold beer.

"Contestant number four! Strut your stuff, baby!"

Channing thrust out her enormous rack, hardened nipples leading the charge. She completely overshadowed the other contestants. She grinned saucily. It was the first time since her thirteenth birthday she hadn't been ashamed of her large breasts.

Amidst catcalls and wolf whistles she sexed it up, shimmying her hips. Stretching on tiptoe to force the tight T-shirt higher up her flat belly. Widening her stance, she spun on her boot heels, bent over, and grabbed her ankles, jiggling her ass and her boobs.

The crowd of men went absolutely wild.

The tease paid off when Moose announced she'd won the Golden Knockers trophy and one hundred bucks.

"Yee-haw!" she yelled and jumped from the bar.

Never in a million years would anyone she grew up with believe Channing would enter a wet T-shirt contest, let alone win first place.

A tiny chorus of Toby Keith's "How Do You Like Me Now?" broke out inside her head and she smirked.

After receiving congratulations from admiring cowboys on the circuit and a few frat brats, she poured a fresh kamikaze in the trophy cup. She toasted herself in the cracked mirror behind the bar and liked what she saw.

She glanced around, half-afraid she'd see Jared storming toward her, intent on spoiling her fun by dragging her off to celebrate her victory in private. The man was seriously antisocial. And dammit, she was having fun for a change.

The Western bar was jam-packed. Jared hated crowds, but he hated leaving her alone in a crowd—especially a group of horny, drunken men. Where could he have gone?

Did she really care?

Sweet, warm breath tickled her ear. "Lookin' for someone, darlin'?"

Channing tilted her head. Colby McKay—king of the rodeo circuit—stared down at her. From far away he looked a total package. Up close he was simply stunning. Icy blue eyes, dark chestnut hair and chiseled features that weren't typical rugged cowboy, but rather, brought to mind the image of a brooding poet.

His toned body spoke of his athletic prowess with horses and bulls; his thickly muscled arms and big, callused hands spoke of his skill with ropes. Mmm. Mmm. He was yummy and he knew it. He also was aware he made her skittish as a new colt.

She flipped her hair over her shoulder, a nervous gesture she hoped he'd misread as dismissive. "Hey, Colby. Have you seen Jared?"

"He's on his cell phone over by the bathroom." The eye-catching cowboy flashed his dimples. "Which leaves you unattended. Which is a damn shame. Dance with me."

Her stomach jumped, a reaction she blamed on booze, and not the intensely sexy way Colby studied her.

Okay, that was a total lie. She *always* acted tongue-tied whenever she got within licking distance of Colby, and his equally sexy traveling buddy, Trevor Glanzer.

Jared had kept her sequestered so she hadn't put truth to the rumors Colby and Trevor were the bad boys of the circuit. She knew they were fierce competitors; they worked hard and played hard—on and off the dirt. She'd seen the buckle bunnies of all ages and sizes constantly vying for their attention.

But she, little city-slicker nobody Channing Kinkaid, had captured Colby's interest.

So, for some unknown reason, Trevor and Colby courted her shamelessly at every opportunity. Sometimes separately. Sometimes double-teaming her with hefty doses of good ol' boy charm. It made her wonder what it'd be like to have them double-teaming her in private.

Whoo-ee. With as hard as they rode livestock? They'd probably break the damn bed frame. Or her.

"Come on, Channing," Colby cajoled. "One dance."

Jarred from her fantasy of becoming a Colby/Trevor sandwich, she stammered, "I-I'm all wet. And I smell like beer."

Colby's hot gaze zoomed to her chest. "I ain't complainin'."

"You will be once I'm plastered against you and getting you wet."

He bent to her ear and murmured, "Nuh-uh, shug. I like my women wet. Really wet. I like it when they get that wetness all over me. All over my fingers. All over my face. All over my—"

"Colby McKay!" Flustered by the image of his dark head burrowed between her legs, his mouth shiny-wet with her juices, she attempted to push him away. He didn't budge. The man redefined rock solid. No wonder bulls and broncs had a tough time tossing him off.

"You ain't as indignant as you'd like me to believe, Miz Channing. In fact—" he nipped her earlobe, sending tingles in an electric line directly to her nipples, "—I suspect a firecracker such as yourself prefers dirty talk."

The subtle pine scent of Colby's aftershave and the underlying hint of aroused male soaked into her skin more thoroughly than the beer. A purely sexual shiver worked loose from her head to the pointed toes of her cowgirl boots.

"Come on and dance with me. Let's see if we can't spread that wetness around a little." Without waiting for her compliance, Colby tugged her toward the dance floor.

"Honky Tonk Badonkadonk" blasted from the speakers.

The second they were engulfed by the mass of dancers, Colby hauled her flush against his firm body. A big, strapping man, he was hard everywhere—from his brawny chest to his powerfully built thighs. No two-stepping for them. He clasped her right hand in his left, nestling his right palm in the small of her back. That single touch seared her flesh like a red-hot brand.

Lord. And the long hard thing poking her belly sure as shooting wasn't his championship belt buckle.

"You okay?"

Channing nodded, even when her head spun with the idea the hottest cowboy on the circuit had a massive hard-on for her—right here in front of rodeo queens, stock contractors, old timers and everyone else.

"See? This ain't so bad, is it?"

"No. Actually, it's really nice, Colby." She rested her cheek on his chest and sighed softly.

"Nice? I'll take that, though, I'd prefer naughty." His hold on her tightened. "Be nicer yet if we were naked," he whispered against her temple.

Naked line dancing. That might be interesting. Gave a new definition to the term *swingers.*

Booted feet shuffled and stomped in the sawdust. Men and women whirled in flashes of bright fringe and glittering rhinestones. Finally Colby spoke again. "Can I ask you something, sweetheart?"

"I guess."

"How'd you end up with Jared?"

Because I didn't see you first.

Channing didn't look up; rather she studied the pearl studs on his plaid Western shirt. "We met after he did a bull-riding exhibition. We got to talking and I told him I wanted an adventure. We hooked up and here I am. Why?"

"So you ain't goofy in love with him? Hopin' he'll put a ring on your finger at summer's end?"

"No." Truth be told, she suspected she'd made a mistake in choosing Jared. Beneath his enchanting Australian accent lurked a moody, possessive man with secrets. She had no idea what to do about it. "Why?"

"This don't seem like your thing."

"What? Traveling on the rodeo circuit?"

"Well, that too. But mostly I was talkin' 'bout a classy broad like you shackin' up with that lyin' slimeball."

Channing glanced up. Instead of acting snappy and defensive, she batted her eyelashes and sweetened her tone. "Why, Colby McKay, I didn't realize you cared about my virtue."

"It ain't your virtue I'm concerned about."

"Then what?"

His hungry gaze captured every nuance of her face, ultimately homing in on her mouth. Heat from his eyes raced down her spine, gathering in her core. She felt more exposed than if he'd stripped her buck naked.

"Jesus. Every time I look at you I lose my damn train of thought."

"Why?"

"'Cause you got the sweet face of an innocent and the body of a high-priced whore."

Her mouth dropped open.

Studying her eyes, Colby gave her a devilish smile and lowered his head. Taking advantage of her parted lips, his tongue darted inside her mouth. No hard, fast kiss. Just a fleeting brush of his soft lips. A lingering stroke of his velvety tongue. His heated breath mingled with hers and her pulse quickened. Everywhere.

Oh. As his talented tongue slid along hers, any pretense of her resistance fled. She savored his taste; a spicy tang of beer, Copenhagen and toothpaste. Another shudder ran through her and she moaned softly.

"Does that shock you, darlin'?" he murmured against the corner of her trembling mouth.

Channing forced her traitorous lips away from his lazy assault. "Does it shock me that you classify me as a whore, same as those buckle bunnies following you around? No."

His eyes flashed blue fire, as if she'd somehow insulted him. "I didn't call you a whore. I didn't call you an innocent, either, but I noticed you didn't focus on that portion of my remark."

"Then explain yourself, Mr. McKay."

"I spend way more time thinkin' 'bout you than I should, Miz Channing." Colby didn't miss a dance beat as he smoothly shoved a firm thigh between hers and waltzed her forward.

Startled by the searing friction of his leg grinding into her crotch, she blurted, "What do you think about, when you're thinking about me?"

"Well, I ain't fantasizin' 'bout holdin' your hand and takin' you to the Sunday church ice-cream social."

"No. Really?"

"Yes'm. Though, my thoughts do tend to wander on how many ways I can take you nine-ways-til-Sunday."

A blush crawled up her neck. "Why do you do this?"

"What?"

"Tease me all the time."

"I ain't teasin' you. I just made my intentions clear."

"No, you talked about your fantasies. Not your intentions."

"That mean you think I'm all talk? I guarantee I'm not foolin' around, Channing, darlin'." He nuzzled her temple, tracking soft, moist kisses up her hairline and back down to her ear. He blew gently. Then he sucked all the air back out.

Channing actually felt the sharp vibration in her pussy. This wild man could make her sopping wet with one well-placed whisper.

"A little haughty, ain't ya?" His fingers slipped under the hem of her shirt. Callused fingertips idly stroked the damp skin beneath the waistband of her jeans on her lower back. "I like your fire. A woman like you could burn a man up. And I'd enjoy every hot second as I went down in flames."

Her breath caught at the eroticism in his simple words and teasing touch.

"Are you trying to see how far you can push me?"

"I suspect you're embarrassed to admit you'd like to be pushed by me. Or tied up, trussed up, any way I want you. At my every wicked whim. And no doubt, shug, I know my way around wicked."

Something about this straight-talking, sweet-talking man made her wild. And horny as hell.

"Colby—"

"Ssh. When you wise up to what Jared really is doin', come talk to me before you do anything rash, okay?"

"But—"

"Promise me, Channing."

"Okay. But why?"

"'Cause, sweetheart, I'm dyin' to show you what you've been missin'."

Another hot burst of moisture exploded in her panties. "What about Jared?"

"Yeah, what about me, mate?" Jared said.

She wheeled around guiltily. Crap. Jared lurked less than two feet away, his hands rested accusingly on his lean hips, as he glared at them.

Colby released her and retreated. "Nothin'. You're a lucky fella, that's all." He tipped his hat to Channing and winked. "Thanks for the dance. See you around. Remember what I said."

Channing watched Colby until he disappeared out the side door, a predatory cowgirl hot on his boot heels.

Jared snagged her hand and jerked her into an awkward embrace. "What were you and King Cheese yapping about?"

"Nothing really."

"You should watch out for him and his buddy, Trevor. Nasty pair, those two."

"What makes you say that?"

Jared tromped on her toe as he twirled her sideways. "Haven't you seen the way the lasses gather around them? Not that I begrudge the blokes for taking their pick of pussy, but crikey. What they expect those chippies to do with not one, but both of them? At the same time?"

What would it feel like, writhing between two hard male bodies? Two sets of rough-skinned hands touching her. Two hot, hungry mouths, kissing, tasting, licking, tormenting every bared inch of her quivering flesh. Two big cocks demanding entrance into her body.

"You listening to me?"

"So, how have *you* seen them doing...things with one woman?"

"Well, yeah. They don't hide it. Ask anyone what they done last year behind the chutes in Cheyenne." He leaned in so she heard the full account. "They had this young chickie stretched out naked over a stack of saddles. Hands tied behind her back with a piggin' string. A bandana covering her eyes."

"Was she there willingly?"

He snorted. "Those kind of women always are."

"What were they doing to her?"

"Using her like a blow-up toy. She was sucking Trevor's cock as Colby nailed her from behind. Then they'd switch, like some kinda Chinese fire drill. Laughing, carrying on. They've no shame, either of them. No respect for women either, if you ask me. Then joking afterwards about that being the proper way to 'break in a new saddle'." His gaze narrowed. "Why? Did that cheese head proposition you?"

I wish. "Umm. No."

"Good. Stay away from their other traveling partner, Edgard. Something about that bloke rubs me the wrong way."

Jared's foul mood required an abrupt switch in the conversation. "Guess what? I won the wet T-shirt contest."

"As you bloody well should have. You've got fantastic tits, love." Jared's hand snaked up her belly. He yanked up the damp shirt and cupped her bared left breast.

Channing squirmed. "Hello? We're in public."

"So?"

"So, if you want to maul me, let's go back to the room." She tugged the shirt down to cover her belly.

"Ah. I see. You can flash these titties to the whole bar, but the minute I want to touch them, they're off-limits? Crikey, I could've stayed in the Outback and gotten that attitude."

An acute sense of unease built. "What is wrong with you tonight? You eat a bad kiwi or something?"

"No."

"Then knock it off."

He laughed harshly. Meanly. "Little Miss Prim and Proper, are we now, love?"

Jared squeezed her nipple hard enough that it brought tears to her eyes. She slapped his hand.

"That wasn't how you were last night."

"How much have you been drinking?"

"Not nearly enough." He puffed up with belligerence. "I oughta be asking *you* that question."

"Why?"

"You know why. A little liquid courage is what you need."

"Need for what, Jared?"

Jared clamped his hands on her hips, spun her until they were back to front and he dry humped her. "A few beers would loosen you up. When you gonna give up this tight ass? It's been a week and I'm bloody well tired of waiting."

Ignoring the burning in her cheeks, Channing twisted from his hold. She latched on to his polyester shirt with both hands, hauling herself up until they were nose to nose. "Lower your voice."

"That bothers you? People hearing you love to do the nasty stuff? Or knowing you're a hypocrite for begging me to use my fingers on your tight little hole, and then pretending it disgusts you?"

Infuriated, she released his lapels. "It doesn't disgust me. The way you're acting disgusts me." She wasn't ashamed of a thing they'd done behind closed doors. But him talking about it as if it were some big joke made her feel used and cheap.

"S'matter? Truth sting a bit, love?"

She stared at him. Who was this cruel man? Something had set him off tonight. Before she could formulate a snappy response, Cash Big Crow sauntered up and tapped Jared on the shoulder.

Cash was another heart-stoppingly handsome cowboy on the rodeo circuit. Native American, short and stocky, with long dark hair he wore in a braid, he had a grin as wide as the brim of his black Stetson. Cash was a little older than the youngsters on the circuit, and a bit bowlegged from years spent riding bulls, broncs and "anything that bucked".

"*Hoka-hey*. Hope I'm not interruptin' a lovers' spat."

"You are," Jared snarled. "What the bloody hell do you want?"

"Whoa, hold on, partner. Just wanted to return this to the lady." He handed Channing her trophy. "You forgot it on the bar. Wouldn't want some other gal to steal it, seeings you worked so hard to win it." He winked.

"Thanks, Cash."

"Oh, and this." Cash held out a silver cell phone to Jared. "You left it in the can."

Jared snatched it. "Appreciate it. Now move along, mate."

Channing had endured enough of Jared and was tempted to ask Cash to take her back to the motel. Let Jared sort out his fit of temper on his own. She wasn't his goddamn babysitter.

"What? You waiting for a tip?" Jared demanded.

"I'm going." Cash took a couple of steps, then turned back. He gave Channing a pitying look before addressing Jared. "Your wife called your phone while I was in the bathroom, that's why I picked it up. She wants you to call her back right away."

Dead silence, ugly as the antelope-horn chandeliers hanging above them.

"Wife?" Channing repeated.

When Jared's gaze zoomed to hers then flitted away, she knew the truth.

The bastard was married. He'd lied to her. Guilt, shame and fury arose inside her.

Jared spun on Cash to chew him out.

Without thinking, Channing blindly swung the trophy and clocked Jared in the back of the head.

He crumpled to the floor.

She froze. Shit. What had she done? What if she'd killed him? Spending her life in a Southern prison wearing orange paper shoes wasn't part of her big adventure.

Clutching the trophy like a shield, she dropped to her knees and accidentally squashed Jared's hat. She gingerly touched his head. A big bump protruded from the back of his neck. No blood though. Good thing she had lousy aim. His chest rose and fell so she knew he wasn't dead.

A sick sort of relief swamped her.

"Hey, slugger, you okay?"

She looked up at Cash. "No. Cash. Please. I didn't know—"

"I figured you didn't, sweets. You don't seem the type to mess around with a married fella."

"I'm not." New experiences did not include becoming a home wrecker. Her stomach churned. "Please get me out of here. I can't stay with him."

"Well, he can't stay here to get trampled. Grab his boots. Let's move him outta the way first before we figure out what to do with you."

After they'd hauled Jared through the sawdust to a dark corner, he came around. He plopped his lopsided hat on and kept his face aimed at the floor.

She doubted the jerk felt any shame. Only anger that he'd gotten caught.

Cash took her aside. "You stayin' at the Silver Spur tonight?"

She nodded and hugged her trophy.

"Get your stuff and head over there. Double lock the door. I'll make sure he don't follow you and cause more trouble. I'll check on you in the mornin'."

"Thank you, Cash."

"No problem, sweets. Just sorry you found out the way you did."

Channing snuck out of the bar without talking to anyone else from the circuit. She unloaded her three pieces of luggage from Jared's truck—and liberated his bottle of whiskey.

A six-foot neon sign shaped like a cowboy boot, announcing *The Silver Spur Motor Inn,* flashed "NO VACANCY". Luckily she'd already secured a room. She dragged her belongings across the highway and let herself into number 111.

Once locked inside, she panicked. What was she going to do? No way did she want to turn tail and run back to the tiresome life she'd fled.

Served her right for trusting someone. It would've been nice, for once in her life, not to have to be so damn self-reliant. Wrong again.

She should leave. Right away. Tonight.

Colby's words surfaced: *Come talk to me before you do anything rash.*

The scared part of her wanted to run to Colby right now. Demand to know why he hadn't told her Jared was married.

But in his own way, Colby had warned her.

Reality check: She doubted this one-stoplight town had a rental car agency or even a bus stop. Nothing she could do about her predicament tonight. She'd deal with it all tomorrow.

A steaming hot shower and three generous slugs of whiskey later, Channing drifted off into an uneasy sleep.

Chapter Two

The woman's lips left a bright red lipstick trail down Colby's blood-darkened shaft as she released his cock. "That's it. Open wider. Like that. Take it all."

The naked brunette bobbed her head. Her soft, hot mouth worked from the pulsing root to the throbbing tip of his cock. The wet sucking sounds coupled with her happy humming moans ricocheted in the tiny humid bathroom as an erotic echo.

Colby sighed and threaded one hand through her long hair, shivering at the sensation of the baby-soft strands teasing the inside of his thighs. The pointed tips of her nipples stabbed his knee as her mouth rocked back and forth, making her big tits sway enticingly.

He slid his hands down her face and neck to roll those tightened nubs between his fingertips. Tugging. Pulling. Twisting. Making them harder. Redder. Wishing he hadn't left those nipple clamps back in Salt Lake. This woman seemed the adventurous type.

She rubbed her slender thighs together, arching into his rougher touch. "More."

"Yeah, me too." He shifted his ass forward on the counter and spread his knees. "Play with my balls, baby." He didn't call her by name because, frankly, he didn't remember her name.

He'd hooked up with her outside the Last Chance Saloon after he'd left Channing with Jared. Frustrated, he'd needed someone, *anyone*, to get him off. As quickly as possible. Sex always cooled his temper. And if he couldn't be with the one he wanted, he'd be with someone who wanted him, even if for the wrong reasons.

This chick knew the score; one night, no promises, and bragging rights that she'd blown the number two All-Around Cowboy on the Mountain and Plains Circuit. She'd gotten right down to business the minute they'd returned to the motel. Shedding her skintight clothes. Fondling his buckle as she dropped to her knees, sucking his dick like a starving woman facing an opulent banquet. Hell, he hadn't even kissed her.

His thoughts traveled to Channing Kinkaid. Jesus. Why was he so obsessed with that little spitfire? She wasn't even his type. But one kiss from her and his cock had gotten hard as a railroad spike.

For a moment he let himself imagine it was Channing deep-throating him. Channing's moans of delight reverberating up his shaft. Channing's sweet-scented hair knotted in his hands. Channing's wanton tongue lapping the come out of the slit in his cock.

Oh hell yeah.

Then long fingernails scraped across his balls and he inhaled sharply, expecting pain. But the woman expertly rolled his sac, knowing exactly how much pressure to use for maximum pleasure. Never missing a lick or stroke with that marvelous suctioning mouth and wickedly skillful tongue.

Good as it felt, much as he loved a no-strings-attached blowjob, Colby just wanted her to finish him off so he could escape.

"Faster," he panted. "Suck harder. Yeah, like that. A few more strokes and you know I'm gonna shoot my load. Then Trevor will take care of you. Got yourself a twofer tonight, baby."

"Mm-hmm."

The bathroom door opened. She never even lifted her head.

Colby glanced over at a grinning Trevor.

"She ready for me yet?" Trevor asked.

"Close."

"Hot damn!" Trevor shucked off his Wranglers and T-shirt. His big belt buckle clunked on the tile. Colby didn't bother to gawk at his friend's naked form. Threesomes were nothing new.

The crackling of a condom package ripping open sounded beside him.

The woman gyrated her hips and moaned, "Yes. Oh please. Please fuck me. Now. From behind."

"After Colby comes," Trevor said. "Don't want you bitin' down on anything important. He's pretty fond of that big cock of his."

She whimpered. Realizing she wouldn't get off until Colby did, she switched tactics, moving her mouth and hand in tandem, faster and faster. Saliva ran down the length of his dick and coated his balls.

That was all it took.

Colby threw back his head. "Come on, work those throat muscles and swallow it all. Ah. Shit yeah."

She gulped noisily. Colby felt her gag reflex kick in, but he was too far gone to care. He held her head tightly, keeping that delectable mouth in place until every last spurt burst from the end of his cock.

Spent, he sagged against the mirror. Breathing hard. “Damn. That was good.”

Colby caressed the woman’s cheek as his dick slipped from between silky smooth lips. By the time he’d opened his eyes, Trevor had already positioned her on the bathmat on all fours.

Her hand was on her dark muff, furiously rubbing her clit. Her sharp white teeth sank into her bottom lip; her eyes were squeezed shut in rapture. She’d tilted her ass in the air for Trevor’s use.

Trevor spread her cheeks wide and rammed into her cunt in one rapid stroke. “Christ, woman,” he growled, “you’re wet. You must really like sucking cock.”

A feminine grunt. “Stop talking and fuck me harder. I’m close to coming.”

“Bossy. I don’t know if I like that.”

“Punish me then. God. Do anything. Just make me come.”

“Maybe this’ll help you along.” Trevor whacked her ass. Four sharp blows on each deeply tanned cheek.

The woman started to climax. Loudly. Shrieking like a wheezing donkey. Thrashing like she was having a seizure.

Colby wondered how much of her reaction was real. Talk about cynical.

Spurred on by her enthusiasm, Trevor fucked her with such ferocity the bathmat skidded sideways across the floor.

Colby watched the scene before him dispassionately. He should be raring to join in. He wasn’t. In fact, his cock had already gone completely limp.

A sad situation at thirty-one; he was sick of trolling for pussy. Same old, same old. A quick fuck and suck, goodbye, then on to the next town. He *was* getting old if he’d been fantasizing about fucking the same woman a different way every night, rather than a different woman the same way every night.

Yeah, that one woman superstar in his lurid fantasies was none other than Channing Kinkaid. A temptress with her gold-flecked hazel eyes. A nymph with a riot of brown curls tumbling between her shoulder blades. A witch's mouth, lush, ripe, the soft pink of peonies in spring. A curvy little body a man could sink his teeth and his cock into for weeks without surfacing.

Where the hell had that romantic nonsense come from?

Channing wasn't his. Although, he had been tempted to spill the beans about Jared's marital status tonight. But he'd decided it wasn't his place. She'd probably shoot the messenger rather than react how he'd hoped—running to him for protection, comfort and wickedly hot sex.

Right. Ignoring the thrashing twosome, he hopped off the counter and left them alone for the big finish.

In the cramped motel room, Edgard was stretched out on the double bed along the wall. He glanced up from watching the PBR Tour on VERSUS. "Done already?"

"Yeah. You getting in on some action?"

"Maybe later."

After Colby dressed he sat down on the opposite bed to pull on his boots.

"Where you going?" Edgard asked.

"I know it's your turn, but I think I'll sleep in the horse trailer. 'Night."

ଔଔ

The next morning Channing leaned on the whitewashed split-rail fence and squinted at the fairgrounds.

What was she supposed to do now? Stuck high and dry in nowhere Oklahoma.

A few trucks and horse trailers remained in the parking lot. The arena was deserted. Most rodeo folk had already headed to the next event. Her stomach growled. She glanced at her watch. Noon.

The "Open" sign blinked at the Last Chance Saloon. She shouldered her macramé purse and trotted across the highway. Maybe they served food. Anything would be better than the vending machine selection of stale crackers and peanuts, or drowning her sorrows in chocolate.

ଔଓ

Colby had finished loading hay for his horse when he heard voices approaching across the paddock. He snapped the locks on the trailer and leaned back against the metal gate bars to wait to see who was looking for him.

Cash and Trevor came around the rear end of the trailer, bickering like siblings.

"It ain't my problem," Cash said. "I'm just glad to see that sumbitch gone."

"Yeah, but he ain't gonna be happy she is. She—"

"Who's gone?" Colby asked.

They both stopped. Trevor gave Cash an uneasy look. "Jared Connelly. He dropped out this morning."

"Why?"

"Seems his wife got wind of his female traveling partner and demanded he return to Australia."

"Serves that bastard right. Where's Channing now?"

Another nervous glance passed between Trevor and Cash.

Colby's stomach muscles tightened. "I said: Where's Channing?"

"That's the thing. We don't know."

He counted to ten. "Did she leave with him?"

Cash snorted. "Not after she smacked him upside the head with her trophy last night when she found out about his missus."

Colby fought a smile. He would've loved to've seen that. "Where'd she stay last night?"

"The Silver Spur."

Damn. She could've been in the room right next to him, listening to some strange chick suck him off. For the first time in a long time, his actions made him ashamed. "What room?"

"One eleven."

"Did you check on her this morning?"

Trevor nodded. "Cash knocked. She didn't answer. So he came and got me and I tried. She wouldn't come to the door for me either. I don't think she's here. The maid wouldn't let us in."

"Did you ask the front desk if she'd checked out?"

Cash and Trevor exchanged a sheepish look.

Idiots.

Colby pushed away from the trailer and headed toward the motel office.

"Hey, Colby. Where you goin'?"

He didn't answer. He just kept walking. And tried like hell not to run.

ഌഌ

Channing nursed a Bud Light in a corner booth. She picked at her second bowl of pretzels and listened to the jukebox wailing another sad song about love gone wrong. In her life even lust had gone wrong.

The cowbell on the front door clanked against the wood as the door opened again, then slammed shut. This was a busy place. Maybe if all else failed she could get hired to sling beer. Her focus strayed to the list of options she'd jotted in her journal, none of which appealed to her.

The bench seat across from her creaked. Thinking Moose had swung by to flirt, she smiled and looked up.

But Colby McKay grinned back at her. "Thought I might find you here, darlin'."

Channing suppressed a feminine sigh. His dimples ought to be illegal. "I figured you'd already taken off."

"I could say the same. I heard what happened last night."

She reached for her pencil. "I'm sure everyone has heard by now." Her gaze narrowed. "Why didn't you tell me Jared was married?"

"Because you'd be pissed off at me thinkin' I had some ulterior motive in tellin' you the truth." He spun her notebook around and studied it. "Which is entirely true. But it don't matter now."

"That ulterior motive why you're here?"

"Yep."

Her heart thudded. She struggled to project an image of absolute calm. "As I'm short on options, I'm open to suggestions."

"Fair enough. Tell me something first, before we get into those options."

"Okay."

"What are you runnin' from?"

It was tempting to hedge or flat out lie. She did neither. "My past. My future. Take your pick."

"Maybe you oughta explain that confusin' comment to this dumb ol' country boy."

She rolled her eyes. "Dumb, yeah right. You don't fool me, Colby McKay."

"And you don't fool me, Channing Kinkaid."

His meaning settled on her thick, sweet and sticky as wild honey.

"My story is not that interesting, actually. I've followed the rules—my parents' rules—my whole life. Just like my older sister, I graduated from an Ivy League school of their choice. Got my Masters degree because that's what offspring of the people in their social circle *do*. My dad lined up a teaching job for me at a prestigious private prep school starting in the fall."

"And?"

She gripped the wooden pencil so tightly it cracked. "And when Mom and Dad introduced me to a wimpy accountant who reeked of Old Spice and old money, and they encouraged me to accept his marriage proposal after *one* lousy date, I snapped. I realized I wasn't living my life; I was living theirs. I needed a break and ran away with the rodeo."

Colby smiled and gently removed the gnawed-on, broken pencil from her death grip. "Regrets about that?"

"Besides my poor choice of a traveling partner? Strangely enough, no."

His thumb swept across the vein on the inside of her wrist, sending tingles up her forearm. "What are your plans now that Jared is gone?"

"That's what I'm sitting here trying to figure out."

"Do you want to go home?"

"God, no."

"Good." Colby angled across the narrow table and repeatedly brushed the back of his knuckles over her cheek. "Run away with me, Channing. At least until we get to Cheyenne next week."

He'd spoken the words she'd wanted to hear. Yet, her sole focus was how the continual rasp of his rough skin on hers caused her insides to quake. Her blood to burn. Her sex to moisten.

Her breathing grew ragged when he trailed those callused fingertips down the gentle curve of her neck. He traced her collarbone with a touch as fleeting as the flutter of butterfly wings. Then he drew circles progressively lower on her chest. All while watching her reaction with his electric blue eyes.

"Naturally, there'd be conditions if I take you on."

Oh yeah. She'd agree to any conditions as long as they included hot, wet, raunchy, shaking-the-rafters sex with him every single night. "You can be damn sure I'll know *exactly* what I'm getting into this time before I go anywhere with you or anyone else like Jared."

"I ain't like Jared at all," he scoffed.

"I know. That's why I didn't smack you with my purse when you showed up."

"I still scare you, though, don't I?"

"A little."

"I shouldn't. We're more alike than you know."

"Hmm. You think that's why I kinda like you, cowboy?"

"Yeah. And the feeling's mutual, shug."

She smiled. "First things first. I can pay my own way to Cheyenne."

Annoyance flitted across his face. "We'll see."

"Is there a sweetie—wife or girlfriend—baking apple pies and waiting for you on the front porch back at home?"

He shook his head. "After this summer rodeo season ends, hopefully I'll have enough points accumulated to qualify me for the NFR in Vegas come December. If not, I oughta have enough to compete in the Dodge Circuit Finals in Pocatello in March. I'll keep up in the points standings by goin' to events closer to home. In the meantime I'll be back in Wyoming to help my dad and brothers run the ranch."

"And more likely than not I'll be teaching on the East Coast."

Something dark shifted in his eyes.

"Then we understand each other?" she prompted.

"For now."

She frowned, not understanding his cryptic answer. "So, about these conditions."

Colby studied her carefully from beneath the brim of his hat. "You'll be in my bed."

Her pulse fluttered. "I figured that much."

"As well as Trevor and Edgard's."

Channing's jaw dropped. "I'd be sleeping with all three of you?"

"No. You'd be fucking all three of us, ain't gonna be much sleepin' involved." Colby scooted forward, his handsome face serious, his blue eyes intent. "Forget about what other people might think, and consider what *you* want, Channing. What you've always wanted but have been denied because it's been against those blasted rules you've followed."

She swallowed hard. "I'm still listening."

"I'm used to havin' a different woman every night if I choose."

"And these women you pick up have no problem being passed between the three of you?"

He grinned. "Shockin', ain't it? What America's youth has come to?"

Despite the surreal conversation, she smiled at his cheeky grin. "What do you do with these willing women?"

"Fuck them. Sometimes one on one. More often than not, two on one. The really darin' gals will take on all three of us at the same time."

How did that work? Which body parts went where? *Don't ask. Act urbane.* She murmured, "Really?"

Colby reached over and twined a curly brown lock around his fingers. He tugged her closer by that hank of hair until his warm breath flowed over her cheek.

"Does that fluster you? Thinkin' of some young, naked woman sandwiched between Trevor and me? With my cock deep in her ass and Trevor's cock in her cunt? And if Edgard's playin' with us, a cock in her mouth, too. Or does that make you wet with want?"

Her vaginal walls throbbed and her clit spasmed, making her slit weep. Images of being pressed between all that hot, hard male flesh. Being overfilled and stretched and used purely for pleasure? Hadn't she secretly fantasized about that very scenario? Giving up all control. Being...*taken.*

A small helpless noise erupted from her mouth.

"What?" Colby asked and sat back. "Tell me what you're thinkin'."

"It doesn't shock me."

His nostrils flared. "It excites you, don't it?"

"Yes. But, I've never been with two guys at once or…"

"Or what?"

Channing paused for him to fill in the blanks.

He didn't. Instead he swiped her beer and took a sip. "Say it in plain English, darlin'. You'd better be able to say it if you want us to do it to you."

She knocked back a fortifying drink and muttered, "I've never tried anal sex." There. That hadn't been so hard.

A secret sexy smile bloomed on his face. "And you want that?"

She nodded, glancing away from the gleam in his eyes to study the sawdust and peanut shells strewn across the floor.

"Then say it," he demanded.

Channing remained mute.

Gently, Colby tilted her face up, placing his lips to her ear. "Say it, sweetheart. I ain't being a jerk. I need to be perfectly clear on what you want." He licked the shell of her ear and blew softly. "Besides. It's sexy as hell to hear those naughty words comin' out of such an angelic mouth."

Channing rubbed her face against the rough stubble on his cheek, lost in the sharp contrast of his male hardness to her female softness. He smelled heavenly. She whispered along his jaw, "I want you to be the first man to take my ass, Colby McKay. I want to know what it's like to be with more than one man. Doing whatever you want to me."

He sucked in a harsh breath. "Whenever we want it?"

The outer door opened and a beam of light slanted across the bar, bouncing off the mirror and blinding her. She scooted away and nestled her spine against the Naugahyde booth. "Within reason," she said. "I'm not into exhibitionism. I'll do whatever you want as long as it's not in front of an audience."

"What constitutes as an audience? Because Edgard and Trevor and I share most everything."

"An audience is any other cowboys on the circuit." She frowned, remembering Jared's description of Trevor and Colby's saddle-breaking exploits.

"I know that look. What have you heard?"

Channing told him.

Colby swore. "That's a damn lie. *Jared* and some fella from Canada did that, not me and Trev. We've done some crazy things, but never nothin' like that. We'd never disrespect a woman that way."

Right then she realized Jared leaving her was a good thing.

He shifted uncomfortably on the creaky bench seat. She could see the outline of his cock through his tight jeans. She squirmed in her already wet panties, imagining all the delicious things he planned to do with it.

"You object to bringin' in another woman into our playtime?"

"Yes. Not something I'm interested in trying."

He lifted a dark brow. "Can I ask why?"

She raised an eyebrow right back. "Besides the fact three cocks will be more than enough to keep me occupied?"

Colby grinned. "Homophobic?"

"Not at all. Girl on girl is just not for me." She chomped a pretzel and pointed the jagged end at him. "And I don't want to watch you fucking another woman either. Is that a problem?"

"Nope." He brushed salt from her chin; his blunt fingertips leisurely traced the outline of her lips. "You've got the prettiest mouth."

Everything inside her went hot and tight. "Then kiss me."

"In a minute. Couple last things I need to know. You'll suck me off, jerk me off, anytime I demand it?"

"Within reason. I'm not going to get on my knees right here."

"Too bad. But sex toys and domination games are okay? I'm wicked good with ropes."

An image arose. Her arms tied helplessly above her head, her legs spread-eagled. A blindfold covering her eyes. A bandana plugging her mouth to stifle the screams of raw pleasure. Powerless and begging under Colby's towering body and punishing hands. She never would've dreamed that scenario would make her absolutely dripping wet. "Yes."

"Would you let me spank you?"

Holy shit. That suggestion caught her off guard. People really did that? And liked it? "Umm. Would you hit me anywhere else?"

Colby frowned. "No. I ain't that kind of man. But there is something about seein' a rosy red ass that appeals to me. And don't discount how sweet I can make punishments when you've been bad, shug."

"This is starting to scare me," Channing muttered.

"Nuh-uh. This is startin' to excite you. So do we have a deal?"

She blurted, "Yes," before she second-guessed herself and said *no*.

"Good. One more thing."

She held her breath. She had a feeling this last question would be the most important one of all.

"Darlin', pleased as I am that everything is up front with us, tell me why you've agreed to all my conditions."

How did she explain without coming across as a desperate ho-bag? But Colby wouldn't judge her. And hiding the truth because she should feel embarrassed wouldn't get her what she craved—this man, in whatever capacity he wanted her—if only for a week.

"Because I'm sick of worrying if I tell a man what I really want out of a sexual relationship that he'll think I'm some kind of deviant. I'm tired of dating guys who see me as their mother, or the mother of their children. Or as a nice girl who's happy with plain-old vanilla sex once a week and doesn't want more. I want more. I want it all. I want to do things that I've only read about. And I want you to teach me."

Colby's fingers stroked her chin, then his hand slid up her jawline to cradle her face. "Believe it or not, I understand wantin' to break free of expectations. I can be the lover who fulfills those desires, Channing. I can push you to the limit. But I'll warn you: I am demandin' and I like to be in control."

"Okay."

"I've got to know you aren't just sayin' this. That you really mean it. That you can handle what I've got planned."

She angled her head and kissed the inside of his wrist. "How can I prove it?"

"Come with me right now. Don't ask questions and don't argue."

"Only if you kiss me again."

"Why you so intent on me kissin' you?"

"Because, *shug*, when we were dancing you made me so wet and hot from that kiss I nearly came all over your leg."

Colby growled and enclosed his mouth over hers. His hot male taste filled her as he forced her lips open and thrust his slick tongue in and out. He gifted her with a grinding kiss that stole her breath and fogged her senses. He sucked her tongue, followed it up with erotic little bites of her lips. Then he retreated, making her chase his tongue back into his greedy mouth.

The kiss softened, sweetened. He explored her reactions, licking her teeth, teasing the roof of her mouth with a fleeting flick of the tip of his tongue. He slid that rough, wet velvet along the inside curve of her cheek and nibbled on her bottom lip. Pulling back to let his breath drift over the dampened spots he'd created, as he brushed soft, yet insistent kisses on the corners of her trembling mouth.

Channing whimpered. Never in her life had she been kissed like that. Her pussy flooded with cream, her nipples were hard as granite, her head spun like a tornado and he hadn't really touched her yet.

What would happen when he did? When they *all* did?

He stared in her dazed eyes with male heat and pride. "I cannot wait to fuck you." His hungry gaze zeroed in on her cleavage. "And those. But first, I've got a little test for you to pass. Come on." Colby dropped ten bucks on the table to pay for the beer.

Holding his hand, she trailed behind him as they crossed the highway and into the arena parking lot. The rodeo grounds resembled an Old West ghost town. He led her to a dirty, white Dodge quad cab hooked to an enormous silver horse trailer.

Edgard and Trevor sauntered over from the corrals.

Her breath caught. Man, they were gorgeous. Edgard Mancuso, Trevor's roping partner, was a darkly handsome Brazilian with the face of a god and the body of a gladiator. And Trevor, an all-American god in his own right, wavy blond hair, rugged looks borne of his Nordic ancestry.

Her nerves kicked in. What if they didn't want her?

"Channing. You're lookin' mighty fine today."

"Thanks, Trevor."

"What's up, Colby?" Trevor asked.

"We've got a bit of a situation. As you've heard, Jared abandoned this little lady. She wants to stay on. I've agreed she can travel with us until Cheyenne…on a few conditions."

"Which are?"

"She becomes our personal buckle bunny."

Trevor grinned. "Sounds good so far."

Edgard scowled at him. "We can get any woman, any time we want. Why do we need just one?"

"Because she's agreed to do whatever we want. And I know you guys have shied away from askin' some of the fillies warmin' our beds to do…certain things."

Edgard glanced away.

"How do we know she ain't just saying she'll do it?"

"Good question. I thought we could test her intentions. If she agrees, and if we're all satisfied, she'll be goin' with us today."

"All three of us? Right now?" Edgard asked skeptically.

"Yeah, we'll start with something easy. She's new at this sort of thing."

Channing's blood began to race through her body with anticipation—pounding and throbbing in some places more than others.

"Whatcha got in mind, Colby?" Trevor asked.

"Let's head into the horse trailer and I'll tell you."

Edgard shook his head. "I'll sit this one out."

The compartment in the horse trailer was bigger—and cleaner—than she'd imagined. A small living area comprised of a two-burner cook top stove, a mini-fridge, a microwave, a sink, and a table and bench seat which sat four. A metal ladder led to an area with a low hanging ceiling and a king-sized mattress. An angular tiny bathroom with a shower, sink and toilet was crammed in the far corner. The space smelled like horseflesh and leather and men.

"Do you live here?" she asked.

"We take turns stayin' in here. Too small for all of us."

Colby flicked on an overhead light. He faced Channing, his blue eyes gleaming. "Take off your shirt, shug."

Did she have the guts to do this? Even when she so desperately wanted it?

Inhaling a slow, quiet breath, her fingers trembled as she unbuttoned the white eyelet blouse.

Colby stood close, Trevor leaned against the back wall, watching.

Down to her white lace bra, she awaited further instructions.

"Good girl. Peel it off. Slowly. Tease me. Make me salivate to get my mouth on those big titties."

Channing reached behind her back and unhooked the clasps. The white satin contrasted against her tanned skin as the straps slithered down her arms. She held the cups in place until the last possible minute and then let the bra drop to the floor.

Silence except for the sounds of heavy male breathing.

"Trevor?" Colby said.

"I'm here buddy."

"You ever seen such a beautiful pair of tits?"

"Can't say as I have."

"Look at those nipples. Big and red as cherries."

Unused to compliments on her body, Channing blushed.

"Touch yourself. Show us what you like."

Channing closed her eyes. She skimmed her palms up her rounded belly, over her ribs, stopping to trace tiny circles around her nipples. She arched her back, lifting her breasts high, squeezing the soft flesh between her fingers. Plucking her nipples. Hard. Much harder than any man had been inclined to.

"What would you do first, Trev? Suck on them? Or slide your cock between them?"

Trevor chuckled. "Suck on them. Bite them. Make her squirm a bit. Then I'd wrap that creamy flesh around my cock and thrust high and hard until the tip reached those pouty lips."

Moisture gushed from her pussy like a water balloon had broken between her thighs. She'd never been so hot, so ready to be touched in her life.

Colby sidled in front of her, cupping a big breast in each hand. He kneaded the mounds, whispered husky, sweet words against her quivering skin, dragging his open mouth across the tops of her breasts. He buried his face in the valley of her cleavage. Flattening his tongue, lapping at the bottom curves.

Locking his gaze to hers, he dipped his head and sucked her beaded right nipple into the wet heat of his mouth. He deftly twirled the left nipple between his fingers as if turning a dial. Hard. Like he noticed she liked it.

Channing clamped her thighs together. "Oh, man. Please don't stop."

"I think she needs more. You wanna help me out here, Trev?"

"Gladly." Trevor latched onto her left nipple; Colby sucked on the right. She couldn't help the keening moan that escaped from the intense pressure. Colby's mouth was more aggressive. Trevor's mouth seemed hotter, his tongue softer as he suckled.

"Can you come like this, darlin'?" Colby asked, his breath tickled her wet nipple making it harder. "Are your tits sensitive enough we can get you off this way?"

"I-it's never happened before."

"A theory we can test another time when you're properly trussed up." He kissed a path up her neck, moving to the side of her body to allow Trevor access to both breasts.

Trevor crushed the globes closer, flicking his agile tongue back and forth between the tight, ruddy nipples.

Colby kissed her. She groaned against his lips. She loved kissing him. He twined their tongues together and lazily tasted the recesses of her mouth. His rough fingertips stroked her spine, sending goose bumps across her naked flesh. His lips slid to her ear and he whispered, "Are you turned on?"

"Yes."

"Is your cunt wet? Are you imaginin' me slurpin' all those sweet juices tricklin' between your thighs?"

"Yes."

"Mmm-mmm, I can't wait. We'll take good care of you in a minute. But for now, I'm dyin' to see your lips wrapped around my cock. Unzip me, Channing."

His buckle clanked as she unhooked his belt. Then he placed her right hand on the placket of his jeans. She scraped her nails along the hardened length. A quick yank and the button popped loose. She slid the zipper down a tine at a time.

Colby groaned.

Using both hands, she peeled back the jeans, delving her fingers beneath the stretchy waistband of his boxers and through the nest of springy hair. The damp, velvety soft tip greeted her palm. She squeezed his cock, mentally cataloguing its size and thickness. A fission of fear appeared. Talk about well endowed.

He hissed. "Come on, don't stop."

Trevor kept working her nipples. The soft kisses vanished as his teeth nipped the pebbled tips. She gasped at the spark of pain and sighed at the soothing lick of his warm tongue.

Channing arched toward Trevor, wanting to concentrate on the exquisite sensations of his talented mouth—her former lovers never paid long, drawn-out attention to her breasts, but Colby elbowed him out of the way.

"On your knees, darlin'." He put his hands on her shoulders and pushed her to the carpeted floor.

"What about me?" Trevor complained.

Colby caressed Channing's face with such genuine affection a lump rose in her throat. "You'll get yours. We're gonna see how good our girl is at multi-taskin'."

A wave of heat rolled through her belly. Her thighs were drenched and clenched.

"Here's the plan. You're gonna blow me while you're givin' Trevor a hand job. Gotta get used to sharin', sweetheart."

She nodded.

"That's my girl. Trev, help her out. Unbutton your own britches."

Colby had wiggled his Wranglers and boxers down to his knees. Channing got her first peek at his cock. A little puddle of drool formed in her mouth. It was by far the biggest dick she'd seen outside of *Playgirl.* Long. And thick. It curved up slightly. Pre-come oozed from the wide purple head. An angry blue vein pulsed on the underside and disappeared between his balls, which hung low, flanked by muscular thighs dusted with dark hair.

Without waiting for permission, the very tip of her tongue circled the weeping tip. Mmm. Colby tasted clean. Musky. Hot and salty. His cock twitched and he sucked in a sharp breath.

She turned and peered at Trevor.

Trevor gave her that killer bad-boy grin. He gently brushed a stray tendril from her damp forehead. "I'd never have pegged you as the kinda girl who'd do this, Channing."

"Which is exactly why I'm here." Her gaze dropped to his big hands, hesitating on his fly. Feeling bold, she challenged, "You shy, Trev? Or are you gonna show me what you've got?"

"I've got plenty to keep you satisfied." He shimmied his jeans over his narrow hips. No underwear. Grinning, he placed his hands behind his head and wagged his dick at her. "Like whatcha see?"

"Mmm-hmm." His cock actually looked longer than Colby's, but it wasn't as thick. The skin was paler, making the dark veins a bigger contrast against the lighter tone of his blond pubic hair. "Come closer."

Trevor shuffled a couple of steps until he stood next to Colby. Without preamble Channing sucked him into her mouth like she was slurping a noodle. Released him. Did it again.

"Hey! You're supposed to be suckin' *me* off," Colby reminded her.

"I need some moisture so I can work him with my hand." She wrapped her fingers around Trevor's shaft and began to stroke. "Like that?"

"Harder."

Channing increased her grip, the twisting sensation echoed in her own body from her nipples to her throbbing cunt.

"Shit yeah. Just like that."

She smiled and faced Colby.

He placed his palms on her cheeks, brushing the head of his cock across the seam of her lips. "Open up. Take me all the way in deep. That's how I like it."

She parted her lips, opening her mouth wide. The broad tip passed over her teeth, rested on her tongue as he kept pushing into her mouth. The cockhead hit the back of her throat and she gagged.

Colby held her in position. "Relax, darlin', and breathe through your nose. You're not gonna choke."

She fought the urge to bite down. Instead, she let the saliva pool on her tongue and didn't swallow.

"That's it. Don't arch your neck so much. You're doin' great. Oh, shug, you're sexy as hell."

The pumping action of her hand on Trevor's cock helped her focus beyond the need pulsing in her pussy. She hollowed her cheeks, and released Colby's dick an inch at a time.

"Jesus, that feels good."

"Tell me about it," Trevor said with a groan. "I ain't gonna last long."

Channing sucked Colby to the root again, burying her nose in his pubic hair. Inhaling his scent. Several more times she deep-throated him. Then her hand circled the thick base of his shaft and she concentrated on the sensitive head, flicking her tongue on his glans on every upstroke.

Colby grunted. “Oh, yeah. Get me soppin’ wet with that greedy mouth. It’s a fucking turn-on that your mouth is waterin’ for me, darlin’.”

No man had ever talked dirty to her or told her exactly what he wanted without sugarcoating it. It didn’t embarrass her; it inflamed her. Her pussy was so wet her juices trickled down the inside of her thighs.

“Faster,” Trevor panted. “Harder. Like that. Goddamn. Yes. More. There it is. God. I’m coming. Right...now. Ah. Shit!”

Channing pulled her mouth from Colby, twisting to watch come jet out the end of Trevor’s pulsating cock and splash on her breasts. She pumped him faster. More white spray arced through the air. The hot fluid dripped off her beaded nipples.

Trevor’s legs shook, his back arched and his handsome face was lost in bliss as she stroked him to completion.

She’d never had a man come on her. Not like that. A feeling of power built and her nervousness disappeared. She bent her head and suckled the reddened knob, relishing the different tastes of these two men.

“Jesus!” Trevor said and jumped back.

“Come on, Channing. I’m so fucking close I can taste it,” Colby growled. “I want you to taste it, too. Trevor got his; now I want mine.”

With both hands free, Channing curled the fingers of her right hand around the thick root and rolled his lightly furred balls with her left. Her mouth glided up until it reached the barrier of her fingers. On every downstroke she increased her suction, building a steady rhythm as she used her teeth on his sweet spot.

"Don't stop. When I tell you, drop your hand and take my cock all the way in your mouth. Oh yeah, here it comes."

His sac drew up; she unwrapped her hand and engulfed him completely, tightening her lips around the base of his shaft.

Colby growled, "That's it. Milk it. Suck every goddamn drop."

Breathing through her nose, she felt his cock twitching on her tongue as he emptied himself down the back of her throat. She swallowed the thick liquid as he kept coming and grinding harder into her mouth. Her eyes watered at the forceful grip he had on her hair, but his hold kept her gag reflex from kicking in. Finally, the pulsing stopped. She unlocked her jaw and released him slowly. And blew a stream of air over his shiny wet shaft.

Colby stumbled back.

Trevor laughed and steadied him. "Whoa, buddy, you okay?"

"Fuck no."

Channing smirked and wiped the back of her hand across her smooth lips. "So, boys...did I pass the test?"

Chapter Three

Channing watched shamelessly as Colby tugged his jeans to his hips and tucked his spent cock back inside his boxers before he zipped up.

Trevor helped her off her knees and gently wiped the stickiness from her chest with a frayed kitchen towel. He slanted his mouth over hers and kissed her, not sweetly, but with fresh hunger and pure male heat. She rubbed the inside of her thighs together to assuage the throbbing ache and Trevor retreated.

She sensed Colby closing in behind her. He lifted her hair and trailed his lips along the curve of her neck. "Shug, that was amazing. We're definitely keepin' you."

"Definitely," Trevor said.

"And you've been a good girl. A very good girl." Colby's palms skated down the front of Channing's body, lingering to plump her breasts higher so Trevor could suckle the taut nipples. "Undo her pants, Trev," Colby said gruffly.

Channing's belly jumped with anticipation as Trevor complied, lowering the zipper and shimmying her skintight jeans down her hips.

The roughened tips of Trevor's fingers followed the elastic band of her plain cotton panties. He seemed to want to dip his fingers into her aching sex, but he was waiting for something.

For a signal from Colby, apparently. It was obvious Colby was in charge.

Colby's right hand trailed over her abdomen, straight through the short curls covering her mound. His middle finger separated the fold of her pussy lips and stroked her distended clit.

"Oh, God. Please. Don't stop."

"Ssh. We'll take care of you. This go-around will be pretty quick since we gotta get on the road, but tonight I promise we'll take our time with you. Spread your legs." In between peppering the sensitive slope of her shoulder with moist kisses, he said to Trevor, "She likes it when you suck her nipples hard."

Channing threaded the fingers of her left hand through Trevor's hair and let her head fall back when Colby's fingers penetrated her pussy. He thrust high, groaning in her ear when he found her absolutely dripping wet. Slow and easy he pumped in and out of her slick channel, sweeping his thumb side to side over her pouting clit. Trevor plucked her left nipple, pulling and twisting it as his mouth closed over the right one.

"Tell me what will make you come all over my hand, Channing," Colby urged against her throat. "I wanna smell that sweet cream."

"Push your fingers in deeper. Faster on my clit. But, lightly. Yeah. Like that. Oh, I'm so close. Yes. Yes. Right there." Light and dark swirls of light exploded behind her lids as the orgasm burst between her thighs. Colby murmured encouragement in her ear, his fingers continuing to plunge and Trevor's rapid sucks on her nipple were synchronized to the blood pulsing in her clit.

She thrashed and squirmed but Colby and Trevor held her tight, keeping their attention entirely focused on bringing her every ounce of pleasure at their command. Shaking and spent, she slumped against Colby's shoulder, breathing hard, dizzy, her body pliant with bone-deep satisfaction.

Trevor continued to lap at her pebbled nipples. Colby circled his fingers inside her, causing another set of tremors to trill through her internal muscles. "Look at me."

She managed to force her eyes open.

Colby slipped his hand from her sex. As he lifted up his hand, coated with her juices, Trevor snagged Colby's wrist and brought those glistening fingers to his lips, licking away every bit of her cream from his friend's hand.

Channing almost came again.

"How does she taste?" Colby asked huskily.

"You tell me." Watching Channing's face, Trevor placed Colby's hand flat on her belly, then layered his own big hand over Colby's and slid both their hands down inside her damp panties, ramming four fingers deep into her wet pussy.

Her breath stalled as those slippery fingers twisted and plunged. Colby brought his hand to his mouth and loudly sucked his fingers clean. Then he angled his head to capture Channing's lips as he kissed her hard, sharing her taste in the most hedonistic, consuming kiss of her life.

With Trevor's fingers still fucking her, and his teeth clamped on her nipple, another orgasm rocketed her body and she whimpered in Colby's mouth.

Finally, Colby broke the kiss and a huge grin spread across his gorgeous face. "Oh, yeah, this is definitely gonna be one fun week."

Colby loaded Channing's suitcases in the horse trailer as Trevor and Edgard performed last-minute checks on the horses. He tamped down the strange need to hold Channing's hand or to constantly touch her in some manner. Talk about acting like a lovesick fool...but there was just something about the woman that brought out his protective instincts.

Edgard ambled to the truck cab. "Horses are loaded. We're ready to roll."

"Who's drivin'?"

"Trevor. I'll navigate if that's okay. I figured you and Channing could sit in the back cab. If she's sharing responsibilities, you'll need to bring her up to speed on what she'll be doing besides warming your bed, *amigo*."

Colby nodded. "What's our next stop?"

"Limon, Colorado. About six hundred miles. Good thing there ain't no rodeo tonight, or we'd already be late for check-in."

"Then let's get on the road." Colby glanced over and saw Channing leaning her elbows on the wooden railing separating the parking lot from the exercise arena, wearing a dreamy expression. He shouted, "Hey, Chan, time to load up."

She turned and tucked the notebook in her hand into the gigantic camouflage messenger bag slung over her shoulder. Her turquoise boots kicked up dust as she hustled toward him, a secret smile tilting the corners of her full mouth.

Colby couldn't help but grin at her and offer his hand when she finally reached him. He brought her knuckles to his mouth and rubbed his lips over them. "Ready?"

"Yeah."

He swept a tendril of hair from her cheek. "You sure about this, darlin' girl?"

She stood on her tiptoes and kissed his chin. “As sure as I’ve been about anything in my life. But one thing, Colby, I’m not a girl.”

“My mistake. You sure enough proved you’re all woman.”

Channing blushed attractively, captivating Colby completely. “Let’s start this adventure, cowboy.”

An enormous, beat-up, red Ford pickup pulled around the back end of the horse trailer and stopped parallel to the cab.

Colby smiled and tugged Channing closer to the rig.

The woman in the truck—Gemma Jansen—was a rough stock contractor from outside of Sheridan. Her husband had died a few years back and instead of selling off the livestock business, she’d taken over and was trying her hand at becoming a rough stock contractor for the Mountain and Plains Rodeo circuit.

Gemma was a true Westerner, a fourth generation Wyomingite, tough, gruff and knowledgeable about everything from land to horse bloodlines. Beneath her salt-of-the-earth persona, sometimes it was easy to forget she wasn’t an old grizzled woman. Somewhere in her forties, she was still a damn attractive woman. It was weird seeing her without her husband, Steve. They’d been married forever. For the first time, Colby wondered if she got as lonely on the road as the rest of them did.

Gemma leaned over and rolled down the dirt-covered passenger window. “Where you boys headed?”

Edgard tipped back his hat and rested his forearm on the oversized mirror. “Limon. How about you?”

“Back home first. There’s a shortage of bucking horse stock in Cody so I’ve gotta get my foreman up there, see if they’re willing to look at any of ours.”

"They'd be damn foolish not to."

"That's what I said. My foreman ain't so sure. And I ain't so sure *his* reluctance ain't borne out of laziness. So I gotta make sure he ain't letting my business go to hell while I'm out workin' this summer. He's the third foreman I've been through in the last eighteen months."

Colby said, "Too bad you can't take Cash with you. He'd convince them guys in Cody to give you a shot. That man could sell wind in Wyoming."

"Like we need more of that." She scowled. "Shoot. One of them crazy tourist traps would kidnap that blowhard Indian, color his face with war paint, put him in buckskin and a feather headdress, trying to pass him off as 'heap big chief'. Cash would surely like that."

"Now, Gemma, that ain't fair. I know you and Cash have your differences, but you cain't argue that he don't know his stock."

A sly smile lit up her face. "My stock sure as shootin' tossed old Cash on his bony ass last night, didn't it?"

Colby laughed.

The driver's side door on Trevor's truck opened and Trevor hopped out. "Hey, my beautiful Gem-stone. How's tricks?"

She snorted. "You're as smooth as a baby's ass, ain't ya, Trev?"

"I try."

"Wasted breath on me. I ain't nearly as tricky as I used to be in my younger years. But I'd be lying if I didn't tell you I had my fair share of lovesick cowboys trailing behind me."

Gemma focused on Colby. "What'd you think of that four-year-old bull, Big Time, last night? You looked damn good on him. Too good. Makes me wonder if I oughta pull him out of rough stock rotation for a while."

"He's gotta good spin. He got all four legs off the ground right out of the chute so you're wrong if you think he's a gimme. He weren't easy at all. Shoot, it's not like I scored a ninety on him, Gem. A couple of the guys said they'd like a chance to test him out. Where's the next place you're bringin' him?"

"Valentine, probably." Gemma's shrewd gaze finally landed on Channing. "Since these boys forgot their manners, I'll just go ahead and introduce myself. Gemma Jansen."

Channing thrust her hand through the open window and clasped Gemma's. "Channing Kinkaid."

"Who're you here with?"

Colby said, "She's with me now."

"Before, I was traveling with Jared. It ended when I found out about Jared's marital status last night."

A single blonde eyebrow lifted. "You didn't know?"

"No, ma'am." She dropped her head, clearly embarrassed.

In a show of support, Colby squeezed the hand he'd placed on Channing's hip.

Gemma gave her an approving look. "Good to hear. Lots of the girls hitching a ride on the wild side don't give a rip about the sanctity of marriage. So if you need a break from the rodeo-injury war stories and the testosterone, come find me. We'll drink whiskey and tell these boys we're doin' each other's hair."

Channing grinned. "Will do. Thanks."

Gemma inclined her head and her straw cowboy hat shaded her face. "Nice day to travel. Behave, boys. Good luck in Limon. See you in Nebraska in a few."

"Drive safe, *senhora*." Edgard thumped the side door and Gemma took off.

Trevor and Edgard conversed in low tones, then Edgard popped the hood of the truck and they fiddled with the engine. Colby opened the rear cab door and gestured for Channing to hop in.

She lifted her satchel over her head, propping it in her lap as she scooted across the leather bench seat. "So what's the plan?"

"Trev's gonna drive until he gets tired and then Edgard will take over."

"What about us?"

Colby kicked aside an empty carton of chocolate milk. "We'll be on tap for next time when we hit the road for Valentine. Today's one of our rare off days so enjoy it while it lasts. Usually, we're rippin' out of the arena the second we get the payouts and headin' to the next event."

Channing scowled at the trash scattered across the floor. "This place is a pigsty."

"Yep."

"Doesn't it bother you?"

"Not particularly."

"Well, it does me. While we're waiting on those two, we're going to pick this crap up and throw it out."

Colby's eyes narrowed. "You ain't our maid, Chan."

"You need one. Besides, I said *we*, not me." Her crafty smile turned into a frown as she picked up a crusty, half-eaten cinnamon roll wedged under the muddy floor mat. "Ugh. Find me something to use as a garbage bag."

He rummaged under the seat until he found one. Shoving cellophane Twinkie wrappers, empty cans of Copenhagen and Skoal, half-full bottles of Gatorade in the clear plastic shopping bag, Colby couldn't recall the last time he'd cared enough to clean up for a woman. Never maybe.

"Do you guys really eat this kind of junk food all the time?"

"No. Sometimes we roll through the McDonald's drive-thru."

Channing chucked a gray athletic sock in the bag. "Here's a warning, this stuff isn't real food. It'll kill you."

"I know." Colby found the matching dirty sock and balled it up and threw it in the trash. "We do have a kitchen in the trailer."

"Do you use it?"

"Not really."

"Well, it's stupid not to. When we get to Limon, we'll go to a real grocery store—not a convenience store—and stock up on real food. Because I can't eat like this."

"Why not? Ain't that part of the appeal of rodeo? Fried Twinkies, nachos, and cold beer?"

"Not for me." Channing dangled a crumpled package of cheddar-flavored Bugles in front of his face. "I'd be easier to jump over than walk around if I shoved this crap in my mouth every damn day."

When she finished tidying up he softly said, "Channing."

Those gold-flecked eyes met his. "What?"

"Get over here and kiss me."

"But—"

"No buts. Now." Colby's strong fingers circled her upper arms and he hauled her across his lap. Before she opened her mouth to protest again, he swooped in for a hungry kiss.

Channing's objection lasted less than three seconds before her hands were gripping his neck and her lithe body was plastered against his. Her mouth was welcoming, hot as sin and sweet as candy.

Colby lifted her until she straddled his lap. His hands inched up the inside of her shirt, softly stroking the trembling muscles of her belly. He loved how quickly she reacted to his every touch. He pulled his lips away a fraction and nibbled her jaw. "I wish you had on that flirty, little, yellow skirt you wore the first time I saw you."

"Colby—"

"Then I could bunch it around your hips and pull aside your panties and stroke your sweet pussy without any barriers. I could get you off in less than two minutes. You'd like that, wouldn't you, shug?"

"Mmm. So confident. Why don't you see if you can't get me off in two minutes through my clothes?"

"You challengin' me?"

"You bet your tight cowboy ass I'm challenging you. Stop talking, kiss me, and put your money where your mouth is." Channing circled her arms around his neck, balancing on her knees, giving him better access to the warm spot between her thighs. She bumped her hips against his stomach, while her eager kisses shattered his control.

This woman drove him insane with her sweetness and fire. Colby scraped his fingernail along the inside seam of her jeans, a lazy assault that made her squirm. He flicked his tongue over hers in the same languid manner, until she whimpered. When he kept his caresses simple and easy, she ripped her mouth away from his on a gasp.

"What are you doing? I think your two minutes are up."

Colby left damp, open-mouthed kisses down the bared column of her throat. God. She smelled like wildflowers. "I've decided since I'm always tryin' to beat the clock on the dirt, I ain't gotta time myself now, or to give into your demands, greedy girl. See, now I'm thinkin' I don't want to rush this. I want you to feel the anticipation, so when I finally slide my cock inside you later tonight, you'll remember how much you wanted it there. How much you craved it."

She whispered, "Don't you want it?"

He tugged her face closer by a chunk of her hair until his hat brim shadowed her eyes. "I can hardly see straight, from wantin' you, Channing. But I'll be goddamned if you'll take this from me because I can't keep my hands off your tempting body. This is my show. You wanted me to be in charge, so I'm remindin' you we're doing this *my* way, understand?"

The hood thunked back into place, shaking the truck frame, breaking the intense moment. The front cab doors slammed shut as Trevor and Edgard climbed in.

Edgard groaned. "Are you guys going to be fucking around back there all day? Because if you are, ride in the horse trailer. It'll be damn distracting to hear your moans and smell sex as we're trying to keep us on the road and in one piece."

"Yeah," Trevor chimed in. "I thought we were waitin' until tonight for any more action?"

"Feeling left out?" Edgard asked.

"Don't pout. It ain't my fault you didn't join in earlier," Trevor shot back.

Great. Colby was acting like a pussy-whipped greenhorn who couldn't think beyond getting in Channing's pants. No way in hell would he admit that weakness to his traveling partners. Instead, he returned Channing to her side of the truck.

"Sorry. Yeah, we got carried away. You sure you don't want me to drive? Because I'm thinkin' me and Channing back here together, even with all our clothes on, is a bad idea."

She snickered.

Trevor gunned the engine. "Hang on, it's gonna be a tight turn to get out of here."

Automatically, Colby and Edgard reached up for the handles hanging from the ceiling as Trevor whipped the big rig around.

Channing smoothed her hands down the outside of her thighs, then busied herself with compacting the trash. She leaned over the front seat. "You guys have any junk up there that needs to be tossed out? It's all picked up back here."

Edgard glared at Colby. "You were making her clean up?"

"Hell, no! I didn't make her do nothin'. Must be a woman thing, it was something she did on her own."

"Well, someone has to do it," she retorted.

"*Gracias*," Edgard said. "I promise we'll try a little harder to keep it tidy now that you're bunking with us, right, *amigos*?"

"Sounds good to me," Trevor said.

Channing set her chin on her forearms, which were resting along the back edge of the front seat. "How are the sleeping arrangements going to work? There's hardly enough room in the horse trailer for two people, let alone four."

Trevor signaled and pulled onto the freeway. "We don't all stay in the trailer. We rent a motel room. It's easier to shower that way. Two of us stay in the room, and one of us sleeps out here. We rotate, so someone is always keeping an eye on the horses."

"Someone meaning me usually sleepin' with the damn horses," Colby grumbled.

"Besides, sometimes we need privacy. A break from each other," Edgard said.

Trevor shot Edgard a strange look.

Channing glanced at Colby over her shoulder. He shrugged at her puzzled expression. She'd learn to deal with the two of them sniping at each other, or she wouldn't. He preferred to stay out of it.

"Like I told Colby, I can't eat fast food all the time. I don't mind cooking if I've got the right supplies."

"And like I told you, we don't expect you to cook and clean for us, darlin'," Colby said testily.

"Especially if you're gonna make us eat vegetables." Trevor shuddered. "Give me jerky and chili dogs over any of that green shit any day."

Edgard nodded. "Don't forget the Mexican delights of Taco Bell."

"Or meat and potatoes," Colby added.

Channing rolled her eyes. She dug in her satchel and untangled her iPod. Once the earpieces were in place, she balled up her fleece-lined jacket to use for a pillow, rammed it in the corner, and closed her eyes.

Instead of gawking at Channing, looking far too tempting even in sleep, Colby dry-washed his face and stared out the window at the landscape, a flat blandness spreading as far as the eye could see. The dirt in Oklahoma was an odd shade of pinkish orange and the horizon never changed from a washed-out, dirty gray.

He missed the brilliant blue Wyoming sky, with snowcapped mountains teasing in the distance. The rolling hills and valleys dotted with clusters of cedar and sagebrush. Herds of antelope running free among the wide-open spaces.

Out of the corner of his eye he saw Channing shifting to get comfortable. She might look little, sweet and innocent, but the woman definitely knew her own mind and didn't hesitate to speak it.

Colby tapped Edgard on the shoulder. "Wake me up when we gas up." He leaned his shoulders against the seat, tugged his battered Resistol over his eyes and drifted off to the familiar sound of the wheels clacking on the highway.

Chapter Four

"Channing?"

She blinked at the late afternoon sunlight streaming through the window and scrambled upright. "What? Where are we?"

Trevor grinned and traced his fingers over her sleep-creased cheek. "We're about an hour outside Limon. Just wondered if you needed to use the bathroom before we get back on the road."

"Wow. I slept for five hours?"

"Four. I've got a bit of a lead foot so we made good time."

"I guess so. Where are Colby and Edgard?"

"Inside. Why? Did you need them for something?" Her skin was so smooth. How long had it been since he'd paid attention to the supreme softness of the skin on a woman's face? Such a contrast from a man's rough skin and stubble.

"No. I was just curious." Channing smiled and angled her head more deeply into his touch. "Mmm. That feels nice. I probably should get out and stretch my legs and visit the little girl's room."

"Let me help you." Trevor clamped his hands over her slim hips and scooted her from the cab. When her boots hit the ground, he slammed the door, and crowded her against the truck bed. "But first, how about one of them sweet kisses, darlin'?"

She rose to her tiptoes and gave him a loud smacking smooch on his Adam's apple. "Like that?"

"You got a mean streak, Chan."

"No, sir. How about if you show *me* how you want to be kissed, Trev, so next time I won't have to guess."

Trevor tilted his black Stetson further back on his head and lowered his face, keeping their eyes locked. When his mouth was close enough their breath mingled, he licked his lips and swept them across hers. Lightly. Softly. Not applying pressure, not nibbling or teasing, not using his tongue, just feeling the warm fullness of her lips parting in expectation of his.

He brought his hand up to her shoulder and lazily rubbed his thumb over the pulse beating in the hollow of her throat. Then he rimmed the inside of her full lower lip with the inside edge of his upper lip. Back and forth, creating friction and heat and moisture. Just that slick, barely-there slide of mouth on mouth made her whimper.

Taking pity on her and himself, he pinched her stubborn chin between his thumb and forefinger and unlocked her jaw to accept the invasion of his tongue.

She responded with such unrestrained passion Trevor knew it was a damn good thing they were in public. As it was he wanted nothing more than to drop his Wranglers to the top of her Tony Lamas and drive into her hot little pussy, right there, next to the gas pumps at the Flying J Truck Plaza.

Trevor forced his mouth away, trying to level his ragged breathing and he rested his forehead to hers. Once he regained control, he stepped back.

Channing smiled and tugged his hat back in place. "Now that's what I call a kiss."

Edgard said, "If you two are done sucking face, we need to get a move on."

"Quit bein' an asshole, Ed. Give Channing time to use the can and get a snack." Trevor waited for him to snap off another smart retort. Instead Edgard scowled and skirted the front of the truck and climbed in the passenger side.

As Trevor watched Channing saunter into the convenience store, he knew Edgard was going to be a problem where she was concerned. Problem was, Trevor didn't know what to do about it.

Colby materialized from the shadows and leaned against the concrete pillar beside the pump. "Everything all right?"

"Yeah." Trevor couldn't meet Colby's gaze. "She's something, isn't she?"

"Yep."

"I think you like her way more than you're lettin' on. So does that mean you're gonna have a problem sharin' her with me, Colby? Actin' all pissed off if Chan and I spend time alone together? If you see me kissin' her?"

"Nah, buddy, there's enough of her to go around. This is what she wants and I think it'll work well for us. But we both know I ain't the one with the jealous streak." Colby pushed away and reached for the windshield cleaner, scrubbing away the bugs and grime with the spongy side, before using the squeegee to slick away the filthy water.

By the time the windshield was clean and Trevor had checked the horses, Channing had returned, looking as fresh as a daisy. She rubbed a shiny red apple across her chest before she took a big chomping bite. Juice dribbled down her chin.

"That apple actually looks good," Trevor said.

"Want a bite?"

She held the fruit to his mouth. Instead of taking a bite, he leaned over and licked her sticky-sweet chin, then swept his tongue over her lips and dipped it into her mouth. "Mmm. I much prefer tasting the apple from you."

Her cheeks were flushed from his attention, but Channing recovered and rolled her eyes before she jumped into the truck.

ᴄᴙ ᴕ ᴙᴕ

After they pulled into Limon, they found a cheap, slightly seedy motel close to the fairgrounds. Edgard and Trevor unloaded the horses, unhooked the trailer, and Colby drove Channing to the Hinky Dinky grocery store outside of town.

She loaded up on fresh fruit, a few veggies. Whole-grain cereal and bread. Lunch meat. Diet soda. And canned soup.

Colby's contribution to the cart was an extra large box of condoms, four cans of Skoal and a case of Bud Light.

Every time she added a new item, her gaze strayed to that box of condoms, extra large, extra ribbed for her pleasure, and she tried not to panic.

She browsed the butcher block and pointed to a chunk of beef. "See? If I had a big crock pot I could toss meat and potatoes in it in the morning, and by the time we stopped, dinner would be done."

Colby brushed a kiss across her forehead. "As much as I've said I don't want you goin' to no trouble for us, slow-cooked beef and potatoes does sound tasty. I miss home cookin'. My ma is a helluva good cook."

Channing bit the inside of her lip. Did she confess to him she really wasn't much of a cook and have him compare her efforts to his mother's?

Colby loaded the grocery bags and talked on his cell phone. They picked up a bucket of fried chicken and all the trimmings and ate the meal in the picnic area outside the motel. It was a beautiful night, not a breath of wind, the humidity tolerable and a silver moon hung low in the sky.

Several other contestants, Brian, Jeff and JJ, all sometime roping partners with Edgard and Trevor, stopped by and the beer disappeared quickly. Just in that short amount of time she realized that these people traveling the circuit were like one big family. Fighting, laughing, fiercely loyal to one another. Not that she'd experienced anything like that in her family life.

Trevor and Edgard returned to the arena to practice roping and Colby tagged along, needing to run his horse.

Channing stayed in the room and indulged in a shower. After she'd shaved and coated her body with lotion, she wondered what would happen when her cowboys returned. Was she supposed to stay naked? Would they prefer another strip tease?

Did she really know what she'd gotten herself into?

The sound of a lock in the door sent her pulse tripping. She shoved the books in her satchel and flipped the page on her notebook.

Colby entered the room first, followed by Trevor. Edgard brought up the rear and he immediately went into the bathroom and the shower kicked on.

Trevor flopped on the queen bed against the wall. "I'm tired."

"I'm not," Colby said. His gaze traveled from Channing's bare toes all the way up her legs to linger on her face. "I'm feelin' *very* energetic tonight."

Yowza.

"Who's sleeping in the trailer?" she asked.

"Edgard," Trevor said.

Did that mean he wouldn't be joining them again? Channing was almost afraid to ask. She was secretly worried Edgard regretted having her along, or worse, that he didn't find her attractive.

As soon as Edgard finished his shower, he bid them goodnight. After Colby cleaned up, he left the room for a time while Trevor took his turn in the bathroom. With every minute that clicked by, Channing became more and more nervous.

Especially when Colby returned to the room with a length of rope in one hand, a bandana in the other, and a wicked gleam in his eye. He said, "Strip. I wanna see you bare-assed naked right now."

Channing nodded, doffed her clothes and stood before him, feeling shy and exposed.

"You're mighty fine, Chan. Come here and turn around."

She crossed the room. The folded red bandana flashed in front of her eyes before everything went dark. A quick pinch on the back of her head and she was blindfolded.

Colby made no move to touch her besides guiding her back to the bed. "Sit here and wait for further instructions. You'll do as you're told. No questions. We clear on that, shug?"

"Yes."

He placed a soft kiss on the corners of her lips and whispered, "Good girl. Don't be scared. We ain't gonna hurt you—" his teeth sank into her earlobe, "—much."

Channing shivered.

The door to the bathroom clicked open and shut. She heard Colby's and Trevor's voices, but she couldn't hear what they were saying. That was probably a good thing.

She swallowed to moisten her dry mouth. Her heart rate kicked up again when humid, soapy-scented air drifted out of the bathroom and she sensed Trevor and Colby standing in front of her.

"Here's the deal, darlin'. We're gonna play a little game of blind man's bluff. You're gonna try to figure out who's touchin' you. If you guess right, you get a reward. If you guess wrong, well, let's just hope you don't have to find out."

Channing went absolutely motionless.

"Lay back on the bed and press your arms together above your head. That's a girl." Scratchy twine wrapped around her wrists several times. Colby whispered, "It ain't too tight, mostly it's to keep your hands out of our way. If you cooperate, we'll leave them loose. The second you try to touch either of us or those hands move? We'll fasten you to the bed frame. We clear on that?"

"Yes."

Trevor said, "Spread your legs wide. I wanna see those heels hangin' off the side of the bed."

She complied.

"You're beautiful, Chan. No matter what we do to you, leave 'em like that until we say otherwise."

Channing had a flash of insight. If they talked, she'd easily be able to figure out which one was doing what. Colby loved to talk dirty, so chances were good he wouldn't be able to keep his mouth shut. She withheld a grin.

Until the music turned on.

Before she could contemplate how she'd differentiate one man from the other in the dark, a hot mouth closed over her left nipple and suckled strongly. Rough fingertips dragged up and down the center of her body. Smoothing over her ribcage and the sensitive bend in her waist. A light stroking over the pulse pounding in the column of her neck.

A work-roughened palm traced her contours, from the arms displayed above her head, down her tensed shoulders. Over the soft curve of her belly, across her hips and the roundness of her thighs. Past her quaking knees, down her calves to her ankles, ending at her ticklish feet. Those maddeningly thorough hands reversed the process with just as much sensual deliberation.

Channing began to shake with pure unadulterated need.

Then those eager hands palmed her breasts, bringing both nipples together to suck and lick and taste. Teeth nipped the tender tips, causing a pain-filled sound to escape from her throat.

The sting was soothed by pursed lips blowing a stream of cool air, followed by a warm, wet tongue lapping and curling around the abused flesh.

"Who?" a gruff male commanded.

Well, shoot. Her chances of guessing correctly were 50-50. "Trevor?"

"Wrong. Turn her over," Colby said.

A hard slap burned across her left butt cheek.

When she protested—"Hey! That stings"—two more smacks landed in rapid succession.

"Keep talkin' and I'll take great pleasure in turnin' this heart-shaped ass rosy red, shug."

Crap.

"Got any other protests?" Trevor asked.

She shook her head.

"Good. Turn her the other way so I can get my licks in, too," Trevor said.

She was rolled to her left side and four solid smacks landed on her right buttock. "Now we're even. Don't make us get out the bullrope, Chan."

The humiliation she thought she'd feel never came. What did that say about her?

Nothing, besides she'd never been wetter or more turned on in her life.

Strong hands gripped her ankles and jerked her body down until her stinging ass nearly hung off the end of the bed. Then a cool, wet tongue licked straight up the center of her pussy.

Her hips shot off the bed.

A warning growl sounded next to her ear.

Then the mouth on her sex began a full-out assault. That clever tongue wiggled deep inside her dripping cunt, licking her from the inside out. Then it zigzagged up to flick little whips of hot velvet across her distended clit. Her blood pulsed and gathered in that little nub, the orgasm danced close to the surface and then the possibility vanished as the teasing mouth trailed away.

Damn. She wanted to demand it return, but she wisely kept her lips pressed together.

Soft kisses circled her mound from the line of her pubic hair, to the crease of her thighs, back down to her vaginal opening. The circle of kisses became progressively smaller. Tighter. Wetter.

Channing tried not to writhe, or to grind her sex into that fleeting tongue. But when that hot, hungry mouth closed over her clit and her swollen pussy lips and began to suck them together, she flat out screamed.

Two thick fingers shot inside and stroked that magical spot as the soft suctioning grew stronger and sent her soaring over the edge of reason and into a climax so extreme she forgot to breathe. She nearly passed out from lack of oxygen to her sex-addled brain.

Once the blood quit rushing in her ears and slowed to a dull throb between her legs, she slumped against the mattress.

A gravelly voice demanded, "Who?"

God. Was she really supposed to care *who'd* brought her to such an intense orgasm? Channing licked her lips and willed her head to quit buzzing.

"Who?" the demand was voiced again.

"Umm. Colby?"

"Very good, shug," he whispered against her throat.

"No, you're very good. That was the most—"

His mouth covered hers; she tasted the musky tang of her own juices on his tongue. Colby kissed her mouth, Trevor's hands roamed over her until she squirmed from the erotic motions. Once Colby released her tingling lips from his, she whispered, "That was...please. I want more."

"Are you supposed to be talkin'?"

"No."

"Then hush up."

The bed dipped. Hands and mouths left her body, leaving her bereft. Tears stung her eyes. "Are you going to punish me?"

"Ssh. Darlin, you're fine. We planned on playin' with you a little more, but the truth is, you've pushed us to the edge tonight and neither one of us is very good at waitin'."

"We want you bad, girl."

Channing smiled at the shaking note in Trevor's voice. "What now?"

Trevor brushed his lips over hers. After twelve short hours she already knew the difference in their kisses, their individual tastes and shape of their mouths. "Now you get your wish to be with us both at the same time."

Her satiation fled and her body seized up.

"Relax. No double penetration tonight, we need to ease you into it." Trevor's knees snugged against her armpits. He spread cool gel over her chest, then he pressed her breasts together tightly in his palms. "I'm dyin' to slide my cock between these glorious tits."

The slippery warmth of his hard shaft eased into the tight valley he created. With every glide, the tip of his cock bumped her chin.

He growled, "Angle your neck and lick the head."

She complied, half-afraid she was doing it wrong, and wanting to do it right because she didn't know how she felt about him coming on her face. Her tongue shot out and curled around the tip. On his next stroke, she let her lips close around the whole head.

"Yeah. Like that. As soon as my balls are ready to explode, my cock is goin' all the way in this pretty mouth."

A fresh rush of moisture gushed between her legs.

Callused hands gripped her hips. "I can smell you creaming, but hang tight, while I get some lube," Colby said. "I don't want to hurt you." Two fingers twisted inside her, mixing the KY with her natural lubrication.

Channing tensed when she felt the head of Colby's cock poised at her entrance. He was a big man—bigger than any she'd ever been with—and even though she couldn't wait to feel him stuffing her pussy full, part of her was a little scared.

"Don't tense up. Once I'm in, it'll feel good. Real good, I promise." As Colby worked his dick in slowly, Trevor began thrusting harder, muttering. Channing wished she could see everything that was happening to her, but the blindfold remained on and her hands were still immobilized above her head.

"Fuck. Here it comes. Open up wide." Trevor released her breasts and cupped one hand under her neck, lifting her higher so his cock slid deeper into her mouth. At the same time, Colby rammed into her to the hilt.

She moaned as hot bursts of come splashed against the back of her throat, a saltier, earthier taste than Colby's. As Trevor rocked against her face, his balls tickled her chin. She swallowed convulsively, feeling the heat and need spiraling through her as Colby slammed into her sopping wet cunt, his hips pistoning faster and faster like a runaway train.

Trevor rolled off her body and began to suck her nipples as Colby reamed her, harder and harder, pulling completely out, and ramming back in until he hit the top of her uterus.

"Darlin', I ain't gonna last," Colby grunted.

Channing arched, whimpering, "Yes, yes, yes," as Colby stroked her clit and she detonated like a nuclear reactor.

He followed right behind. Her strong interior muscles clutched his dick like teeth, keeping his pulsing shaft submerged inside her after he'd shot his load.

Breathing as hard as she was, Colby crumpled against her.

He rested his head on her belly as Trevor untied her hands and rubbed her wrists to get the blood flowing again.

While she tried to assess the delicious damage the men's passion had inflicted upon her unsuspecting body, Trevor leaned over and kissed her, gently removing the blindfold.

"Thank you, darlin'. Plenty more of where that came from. But get some sleep. I'm gonna go check on Edgard and make sure he ain't getting shitfaced with the horses." Trevor slipped on his sweat bottoms, leaving his broad, sweaty chest bare, and exited the room before she caught her breath.

Colby eased his spent cock from her with painstaking slowness. He disposed of the condom and shut off the lights. He picked her limp body up and hugged her close as he flipped back the covers and then slid them between the cool sheets.

"I'm so tired," she murmured.

He kissed the top of her head. "Sleep. You deserve it. You're gonna need your strength for tomorrow because I can't wait to have you again. And again. You're gonna be as bowlegged as Cash by the time I get through with you."

Channing sighed dreamily. But she wasn't ready to drift off into la-la land yet. She wanted to know everything about Colby McKay. "Tell me about your life on your ranch in the wilds of Wyoming."

Colby dragged his fingers up and down her spine. "It's like heaven and hell rolled into one. Parts of the land are beautiful; parts are butt ugly and barren. But the whole shebang has been in the McKay family for one hundred and twenty years, so it's home."

"You ever lived anyplace else?"

"Nope. Never wanted to. I've never wanted to do anything with my life besides work on the ranch and rodeo."

She listened to Colby extol the virtues of rural living and the frustrations. She wondered what it would be like to be so...connected. To the land. To your family. To your neighbors.

"What about you?" Colby prompted. "What's it like livin' with a couple million people around you all the damn time?"

"Lonely."

"Seriously?"

"Yeah."

"Even living in the least populated county in the least populated state I was never lonely growin' up. Too many brothers and cousins. Though I'd like to have punched 'em most days, we get along great now."

"Tell me about them."

He sighed. "Another time, okay? You need to stop chatterin' and—"

"Please? I've got my second wind." She yawned.

"Right. You don't have to uncover all my secrets tonight. Go to sleep, Chan. I'll tell you anything you want to know tomorrow."

"Okay. I'm holding you to that, cowboy." She snuggled into him and conked out.

Chapter Five

Warm, wet kisses started at her hairline and trailed down the inside curve of her neck to the slope of her shoulder and back up the other side. Stuttered breathing caused her pulse to flutter and the tiny hairs on her nape to stand at attention.

Channing tried to turn into Colby's embrace, but he held her in place.

"Morning. You slept good. We plumb wore you out. I don't think you moved at all after we stopped talkin' last night." He lightly bit her biceps. "I never would've dreamed you're so damn cuddly."

"Sorry."

"Don't apologize. I loved it. Especially those sweet snores comin' from your sinful mouth. Lord. I've been watchin' you sleep for the last ten minutes, wishin' you'd wake up. As you can tell, I kinda got tired of waitin'."

She blushed and attempted to roll over. "Colby—"

His big palm landed between her shoulder blades and he pushed her flat to her stomach. "You sore?"

"A little."

"Well, I'll try to be gentle, but damn, I want you like this. All warm and sleepy and soft." Colby brushed his mouth over her ear. "Sometimes I wake up with morning wood, but never like this, like an iron bar. You do this to me, Channing. Only you." He ground his rock-hard cock into her hip. "Don't move. I'll be right back."

No matter what he thought, in no way was Channing relaxed now. She closed her eyes and inhaled. Colby's musk, the sweeter perfume of her arousal and the scent of last night's sexcapade lingered in the room and on the sheets and she was instantly aroused. She heard the crinkling of a condom package being ripped open.

The bed swayed and Colby slapped both her ass cheeks. Her immediate protest of "Hey!" was lost as he tongued the hot marks, then dragged that wicked, wet tongue up her spine.

"On your knees, darlin'. Stretch your arms above your head."

Channing kept her cheek pressed into the mattress as Colby hiked her hips higher and propped a folded pillow beneath her belly. He widened her base as his knees slid between her calves. His whole hand skated up and down her backbone in a sweetly soothing manner. Then she felt two fingers lightly stroking her pussy, from her clit to her vaginal opening before those slick digits slid in deep.

"It's okay, just lubing you up. I know you're a little tender. This will help get you ready for me because I ain't gonna wait. I want you right now."

The fingers left briefly and returned, colder, and even slipperier than before. Her sex bloomed and opened for him like a flower.

"God, you look pretty, all those creamy pink curves stretched out for me to feast on. You're about the sexiest damn thing I've ever seen, Chan."

This man redefined sweet talker.

Colby angled closer and kissed the sensitive spot behind her ear. "Ready?"

"Mmm. Yes."

"Good." His hipbones brushed her ass, and he spread her wide as the thick head of his cock poised at her entrance. Colby didn't ease in. He thrust to the hilt in one swift movement.

Channing gasped—not so much at the glint of pain bordering on perverse pleasure, but at the male need pulsing from him and how her body immediately softened further, eager to answer the mating call of his.

"I can't go slow. This will be hard and fast. Jesus. This hot, tight pussy makes me fucking crazy." His hands curled over her hips and he slammed into her like a man possessed.

His heavy balls slapped her clit, his pubic hair tickled her ass and she lost her mind in the heady reaction of his absolute desperation for her. It humbled and amazed her how quickly he'd amassed intimate knowledge of giving her exactly what she wanted without her having to play coy. Without her having to beg him. Without her having to worry about him saying no and thinking she was a perverted sex fiend.

Long, thorough stroke after long stroke of his rigid cock and her breathing became ragged. She teetered on the edge of climax, craving that rush as that elusive point dangled within reach. His right hand left her hip. She felt a coolness sweep over her rear hole and then a slight burning sensation as a thick finger breached the puckered opening.

"Oh, God."

"Do you like that?" His slick finger pumped in and out of her ass in time with his cock pounding into her cunt.

"Yes. I never thought this would feel—"

"Your body knows what it wants even if your brain is tellin' you it's wrong." A few more deft strokes then his finger slipped from that tight hole and she whimpered at the loss of fullness...until he returned with two fingers, stretching deep inside, making her muscles clamp down even harder around his marauding fingers.

"I can't wait to grind my cock in here. Jesus, you're so fucking tight. So fucking silky and warm. So fucking...perfect." Colby grunted, and a hoarse shout echoed in the room.

She felt his balls draw up as he came. The twitching end of his cock coupled with the rhythmic stroking of his fingers in her ass sent her rocketing to an orgasm so intense, when she sagged against the pillow tucked under her belly, that accidental brush of the stiff fabric across her swollen clit increased the strength of her climax tenfold. She screamed until she ran out of air.

His fingers slipped from her darkest recess, yet his cock stayed buried to the root. Colby collapsed on her back, pushing them both flat to the mattress. The solid weight of him should have crushed her, but as she had no breath left in her body, it didn't matter. She reveled in the realization he was as bowled over by the passion between them as she was.

Eventually, tender kisses tracked her sweat-covered hairline. "You okay?"

Channing grunted but couldn't find the energy to move.

Colby chuckled. "Darlin', you are amazingly sexy all the time, but in the morning especially. If we were home at the ranch I'd never get up on time to get my chores done."

She grunted again.

"You hungry? You want me to rustle up something to eat?"

"If I ever remember how to work my body again."

"I can work you over real good again—" his teeth sank into her shoulder blade, "—if you want."

That telltale twitching of his cock stirring within her spurred her to move. "Maybe later. Get off me, cowboy."

He placed a gentle kiss on the back of her head. "Thanks for lettin' me be rough and raunchy with you this morning. Most women hate it." Immediate silence. "Shit. Sorry. I've got a big mouth. Sometimes I'm not tactful at all, talkin' to you about other women, right after we've...never mind." He lifted his hips and pulled out of her body.

The room reverberated with tension.

Channing rolled over. Colby had a sheepish expression on his face, like he expected her to chew him out for his overzealous amorous behavior. Feeling oddly protective of him because of the vulnerability she'd glimpsed, she grabbed the back of his damp neck, bringing her mouth to his for a steamy kiss.

"I'm not like most women, Colby McKay. I like the raunchy side of you. I like the fact you don't treat me like a China doll and want me to show you my wild side, too."

He grinned shyly and smooched the tip of her nose. "You're sweeter'n ten pounds of sugar. Get dressed or I won't be responsible for what happens next. We're already runnin' late." Whistling off-key, he disappeared into the bathroom.

ঙ্গ

Voices drifted out the back end of the horse trailer.

"No. There ain't nothin' wrong with this rope. Leave it be."

"Come on, Edgard, it's a frayed piece of crap. Either you toss it in the garbage or I will."

"This rope is not what's causing the problems, *amigo*."

"What the fuck is that supposed to mean? You think it's *my* fault that you can't get a bead on anything that moves faster than my crippled-up grandma?"

"I'm going to make you pay for that, Trev. One way or another, easy or hard—"

Channing cleared her throat. "Knock knock."

Silence.

"I know you guys are in here, I heard you arguing. Hell, everyone in Limon heard you arguing. Am I interrupting something?"

"Yes," Edgard said at the same time Trev said, "No."

"Oh, well...I won't be long. I just need to eat some breakfast and then I'll get out of your hair and let you get back to it."

The trailer shook as Trevor stomped out. Another round of heated words was exchanged outside, followed by harsh silence.

Edgard climbed into the living quarters and watched Channing dump Raisin Bran into a bowl and pour milk over it.

She looked up at him and smiled warily. Good god. He was magnificent even when he scowled. "Want some?"

"Sure. If it is no trouble."

"Not at all." She slid the bowl at him and motioned for him to sit at the dinette. And she sat across from him and dug in.

"I didn't hear Trevor come back to the room last night. Were you guys beating the shit out of each other or something?"

Edgard's spoon froze halfway to his mouth. "No. Why would you say that?"

"Seems like you guys are always fighting."

He shrugged and resumed eating. "It goes with the territory. Especially when things aren't going well."

"Meaning?"

"We've lost our rhythm and we've dropped in the standings in the last two weeks. No money. Tempers are short."

"I'm sorry."

"It happens."

Channing stirred her cereal, half-tempted to abandon it and this awkward conversation.

Edgard sighed. "What?"

She met his dark gaze. "You don't want me here, do you?"

A heavy pause weighted the air as he considered his answer. "What makes you think that?"

"Besides the fact I'm a sure thing who's supposed to fill your every forbidden fantasy and you haven't so much as held my hand?"

He smiled but it didn't reach his coal black eyes. "Not exactly the shy, retiring type, are you?"

If he only knew she usually cowered in the corner. "Am I too forward? Is that why you don't like me?"

"Channing, I like you fine. I've just got a lot on my mind that has nothing to do with you, okay?"

"Okay. So I don't disgust you?"

"No."

"I thought Colby said you three shared everything."

"Not everything."

"But even if I'm...not your type and you're not attracted to me or whatever, I'd...oh forget it."

He sighed again. "No. Spit it out."

"I'd still like to be your friend, because like it or not, you're stuck with me for the next week."

A ghost of a gentle smile. "You clicked with Colby pretty fast, didn't you?"

"Yes." She wanted to ask him why he didn't mention she'd also clicked with Trevor—with everyone besides him.

Edgard snagged her hand and gave her knuckles a quick kiss. "No wonder Colby calls you *shug*, you are very sweet."

She blushed.

"Are you coming to the performances this afternoon?"

"I planned to. Why?"

"I'm hoping that now that you're traveling with us, our luck will change." He stood, went to the sink and rinsed his bowl and spoon. "I'll see you later."

Channing stared after him for the longest time, not entirely understanding what had happened, or if anything had changed.

Chapter Six

The afternoon was scorching hot in the rodeo stands. Channing had coated her bare arms with sunscreen and was glad her lightweight and light-colored cowboy hat deflected the worst of the sun's rays and allowed the slightest breeze through the finely woven straw to cool her head.

She sipped her iced tea and shifted, yanking down her yellow skirt. Her legs stuck to the wool blanket she sat on, but it was better than the back of her thighs getting seared like raw steaks by the metal bleacher seats.

Edgard, Trevor and Colby had paid their entry fees, pinned their numbers to their backs and gone off to prepare to rodeo, leaving her free to explore the grounds before the action started. Since she didn't know any of the wives or girlfriends on the circuit, she had no choice but to sit by herself.

The rodeo announcer's voice boomed from the loudspeakers. "Next up in saddle bronc riding is Colby McKay, the Wyoming cowboy from Sundance. Colby is currently ranked eighth in saddle bronc riding competition in the Mountain and Plains Circuit, with 8,712 cumulative points. He's also in the number two position this week in the All-Around standings. Ooh, and looky here, rodeo fans, Colby's draw today is the three-year-old named Elway, a bronc from the Sutliff Rodeo Stock Company out of Livingston, Colorado."

Channing focused the binoculars on the chutes across the arena. The gatekeeper waited in front of the metal gate, rope in hand, watching for Colby's signal. From this distance the only thing she could see was the top of Colby's brown cowboy hat. Then his free arm flew up, the gate opened and out he came, holding on for dear life as Elway tried like hell to buck him off.

But Colby was beautiful, sheer poetry in motion as he dipped and glided with every hop and bounce of the horse. His feet spurring, the red metallic fringe on his chaps fluttering. His counter movements were synchronized, almost as if he sensed what direction Elway planned to go before the horse himself even knew.

Colby stayed on the full eight seconds. He untied his hand and launched himself onto the pickup man's horse, just as smooth as if he'd done it a million times.

Not a million, but thousands, and that probably wasn't much of an exaggeration. The crowd applauded. Colby waved his hat in acknowledgment as he sauntered back to the holding pens, squinting at the scoreboard, studying his ride on the big screen.

Channing held her breath and waited for the score—half for the horse's performance, half for the rider's. Finally a red 78 flashed to another smattering of applause and the next rider was announced.

The score put Colby in second place. As he was the sixth rider out of twenty, there was a good chance he'd get knocked down even farther in the standings. With this being a one-day rodeo, he had no chance to return tomorrow for a second go-round and the short go directly after that. Only the top five finished in the money.

She knew he wouldn't dwell on his performance. Unlike the other competitors, he wasn't finished with his events. He still had to compete in tie-down roping and bull riding. Trevor and Edgard both competed in tie-down roping but not bull riding.

Although bull riding tended to be the most exciting part of rodeo, it was also the most dangerous. And she remembered that like lots of other older competitors, Colby hadn't embraced the facemask equipment so many of the younger riders used. He wore the protective vest that would shield him from getting gored by the bull's horns, but he refused to put his face in a cage.

Why hadn't the potential dangers bothered her when she watched Jared ride?

She dug out her notebook and jotted down her observations as she waited through the other events, bareback riding, steer wrestling—also known as *bulldogging*—and the event Trevor and Edgard were entered in, team roping.

Trevor was the header, which meant he was out of the gate first, and his job was to rope the steer either around the horns or around the neck, while Edgard's job was to catch the steer's feet in his rope. If they were successful and caught the steer properly, then they had to face each other on their respective horses and the steer had to stay on the ground for the judge's call.

Team roping was tricky. If the horse took off before the steer broke the barrier, then they received no score. Not to mention the difficulties in the speed of the various steers and the ability to hook both horns and feet—without missing.

Channing leaned forward when she saw Trevor and Edgard in the holding pens, working their ropes, circling the area on their individual quarter horses. Finally, it was their turn.

The rodeo announcer said, "Next up, Edgard Mancuso and Trevor Glanzer. Trevor is currently twelfth in the standings, down from his high point of third last month. These guys have had a run of bad luck lately. Let's hope this steer from Martinson Brothers out of Rapid City gives them an opportunity to win some money. Both these cowboys are the real deal folks. Edgard's family owns a large cattle operation in his native Brazil, and everyone recognizes the name Glanzer. Trevor's father, Tater, was world champion header twenty years ago. And…they're off!"

Trevor's horse, Chess, put on a burst of speed as the rope circled above Trevor's head. He hooked one horn and, lickety-split, Edgard caught the back legs and the steer went down. The crowd cheered.

But the scoreboard flashed NO SCORE because Trevor had broken the barrier. Channing saw the disappointment and frustration on both their faces as they waved stained work gloves to the crowd and followed the pickup men through the back gate and around the outside of the arena.

Trevor and Edgard were out of the money again. It'd be interesting to see what their mood would be like tonight. They were sniping at each other before they'd lost.

Colby was first up in the tie-down roping.

Again the announcer rattled off Colby's stats. She wondered if he listened or if his focus was solely on the job at hand.

Channing remembered overhearing Colby being interviewed by a cub newspaper reporter in one of the first small towns they'd visited on the circuit. How he'd told the woman the reason he competed in three events, rather than two as most All-Around Cowboy contenders preferred, was because his real job—ranching—demanded he could accurately rope runaway steers and have no problems riding a variety of horses, which was why he picked saddle bronc and tie-down roping as his main events.

Then when she'd asked why he'd take a chance on bull riding, he'd grinned and said bull riding was just for fun, because in real life on the ranch no one was stupid enough to tangle with a bull.

Channing was closer to the action at this end of the arena and didn't need the binoculars. The black calf cleared the barrier and Colby's horse, King, hunkered down, dirt clods busting beneath the flying hooves. With his rope circling the air, Colby caught the calf. He launched himself off the horse with his piggin' string clamped between his teeth, knocked the calf to the ground, and flipped him on his side. The rope in his hands was a blur as he tied and then threw his hands in the air. The clock stopped.

King backed up, pulling the rope taut as Colby stood, and heaved himself back in the saddle, waiting the requisite six seconds so the judges could verify the tie held.

The calf squirmed but stayed down. The time read 4.7 seconds. The crowd whooped and hollered, and Colby waved as he reined King around and out of the arena.

Channing flipped open her program and wrote the times down next to the rest of the competitors. So far, Colby's time held the top spot. She knew that almost more important than the money was the points accumulation, which would keep his position in the All-Around race. Edgard's time was 8.7 and Trevor ended up with no score.

Barrel racing was the next event. She recognized some of the women. Cowboys loved real cowgirls, especially when they looked like rodeo queens but could ride and rope as well as a man. Channing also knew that gossip about who was riding who outside the arena ran rampant on the circuit. Few of the participants in the "wholesome family values" events of pro rodeo were squeaky clean. Musical horse trailers seemed to be the game of choice to stave off boredom.

As Tara Reynolds, reigning barrel racing circuit champ, cemented her first place in the standings by an 11.9 run, Channing tried to recall whether she'd heard gossip about Colby or Trevor taking Tara and her tiara for a tumble.

Finally, the bull fighters came out and loud rock music blared from the speakers. The excitement of the crowd increased, beer vendors zipped through the stands more frequently. And from where she sat, it appeared more guys hung out by the chutes.

The bulls shut out the first ten competitors. Colby was up and he'd drawn Black Bart, a nasty bull, who'd gone unridden in the last seventeen outs. Channing remembered Jared getting tossed on his head right out of the gate when he'd tried to ride Black Bart. She leaned closer, not realizing she was chewing her lip until she tasted blood.

She had to calm down. The rodeo season was long and injuries were plenty. She had to trust Colby knew what he was doing.

Trevor was behind the chute helping Colby get situated on the bull, holding the bullrope while Colby rosined up his glove. Trevor's foot came over the barrier and he pressed down on the bull's hind end in an effort to get him to stand up. It must've worked because Colby's free arm gripped the metal bar. A couple of solid shifts on the bull's back, he nodded his head rapidly at the gate man and the gate flew open.

Man and bull burst out in a cloud of dust. Black Bart spun hard to the left, then countered with a spin to the right. Colby bumped along, his free arm high above him, but on the last switchback, Black Bart's hips canted to the right and Colby slid over sideways, catching air as he sailed from the bull's back.

He hit the ground hard on his shoulder, spun around to his feet to see where the bull was, and raced pell-mell to the fence as Black Bart charged him, weaving around the bull fighters, horns down, aiming for Colby.

But realizing his prey was gone, Black Bart stopped abruptly. His balls and jowls shook with anger and long streams of white snot flew from his nose as he trotted over to the livestock pen.

Colby reached out for his bullrope and watched his ride on the big screen. The clock had stopped at 5.2 seconds. He climbed over the railing and disappeared.

She wondered if he was commiserating with other riders who'd eaten dirt. Was he having his shoulder checked out in the medical tent?

Now they just had to wait for the payouts. Then they'd be on the road headed to Greeley for the two-day event there.

Channing didn't know if she was supposed to head back to the horse trailer or wait in the stands. Jared had never wanted her around his rodeo pals or sponsors, now she knew why.

But things were different with Colby and Trevor at least. Except the devil on her shoulder whispered maybe they'd prefer she'd stay in the background, too. After all, she was scarcely above buckle-bunny status.

As she debated, Cash Big Crow spotted her and lumbered up to where she stood.

"*Hoka hey.* How come you're up here by yourself, pretty lady?"

She laughed. "Where else am I supposed to be? What are you doing?"

"Nothing much."

"Nice ride, by the way. Did you finish in the money?"

He scratched his head. “I think so, that’s why I’m hangin’ around.” He peered over her shoulder to the commotion in the parking lot behind her. “You know who Gemma Jansen is?” Channing nodded. “Have you seen her lately?”

“Yesterday. She was headed home.”

Cash’s eyes narrowed. “Home? Why?”

“She said something about her foreman not doing his job at her place. Then I think she planned on taking bucking horses to Cody before she headed to Valentine.”

“Alone? Goddamn her. That woman’s got no business travelin’ all over half the damn country by herself—”

“Unlike you. You’re perfectly entitled to do whatever the hell you want, right?”

He grinned guiltily. “Sorry. I really ain’t a chauvinist. It’s just she’s so damn stubborn she won’t ask for help from nobody.”

“Channing!”

She whirled around and saw Trevor hanging on the fence.

“Colby’s been lookin’ everywhere for you. Time to go, girl.”

“Be right there.” She smiled at Cash. “See you in Greeley.”

ঔঌ

Colby paced back and forth. Grumbling to himself. Would it be too goddamn much for her to be around when he needed her?

“Colby? What’s wrong?”

He slowed his angry breathing as he stalked to where Channing had paused by the contestants’ entry gate.

“You have a pained look on your face. Are you hurt?”

"No. Where the hell have you been?"

She frowned. "In the stands watching the rodeo."

"Just off enjoyin' yourself?"

"Yes. Why? Isn't that what I'm supposed to do?"

"No."

"No? What's the matter with you?"

Colby grabbed her arm and bent down until they were nose to nose. "Why weren't you in the spectator stands with the other wives and girlfriends *enjoyin'* the rodeo from there?"

"What? Because I-I—"

"I searched for you after every goddamned event. You should've been there. That's where I expect to see you from now on, do you understand?"

Channing threw off his hand. "Then maybe you should've given me a ticket, because I sat by myself on the other side of the arena like I always do."

"Always?"

"Yeah, always. What's the big deal?"

"The big deal is me wonderin' why don't you want to sit where you're supposed—"

"Supposed to what?" She speared a finger into his chest. "You took off and left me the minute we hit the check-in booth. I've never been here. I've never been to any rodeo with you, remember? What was I supposed to do? Stand around like some floozy and wait for you to make up your mind on whether I was good enough—"

"Stop talkin' right now."

"No. You don't get to order me around when you abandoned me. I don't know why the hell I'm surprised that you don't want people to know you're with me."

He was too pissed off to speak.

She blithely continued, "I'm used to being the cause of embarrassment. I am aware I rank well below the rest of the more knowledgeable buckle bunnies trailing after you like lovesick calves—"

"I'm warnin' you, Channing, stop chatterin' like a goddamn magpie and listen up right now. Didn't Jared—"

"Jared was just as worried about what people might think of us being together as you are, cowboy. So, despite your claims to the contrary, you're more alike than you know."

Shit. Colby stepped back and squeezed his eyes shut. He'd forgotten Jared had kept Channing sequestered so no one blabbed to her about his wife. Therefore, Channing wouldn't have known a certain amount of seats were set aside at every performance for family and friends. When he reopened his eyes, she was stomping off.

"Channing, come back here."

"No," she tossed off over her shoulder.

"I'm warnin' you, girl, you don't want to make me mad."

"Tough shit, tough guy. Suck it up and walk it off."

People around them stopped and stared, nudged each other and chuckled, giving Colby a wide berth.

"Last chance," he yelled.

Channing flipped him the bird without turning around. In fact, she ran away from him like her boot heels were smoking.

He was going to paddle that sassy little ass but good.

"Too bad you didn't bring your piggin' string. She sure is fit to be tied. You tryin' to keep her on a short rope or something?"

"Shut the fuck up, Cash."

"What's the problem?"

"None of your goddamn business."

"Trouble in paradise already? Is this about why you're makin' her sit by herself instead of in the VIP stand?"

"I didn't make her do nothin'."

"Really? I saw her up there, all alone, lookin' sad and lost, poor thing."

Colby clenched his teeth together.

"I never pegged you for that kind of guy."

"What kind of guy?"

"The kind who's afraid what snotty comments the other fellas' womenfolk might say to her about travelin' with all three of you."

"Hell no, I could give a shit about that."

"Then what's goin' on?"

"What I do, or don't do, to her or for her, ain't your concern. She knows—"

"No, she don't know nothin' about behind-the-scenes rodeo protocol for contestants and their families, and that, my friend, *is* your fault. After being treated like Jared's dirty little secret, maybe you oughta make it clear you don't expect to treat her the same way, eh?" Cash sauntered off as regal as a Lakota elder.

Shit. Colby kicked a clod of dirt. Hard.

Colby wended through the crowd, dodging kids, horseshit and the rhinestone sparkle of low-cut blouses as several buckle bunnies vied for his attention. A stolid woman and small boy all but tripped him to get him to stop. "Hey, are you Colby McKay?" the youngster asked.

"Yep."

"Oh wow, can I get your autograph? Please?"

"Sure thing." He hunkered down and snagged the program from the boy's grubby little hand along with the proffered pen. "Who do I make this out to?"

"Mitchell."

"You a big rodeo fan, Mitchell?"

He nodded somberly. "Some day I'm gonna be the number one All-Around Cowboy, too."

Colby didn't have the heart to tell the kid he was currently stuck in the number two position. Again. "Good plan. Good luck. See you on the circuit someday." Colby smiled and patted him on the top of his blond head. When he looked around for Channing, he wasn't surprised she was long gone.

Damn fool woman.

Didn't want people to know they were together. Embarrassed by her. Right. The little hellcat had even flipped him off! He seethed and knew there was only one way to handle this.

That woman was in a whole mess of trouble. He'd show her exactly how he dealt with breaking in headstrong fillies.

Chapter Seven

Edgard was slumped against the wheel well on the right side of the horse trailer, eating sunflower seeds. He straightened up when he saw Colby barreling toward him.

"Is she in there?" Colby snapped.

"Yeah. So is Trevor. She seemed pretty upset. What did you do to her?"

"Nothin' compared to what I'm *gonna* do to her."

Laconic Edgard vanished and he shifted lightning fast to block Colby's access to the living quarters.

"Move it, Ed, unless you plan on helpin' with Channing's punishment."

His left eyebrow winged up at the word *punishment*. "Maybe, *amigo*, you should walk it off and let Trevor calm her down first before you go busting in there like an angry bull."

"The fuck I will. Move."

"No."

"You're startin' to piss me off, Mancuso."

"Yeah? Well, you know what? I don't like the look in your eye, McKay."

"So?"

"So, I think I will help you after all, just to make sure you don't get carried away."

"Me?"

"Yeah, *you.* Miz Channing is a lot more delicate than you give her credit for and sometimes your punishments are just plain mean. And maybe she ain't the only one who oughta be reprimanded." Edgard spun and flung open the door.

Stung by the truth, Colby muttered, "Great," and followed Edgard inside the dark trailer.

Channing's arms were folded over her chest and her haughty little butt rested against the kitchen sink. She jumped when Colby slammed and locked the door behind him.

"What's going on?" Trevor asked.

"Strip," Colby said to Channing.

"What?"

"I said strip. Now. Don't make me tell you again. You really don't want to add another punishment to the one you've already earned, do you darlin'?"

She swallowed hard but the look in her golden eyes was decidedly defiant. "Punishment?"

"What in the hell are you talkin' about, Colby?" Trevor demanded.

Colby pointed at Channing. "Not only does Little Miss think we're embarrassed to be seen with her, when I tried to talk to her outside the gates, she got smart with me and stormed off. So, since she don't want to talk, the time for talkin' is over. Start strippin'."

"Channing, girl, you didn't do that, did you?"

She nodded warily at Trevor.

Trevor stood and stretched. "Ah, this is gonna be an interestin' afternoon. What do you want me to do?"

"Find the ropes and that set of clamps." Colby flashed his teeth at her. "Lube would be good, too."

"You're helping him?" Channing said to Trevor.

"Yep. We ain't gonna listen to nobody talkin' you down, least of all you doin' it to yourself. And when Colby or I or Edgard want to talk to you, it'd be in your best interest to listen up. You'll learn there will be consequences. You heard him. Strip." Hiding the devilish twinkle in his eye, Trevor unlocked the door separating the living quarters from the horse stalls, and rummaged around in the tack closet.

She was frozen in place.

Colby watched and waited for her reaction.

"But—"

"No buts. You said you'd do whatever we wanted. That means you don't get to ask questions. Or argue, especially when you've been bad."

Edgard sidled in front of her and gently stroked her cheek. "Listen to me and let me help."

"You, too? But I thought you didn't want—"

"It is not for you to question what I want. It is for you to do as you're told."

Colby frowned at Edgard's surprising response.

"But I'm scared."

"Sweet thing, none of us would ever really hurt you. But you have to understand there is a price for insolence. No backtalk. Ever. That don't mean you can't speak your mind, but you don't get to dress us down in public. Ever." Edgard stroked her neck, sweetly, like they'd been lovers for years, and nuzzled her temple. "Take off your clothes. I'm sayin' this for your own good and as your friend."

Her shaking hands fumbled with the button before the swishy skirt fell to the floor. The T-shirt was next, leaving Channing clad only in a bra and panties.

Colby's cock grew impossibly harder at her exposed creamy skin and her hesitation. "Leave the boots on," he said gruffly. "Everything else, off."

She wouldn't meet his gaze as she shimmied the lemon yellow panties down her taut thighs and whisked off the matching bra.

"Beautiful." Colby ambled to stand beside her, squeezing his hands in fists to keep from touching her. "We're gonna condition you. So you'll know why it pisses me off that you'd ever be foolish enough to think you'd embarrass me. Or any of us. Why you never, ever get to talk to me that way in public again." *Even if I sort of deserved it.* He called over his shoulder, "Trev? Where are those goddamn ropes?"

"Right here. We lost the last set of clamps, remember?"

"Looks like we'll be makin' a trip to the adult toy store soon." He withheld a wicked smile at Channing's wide-eyed stare. "Tie her hands behind her back with that one; give the other one to me." He smacked it on his palm twice and Channing jumped.

Trevor nodded and twirled her around. Once he finished securing her, Colby said, "Ed, grab the mirror out of the bathroom." He led Channing to the square dining table and stretched her across the surface, belly down.

"This is cold!"

Colby couldn't help but shape his hands over her silky flesh, drawing a shudder and a fresh set of goose bumps across her soft skin. "You'll get used to it."

When Edgard returned with the mirror, Colby tilted it against the plaid seat cushion so Channing could see the smooth line of her back and the intriguing curve of her ass.

“What are you doing?”

“Hush, or I’ll gag you. Watch the mirror. If we see you lookin’ anywhere else, the punishment starts over from the beginning, understand?”

She nodded.

Using the soft, frayed end of the old cotton rope, Colby swished it across her shoulder blades. He flicked it over the top of her arms. The ticklish bend of her torso. Trailed it up and down her spine softly, like a feather. He crisscrossed it over her legs. He performed the caress a dozen times, watching her squirm more thoroughly with every pass. Smelling her excitement with each pass.

Then he snapped his wrist and whipped the rope against her ass, each cheek, ten times in rapid succession.

Channing gasped.

He angled his face near her head. “Listen up. I’m not embarrassed by you.”

She didn’t answer.

Colby flicked the rope on each cheek again. “Repeat it back to me.”

“You’re not embarrassed by me.”

“Good.” He dragged the silky end of the rope down her butt crack. “Say: I want you around.”

She hesitated.

Three whips this time. Her cheeks flexed. “I want you around. Say it.”

“You want me around.”

"You're learnin'. Last thing. You wanna dress me down, do it in private." Four sharp cracks.

Channing groaned.

"Say no backtalk."

"No backtalk."

"See? That ain't so bad." Colby whispered in her ear, "Tell me the truth. Don't you like that little spark of pain with your pleasure?" He added five more strokes to each cheek.

Her gaze darted to the mirror and the stripes that'd bloomed on her flesh. Not ugly raised welts, just pink strips, which contrasted with her pearly white skin.

"Now, isn't that pretty?" he murmured, skimming his rough palm over the quivering globes of her butt. "Warm. Soft."

She whimpered.

"Ah, shug, I told you that you wouldn't be cold for long. You feelin' the heat yet?"

A tiny nod.

"You've been a good girl, takin' your licks with no complaints. Let me take the sting away." Colby slid her body down the table until the tips of her pointy-toed turquoise boots hit the carpet. "Spread your legs wide. I wanna see if your pussy is the same color as those lovely stripes on your ass."

"What do you want me to do?" Trevor asked.

"Get that mirror to the right angle and make sure she watches everything I'm doing to her." Colby dropped to his knees. He cupped her butt cheeks and looked his fill. The blood-darkened pink of the hood covering her clit peeked out from between her ruby-red pussy lips. The lighter salmon color of the opening to her cunt gave way to mauve of her puckered rosette. He closed his eyes briefly and inhaled the heady aroma of her excitement.

Then Colby buried his face into the paradise between her soft thighs. Licking her sweet syrup, sucking her inflamed clit, losing himself and his anger in her taste and her feminine heat. He made soft humming noises against that little throbbing nub until she began to grind that warm wetness into his face.

When he sensed the change in her breathing and the sudden tension in her muscles, he removed his mouth and pulled back, leaving her panting for more, hanging on the cusp of an explosion.

Their eyes met in the mirror. "I want you, Chan. I want you bad. I always want you. Say it back to me."

"You want me bad. Please—"

He growled and smacked her ass. "Say it right this time."

"You want me. You want me bad. You always want me."

"Goddamn right. Don't forget it." Without looking away from her, he said, "Edgard. Drop your pants and move to the head of the table."

Clank clank echoed as Edgard freed the metal catch on his big belt buckle. Then the tinny sound of a zipper releasing and the rustle of denim, followed by muffled footsteps filled the stillness.

To Edgard, Colby said, "Make sure she knows you want her, too."

"But—"

"Do it," Colby hissed. "Suck him off, Channing. Make it good. Make me wish it was my dick deep in your mouth."

She blinked at him twice before focusing on Edgard.

Edgard rubbed the weeping end of his cock over her lips, murmuring to her, threading her curly hair through his fingers. She opened and swallowed him in increments. Finally, Edgard's rosy meat disappeared completely between Channing's full lips, a second later that wet cock slid back out.

She was so fucking sexy Colby found it hard to breathe.

Edgard's hips picked up a continual rhythm. He whispered foreign words to her, which heightened the intimacy of her moist sucking sounds and the stuttered male breathing clouding the small space.

Jesus. Colby didn't want to watch. He wanted to participate. More than anything he wanted to go back and fix things so they returned to the way they were this morning. He sensed Trevor behind him, waiting for further instructions. Trevor knew the score, knew it was Colby's show.

"Give it to her however she wants it, Trev. Just make it good for her, okay?" Colby adjusted his iron erection and turned for the door.

"What about you?"

"I'll get the horses ready to load. We need to leave soon."

Channing stopped and cranked her head around. "Colby?"

Colby locked his gaze to hers. "This is my punishment, because I want you like crazy, darlin', and I'm walkin' away with my cock tucked between my legs. I'm sorry. I never should've left you to fend for yourself, especially after the way Jared treated you. The last thing I am is embarrassed that you're with me. I promise it won't happen again. Have fun with these boys. Let them show you how worthy you are. I'll see you later." The door clicked shut behind him.

Half an hour later his hard-on still hadn't deflated. It was going to be a long-ass drive to Greeley.

Chapter Eight

Colby drove. Trevor navigated. The traffic around Denver was a nasty snarl, so the mood inside the cab was subdued.

They pulled into another family-type "motor inn" and, immediately, Colby hopped out to take care of the horses. Edgard helped, leaving Channing and Trevor to check in. As soon as they had the keys, Trevor left her, too.

Once she'd unpacked, Channing realized all of her clothes were dirty and she set off in search of a laundry room. While the loads washed, she wrote in her journal, pouring out her frustration. With Colby. With Trevor. With Edgard. But mostly with Colby and his disappearing act today.

Yeah, she'd been furious with him for getting pissed off at her for something that wasn't her fault. Then demanding her obedience. After he'd had her submission and had spanked her ass, licked her sex like a starving man, consequently turning her into a trembling pile of fuck-me-now pleading whimpers, he'd walked away. Walked away!

True, he hadn't exactly left her high and dry. Trevor had fucked her thoroughly, making sure she came twice before he gave into his own needs. But it'd been just plain weird to give Edgard a blowjob. First off, he wasn't circumcised. Second, he didn't come in her mouth, but in his own hand. She got the feeling he was disappointed in her performance. Like he expected...better. Like he couldn't wait for it to be over.

Yeah. That'd give a girl a complex.

Oh sure, he'd whispered sweet nothings in her ear in that sexy Portuguese accent while Trevor nailed her from behind. But Edgard hadn't kissed her. Or touched her body anywhere besides her face. Nor did he make a big deal about her breasts—most men went crazy kissing and fondling, sucking and biting her nipples. Since her hands had been bound, why hadn't he helped Trevor get her off faster by rubbing her clit? She knew if Colby had been in the room, his hands, his mouth, his cock—his undivided attention would've been all over her.

The rest of the interlude had scarcely lasted twenty minutes. Yeah, she'd enjoyed herself, and Trevor was a caring lover. But the truth was, she'd missed Colby.

What kind of idiot did that make her? They'd only been together two days and she'd already attached herself to him like one of those pesky sticky burrs that get caught up in horses' tails.

And yet, she knew in her heart Colby had been mortified by his own behavior. Not the little whipping he'd given her, but letting her sit alone. Not knowing that she hadn't known any better and blaming himself.

The man was unbelievably sweet when he wasn't being a pain in the ass.

The two loads spun and she tossed them in the dryer along with a perfumed dryer sheet. As she sat at the chipped Formica table, the words on the paper changed from angry to speculative—instead of writing about herself, she wrote about him. Them. The folks she'd come across in her travels, salt-of-the-earth types, so far removed from the salty-tongued people she'd grown up around.

Her mind drifted to a series of vignettes she'd tucked away in her subconscious. An older couple she'd seen in the beer line sneaking foamy kisses. A cowgirl hiding her tears as she currycombed and talked to her horse. The bruises on a youngster's arm as he practiced bulldogging on his border collie. The broken look on a young cowboy's face as he looked longingly at the steel gate separating the contestants from the wannabes.

Real life. Real people. Channing realized this sabbatical wasn't about getting away from her parents' expectations, acting the rebel, hiding for a time and then (grudgingly) accepting her destiny. This trip would be the defining point in her life.

The dryer buzzed, jarring her from her reverie. She looked around and smiled. Never in a million years would she have believed she'd experience a catharsis in a dingy laundry room in Colorado.

She folded her clothes and repacked them in her small rolling suitcase and dragged it back to the empty room. Ten minutes later she was still bored. No one told her she had to sit and wait for the trio to return. She was perfectly capable of finding her own entertainment.

After a quick fix of her hair and makeup, Channing ventured into the warm night. Traffic whooshed by. Instead of the heavy fumes of exhaust, she smelled pine. Muffled children's shrieks ricocheted from the outdoor pool behind the motel office. Up the road on the left she spied a couple of fast food places...and the neon sign of a bucking bronc boasting an honest-to-God, Western honky-tonk.

Yee-haw. No brainer which direction she headed.

ଔଓଔଓ

George Strait blared from the speakers. Pitchers of beer were refilled almost as quickly as they'd emptied. The bar was elbow to elbow with cowboys of all ages, shapes, and sizes. Hats of all colors. The cowgirls weren't as plentiful, so Channing had spent a goodly amount of time fending off advances. She began to question the wisdom in coming here alone.

She'd managed to choke down a burger—no fries—in between sips of a Fat Tire beer. The music was good, people were dancing up a storm and she probably would've been having a great time if she'd known a single soul. Instead, she was an outsider.

Alone again.

Channing crumpled her bar napkin and decided to call it a night. She spun her barstool around, right into Cash Big Crow.

His mouth creased into a grin that lit up his whole face. "Channing. I wondered if that was you. Where are the guys?"

"I don't know. They dumped me off at the room. When I became bored waiting for them I went looking for food and fun."

"Don't imagine Colby's gonna be too thrilled when he finds out you've been here alone."

She leaned forward and whispered, "So don't tell him."

Cash chuckled. "No comment, but I ain't got a death wish for keepin' something from him that he's got a right to know."

A right to know. She scowled.

"Any contests going on so's you can add to your trophy collection?"

"Nah. One trophy doesn't a collection make, Cash. Unlike you guys always chasing after that next shiny buckle and payout, I'll quit while I'm ahead."

"Good plan. So, you wanna take a spin on the dance floor? I promise I don't do none of that fancy footwork like you see at powwows."

Playfully, she tugged his braid. "Sure."

Cash was an excellent dancer and they laughed and two-stepped through four fast songs. Needing to catch her breath, Channing led him off the dance floor and he disappeared to answer his cell phone.

She rested against a wooden pillar and observed the action on the dance floor. One couple in matching Western shirts had to be in their eighties. She wondered how long they'd been together. If they had a big family, a ton of grandkids and great-grandkids. Or maybe they'd been high school sweethearts and after spending their lives married to other people they'd found each other again.

A scratchy male voice said, "You wanna dance?"

Channing didn't turn around. "No. But thank you for asking."

"Why not?"

The boozy breath got a whole lot closer.

"I just don't." *Take a hint, buddy.*

"Think you're too good for me? You can dance with that dirty injun, but not with me?"

Don't rise to his taunts. Just ignore him.

A gummy hand circled her upper arm and jerked her sideways. Channing tried to pull away but didn't have much leverage against his strength. Too bad she didn't have her trophy, she could just clock him a good one.

"Maybe we oughta have our own private party. Outside. I got a big quad cab. The seats are plenty soft."

She fought the rising panic. There were lots of people in here. Someone would notice this beast strong-arming her out the door, wouldn't they? Surely, Cash would be back soon. Channing forced herself to look at the asshole harassing her, rather than cowering.

The guy's smile was as greasy as his hair. His eyes were as hard and mean as his grip. "Maybe I oughtn't ask. Maybe I oughta just take what I want." His grimy, crooked finger slid down the center of her body, between her breasts to her belly button. "I think you'd like that."

She shuddered with revulsion.

"Or maybe you oughta get your goddamn hand offa her before I rip it clean off your body."

The greasy guy tipped his head back and glared at Colby from beneath the rim of his filthy baseball cap. "I saw her first. Find your own bunny, sheep boy."

"Get your fucking hand off her right now. I ain't askin', I'm tellin' you and I won't say it again."

Recognizing the menace in Colby's tone, the man's hand dropped like a rock. "Have at her. We'll see how damn tough you are when her injun boyfriend comes back and gut stabs you." He sneered and staggered away.

Channing launched herself at Colby, hiding her face in the warm curve of his neck.

"Hey, now, darlin', what's this? You okay?"

She shook her head.

He sucked in a harsh breath. "Where did that slimy fucker touch you? I'll kill him."

Again she shook her head.

He cupped her face in his hands and tilted her face toward his. "What then?"

"Oh God, I'm so glad you're here. It was stupid of me to come by myself but I was bored and lonely and hungry and you were mad at me and I know I'm supposed to be a tough and independent woman—"

Instantly, Colby's mouth covered hers. His kiss was a mixture of comfort and sweetness and protection. When he broke away, Channing felt tears pooling in her eyes.

"I'm sorry for today. I just don't know what I'm doing half the time. I'm just not a very good cowgirl. I didn't mean to make you mad."

"Ssh. We'll figure it out. Come on. Let me hold you until you calm down some." He maneuvered her onto the dance floor, twined her body around his to his liking and they swayed to the strains of "Love Can Build a Bridge".

"Better?" he murmured.

"Much. Thank you."

"No problem. I'm sorry about today too, shug."

She nodded and snuggled closer.

When the song ended he whispered, "Am I gonna have to kick someone else's ass tonight?"

"No, why?"

"Mr. Grabby said something about your injun boyfriend."

"Oh. He meant Cash. He was hanging out with me for awhile."

"Remind me to buy him a beer to thank him for lookin' out for my best girl."

Channing slanted back and studied Colby's face, hidden in the shadow of his cowboy hat and the dimness of the bar. "Am I really your best girl, Colby?"

"Goddamn right you are. You're my only girl."

"I don't like fighting with you."

"Same goes, darlin'."

Relief made her reckless and she ground her pelvis against his and discovered he was already hard. "Mmm. Maybe I need a refresher on the responsibilities of being your best girl. You can leave out the ass whooping this time."

"Channing—"

"I hated the way you left me today, and we didn't get anything resolved, especially after the way you put your mouth on me, I was so close to coming—"

Colby growled and clamped his hands on her gyrating hips. "Unless you want me to fuck you right here on the dance floor, knock it off, Chan. I'm not kiddin'."

"I'm not either. I missed you. Let me show you how much." She stretched to her tiptoes and brushed her lips across the pulse thrumming in his throat.

Tonight he was clean-shaven. A subtle piney scent teased her from beneath his starched shirt collar. She loved his smooth, square jaw and the way he considered her from beneath his ridiculously long dark eyelashes. She loved how his nostrils flared when he was aroused and the determined set to his mouth just before he kissed her. Everything about this sturdy, sexy, sweet man intoxicated her.

In between nibbling bites on his neck, she whispered, "I want to be with you, Colby. Running my hands over your skin as your rough flesh rubs against mine. Digging my heels into your tight little cowboy butt as you slide in and out of me. Looking in your gorgeous blue eyes as we're barely a breath apart. Tasting your kisses. Seeing those dimples wink at me when I do something that turns you on. Your sweat mingling with mine, how it lets our bodies slide together perfectly—"

"Enough," he said hoarsely. "Jesus, I only got so much willpower where you're concerned."

"And that's bad because?"

"Because I gotta cool down or it'll be over before it even starts. Damn, girl, I need a diversion."

Rather than towing her from the dance floor like a man on a mission to get her naked, he sauntered to the back corner of the bar by the dartboards and introduced her to some of the other guys she'd recognized from the circuit.

Normally she wasn't tongue-tied in social situations but tonight she felt shy. Especially when Colby plopped down and rather than finding her another chair, he pulled her on his lap. Her butt straddled his thigh, high, near his groin.

A beer bottle dangled from his fingers and if she wanted a drink, he held it up for her to sip. She swore the heat from his lips left an impression on the glass, and her own lips fit that dent perfectly.

His insistence on catering to her and showing every one of his pals they were together didn't make her feel like a piece of property. It made her feel special. Like she belonged.

Colby and the guys talked specifics on their rides and times and pros and cons of certain rough stock. Channing paid close attention because it fascinated her. The other women didn't seem to care. Because they'd heard the stories a million times? Or because the dirt on rodeoing full time was old hat to them?

Cash swung by to make sure she was all right before he bid the crew goodnight. The hardcore partiers—young, fresh-faced cowboys barely old enough to shave—gave Cash a rash of crap for being an old timer. Cash winked at her and took it in stride. Channing noticed Cash politely excused himself from the clutches of several buckle bunnies and left alone. What was up with that? Very few cowboys opted to say no to willing female flesh. Ever.

During the latter part of the conversation with a group of tie-down ropers, Colby started lightly stroking the exposed skin on her lower back where her shirt gapped from her skirt. An idle, fleeting touch, which should've been comforting but packed a powerful punch of sexual promise. Every lingering caress of his blunt, rough finger felt like he was stroking her pussy. Didn't take long for her panties to become soaked through.

Sighing, she wiggled closer to his chest.

He subtly inched away, only to continue battering her senses with the lazy assault.

Two can play this game, Channing thought. When she rhythmically clenched her butt cheeks together on Colby's thigh, he stood so quickly he almost knocked her on her ass.

Amidst catcalls and high-fives and suggestions for positions (spread-eagled across the horse trailer hitch?) they exited the rowdy bar.

Outside in the chilly mountain air, she shivered in her thin T-shirt. Colby didn't notice. They didn't talk at all until they cleared the main thoroughfare and were hidden in the shadows of the motel outbuildings. Pine trees towered above them. Moonlight was conspicuously absent.

Colby twirled Channing around, pressing her back against a metal shed as he devoured her with his lips, teeth, and tongue. His hands squeezed her breasts, his thumbs rasped over her hardened nipples, his knee separated her legs and he ground his brawny thigh into her crotch.

His lips slid to her ear. "I can't wait. I've wanted you all goddamn day. 'Bout killed me to walk away from you earlier, leavin' you with them. I can't think but for wantin' you. Right here, right now, Chan. Darlin', say yes. I'm dyin' to feel you around me."

"Yes. Yes. Please, Colby."

"Wrap your legs over my hips." He lifted her off the ground. "Have I told you how much I love this naughty little skirt? Mmm-mmm. Gotta 'preciate this easy access." His thumb swept the damp cotton of her panties, and then wiggled under the elastic leg band. Finding her already hot and slick, he groaned. "Shug, you heat up as fast as my woodstove. Makes me a crazy man that my touch makes you so wet."

Frantic from his sexy admission, Channing tugged on his championship belt buckle. The zipper slid down fine, but the skintight Wranglers were a problem. "Maybe you should start wearing skirts too, cowboy, because there ain't nothing easy about getting these jeans off. Did you borrow a pair from Dwight Yoakam? Damn, these things are really snug."

Colby laughed. "More snug in some places than others."

"It's not funny! Help me."

"Hang on." He set her down, hooked his thumbs in the belt loops and yanked. Stiff denim and the soft flannel boxers slid down to his knees. He picked her back up and practically threw her against the building.

That supremely hot, long male flesh teased her belly, trailing a bead of pre-come above her navel. She arched, wanting that hardness buried deep in her molten core. Now.

"Stop bouncin' around." Colby peeled her T-shirt and bra up and feasted on her nipples. "God, I love your tits." He sucked powerfully enough to leave a mark. "I want to spend hours—"

"Not hours and especially not now. Geez, afterward you can play with them until they fall off, but right now, fuck me, Colby. Just bend your knees and slide it in deep."

"You sure have a dirty mouth. It's one of the things I like best about you. Well, besides this."

He shifted his hips, hunkered down to a shallow squat, and just like that, he filled her in one mighty stroke. He caught her whimper in a tongue-tangling kiss.

The potent sensation of his cock thrusting inside her, sleek and thick and hot, made her forget her first foray into exhibitionism and everything besides satiating her sexual greed for this man.

He fucked her slowly, steadily and seamlessly. The jagged line of pubic hair above his cock abraded her clit, creating friction so profoundly delicious she couldn't concentrate on their kiss and she had to break it off.

Channing gasped for breath. Her mind spun and her head fell back against the cool metal, giving Colby total access to her neck. Like a heat-seeking missile, he zeroed in on the sweet spot; his moist lips left a tingle on her skin that burned hotter with every flicker of his scorching tongue. "Oh, God, like that, don't change a thing."

"Not even like this?" On the upstroke he canted his pelvis slightly and that extra concentrated pressure did the trick.

Her pussy clenched, that liquid pulsing began slowly, picked up speed like a runaway semi-truck, faster and faster and faster and then roared through her as she shattered.

Colby shifted again, grinding side to side as his teeth nipped the cord straining in her arched neck. "Come on, darlin', take me with you this time. Bear down, bring me deep as you can." As he pressed her knees out, she countered by squeezing her interior muscles.

"Goddamn. Yeah. That's it, Chan, hang tight." He didn't plunge faster, he just let her pulsing body coax the orgasm from him, pulling him deeper as they rocked together with sweet intensity.

Spent, a single satisfied shiver traveled through him and she felt it as deeply as if her own body had generated it. With his face nestled against her collarbone, his labored exhalations cooled her dampened skin.

He muttered, "Shit."

"What?"

"No condom."

"Oh shit," she said.

"Yeah." He angled back to look at her, apparently not caring that his hat was completely cockeyed. "Bad timing, huh?"

"Maybe not." She dipped her head and studied the alabaster snaps on his shirt.

"What?" He tipped her chin back up. "Darlin', what's wrong?"

"Nothing, really. Okay, I mean, there is something, it's not wrong per se. I have a confession to make and I don't want you to get mad at me."

His eyes narrowed. "What?"

She blurted, "I'm on the pill. You probably figured out I don't have much sexual experience and I've heard such horror stories about the STDs floating around out there that I wanted to make sure that I was always protected on all fronts. And damn. I'm sorry. After what happened with Jared, it just seemed safer to keep that information to myself."

"Ssh, darlin', stop babblin'. You don't have to be defensive with me, all right? Believe it or not, I understand. And if it'll ease your mind, I ain't been with a woman without wearing a condom since I was a green lad of about sixteen."

"So you're not mad?"

"Hell no."

Channing closed her eyes. "Good. Thank you."

"Can I ask you something?"

"Sure."

He shifted his hips, and a stream of moisture trickled down as he eased his spent cock out of her tender body. "When it's just you and me, can we skip the rubbers? 'Cause I sure like really feelin' you—just you—bare against me. There ain't nothing like it in the world."

She rubbed her cheek along his. "Sure. Speaking of you and me...where am I sleeping tonight?"

"Maybe the question oughta be where do you *want* to sleep tonight?"

"With you." She felt him smile against her cheek.

"Good answer. We're bunkin' in the horse trailer. You need anything from the motel room before we hit the hay?"

"Just my toothbrush now that we've got that pesky condom issue cleared up."

Colby chuckled and pressed a soft kiss on her forehead. "You sore?"

"A little."

"Mmm. Have we really only been together a coupla days?"

She stiffened up. "Yes. Why? Is time dragging?"

"No. On the road, time usually drags like an old dog. But it seems like you've always been around. I'm glad you're here, darlin'."

Probably not the first time he'd said such sugared words, but she'd take it since it was the first time anyone had ever uttered them to her. She grinned. "Me too, cowboy."

Chapter Nine

Colby was up early the next morning. As much as he wanted to start his day off with a bang and loll in bed with Channing, he knew she was sore. With good reason. He couldn't get enough of her.

He kissed her exposed nipple, grinning when she purred and snuggled into him. Damn distracting woman.

Fortified with free coffee from the motel lobby, he knocked on the door to the room. "It's Colby. Open the damn door."

A click of the slide latch moving and then Trevor swung open the door. "Hey. What's up?"

Colby peered over Trevor's bare shoulder at the rumpled bed. "Where's Edgard?"

"Shower. He'll be out in a minute. Before you ask, he's already checked on the horses this morning." Trevor yawned. "Where's Channing?"

"Sleepin' in the horse trailer."

"Is she okay?"

"She is now." Colby sipped his coffee and flopped in the chair by the windows. He told Trevor what'd gone down the previous night. "So, I don't want her goin' nowhere alone. She snuck off for that rowdy bar down the street and some greasy trucker was sniffin' around."

"You set him straight?"

"Damn right."

"Did you get everything straightened out with her?"

Colby grinned. "Damn right. Why you think she's sleepin' like a baby?"

Trevor high-fived him. "Goddamn, Colby. If there was a woman alive who could change my wicked ways and make me want to settle down, it'd be her."

"Amen, brother. But you'd have to fight me for her. So you understand why I want us all to keep a better eye on her."

"Keep an eye on who?" Edgard said as he cracked open the bathroom door.

Colby relayed the scene from the bar.

It was a typical morning. They talked rodeo. Advice was offered and taken. Aches and pains were detailed. When Trevor and Edgard began to argue strategy, Colby made his getaway. He refilled his coffee and stopped to chat with a couple of young bull riders from Utah before he went to check on Channing.

In the horse trailer, Channing sat slumped over the table, naked, listlessly stirring her half-eaten bowl of Raisin Bran.

He ran a hand down her bare back. "You okay?" he asked as he sprawled in the chair next to her.

"Tired. Damn virile man," she grumbled.

"Was that a complaint?"

"No. But when you said we should officially 'break in' the bed in this horse trailer, I didn't think you meant literally break the damn bed. I think I have bruises on my back and butt from the mattress springs."

"You bring out the beast in me, darlin', what can I say?"

"Say you have a coffee maker hidden around here someplace."

"Sorry. We don't."

Channing groaned.

"But I will let you have some of my coffee." He grabbed a Styrofoam cup and poured half his lukewarm coffee into it. Then he slid it next to her cereal bowl.

"Thank you." She downed it in one swallow. "The next time we pass a Wal-Mart I'm jumping out. I don't care if we've got the horse trailer fully loaded and the governor aboard. I'm buying a coffee pot and a jumbo can of coffee. I'm not fit for human company without my daily infusion of vitamin caffeine."

"Missin' Starbucks, are you?"

She shot him a dirty look. "Are you serious? Their coffee tastes like strained dog shit. Plus, who's dumb enough to pay four bucks for a cup of burned coffee?"

"Lots of folks, apparently. Them damn stores are everywhere. You'd think those people were drinkin' liquid gold, they're so obsessed with havin' that same brand every morning."

"Not me. They're a bunch of sheep. Give me a plain old cup of joe—black—and I'm a happy camper." Channing snickered. "Or I'd be happy if this camper had a Mr. Coffee."

Colby smoothed a wayward curl behind her ear. "We'll get you fixed up. I can't have my best girl cranky at the crack of dawn, now can I? You comin' to watch us today, Chan?"

"Of course. Provided you show me where I'm supposed to be sitting." A sneaky smile curled the corners of her mouth. "I'm not up for another round of punishment. My ass is still a little tender from that whippin' yesterday."

"Too bad," he muttered.

"Too bad what?"

"That your ass is tender."

"Why?"

He stared at her from beneath lowered lashes. "You know what I'm talkin' about."

"Was that a hint?"

"A very broad one." He stood, sorry he'd initiated the conversation so early. "Your ticket will be under my name at the box office. I've got to get goin'."

"Aren't you eating anything?"

"I never eat before I compete."

Channing smiled again. "Pity."

By the calculating look on her face, he knew she hadn't been thinking about him eating food. "You are one naughty girl, ain't ya?"

"You bring out the worst in me, but you don't think I'm nearly naughty enough."

An awkward moment filled the air.

"You wanna explain that, Chan?"

"Maybe."

He growled. "You're mighty close to earnin' another punishment. I think you liked gettin' your sweet butt whipped."

"Wrong. Well, sort of. But I tell you what, cowboy, I'll make you a real sweet deal."

Colby had to remind himself that she was still pretty shy about telling him what she wanted in bed. "I'm listenin'."

"I'll forget all about my sore ass, and let you have your wicked way with it tonight...if I see a ninety-point bull ride out of you today."

Holy shit. So much for her supposed shyness. "No foolin'?"

"Nope. But if you get anything less than a ninety, you have to trot your tight little cowboy behind right over to Wal-Mart, still wearing your sexy chaps, your back number and arena dirt, and buy me a coffee pot. A *nice* one."

"You got yourself a deal, darlin'."

"One other thing."

His gaze narrowed. It figured there'd be conditions.

"If this does come to pass tonight, for my first time, so to speak, I'd rather not bring in Trevor and Edgard. I'd rather this stayed...between us."

"Why just us?"

"Because I feel safe with you."

Colby cupped her face in his hands and kissed her soundly. The woman constantly surprised him. "Okay. But there's one thing you need to do for me when I nail that ninety-point score."

Her teasing smile froze. "What's that?"

"Bring lots of lube. 'Cause it probably ain't gonna be no easy ride." He grinned and scooted from the trailer before she smacked him.

Wouldn't his mama be scandalized by his raunchy behavior and dirty talk?

Almost on cue, his cell phone rang. "Yeah?"

"Is that any way to greet your mother, Colby West McKay?"

"No. Hey, Ma, what's up?"

"I just wanted to double-check on you since I never hear from you. Make sure you weren't lying in a ditch someplace in some godforsaken redneck state."

He rolled his eyes, knowing he wouldn't dare do that in front of her. "Sorry. Don't take it personal. I'm either too busy or too damn tired. I ain't callin' nobody lately."

"Not a valid excuse and it makes me worry. Seems nobody's calling me. I haven't heard from Cam either."

"Cut him a break, Ma. He *is* in Iraq," Colby said dryly.

"Fine. I'll cut him one, but not you. Got new injuries I should know about, son?"

"No."

She switched tactics and chatted about his baby sister Keely's latest wild exploits. How his older brother Cord and his nephew Ky were faring in the wake of Cord's recent divorce. Seems his brother Colton had purchased another couple thousand acres of grazing land directly west of their ranch. Then she admitted she hadn't heard from his youngest brother Carter recently and she was feeling left out of her sons' lives.

"Ma. You're gonna see me in Cheyenne in a few days to see that I'm just fine."

"I know. So, what happened in Limon?"

Colby told her the nitty-gritty details about the events he'd lost and placed in, how those wins and losses affected his overall standings. He touched on Trevor and Edgard's professional troubles—but he didn't mention Channing at all.

After he'd hung up he wondered why. Because this thing with Channing was new? Because it wasn't permanent? Or because he was a chickenshit because it was special and he didn't want to jinx it?

His mother knew him better than anyone. She was pretty much in the dark about his on-the-road, wild exploits and former sexual hi-jinks, but she'd always seemed to read between the lines. She had a better understanding that "boys will be boys" than his more traditional father did. The fact that he'd hooked up with a woman would be big news to his family. And at this point he didn't want his mama zeroing in on what was happening between him and Channing.

Don't you mean, between you and Channing, and Trevor and Channing, and Edgard and Channing?

He told that smarmy little voice to shut up.

Sure, he was sharing her with them, but when it came right down to it Channing preferred him. He knew it. She'd admitted it and neither Trevor nor Edgard would be surprised by it. But the bottom line didn't change. They'd part ways at Cheyenne.

Colby didn't have time to dwell on future events. He had a competition to prepare for. Tonight, the reward would be sweet indeed. He packed his gear bag, grabbed his saddle and hitched a ride with Cash to the rodeo grounds.

☙❧

Trevor paced in front of the motel room, seething. How dare that know-it-all asshole continue to insist the problems dogging them in the arena were somehow his fault? So maybe he was a little tense, but who wouldn't be after a losing streak that now reached into double digits? The fact Edgard continually pointed it out and suggested maybe it was time for them to consider other options, flat out pissed him off.

Trevor didn't have any other options. Like Colby, this was his last shot at making the National Finals Rodeo. Trevor's father, the infamous Tater Glanzer, was sorely disappointed in his son's lack of a NFR title, despite the fact Trevor had won five circuit titles. And good old dad had been insistent that this be

Trevor's last year—mostly because Trevor's younger brother, Tanner, had a much better shot at bringing home that all-important national tie-down roping title.

Then Trevor would be stuck working with the old man all the time.

The thought of continually hearing his father berate him, the expectation that Trevor would permanently give up the rodeo lifestyle and his freedom made Trevor sick to his stomach. His family had never paid much attention to him besides to instill the obsession with rodeo within another member of the Glanzer clan. They sure didn't understand him. There were things about him that would cause a rift between them that could never be repaired if they found out.

So even if he and Edgard were losing ground in the individual standings, he'd rather stay on the circuit, rather than head home and deal with the questions and comments from his family on his future plans.

Edgard didn't understand his dilemma. Neither did Colby. They both had utter acceptance from their families. Once again, he felt completely alone. Scared that somehow the choices he'd made would come back to bite him on the ass.

The door to the room opened and Edgard glared at him from inside the doorway. "You ready to walk over to the arena?"

I don't need you to hold my goddamn hand. Trevor smiled tightly. "You go ahead. I've got to get something out of the horse trailer first."

Without waiting for Edgard to protest, he stalked off across the motel parking lot.

As Trevor barged in the horse trailer it never occurred to him to knock.

Channing sat buck-ass naked at the little dinette table.

She gasped. It was cute how she tried to tug the sheet from the bed around her nakedness. "Trevor! What are you doing here?"

"This is my horse trailer. Maybe I oughta ask you what you're doin' eatin' breakfast naked as a jaybird?"

"I-I just woke up."

"Ah. So Colby already took off to check in?"

"Umm. Yeah."

He waggled his eyebrows. "I've got you all to myself?"

"It would appear so."

"Hot damn. I knew there was a reason I came here." His gaze made a slow sweep from her pink toenails to her tangled mane, sticking out of her head at all angles. Finally his eyes zeroed in on the short dark curls peeking between her thighs. "And now I know *exactly* what I want for breakfast."

"But—"

"No buts. Since Colby ain't here, I'm callin' the shots."

"Okay. But I do want to be honest and let you know I'm a little sore from yesterday. I—I'm not used to that. Any of it."

"Then I best kiss it and make it all better, huh?"

Channing swallowed hard.

"Do I make you nervous?"

"Only if I see a rope in your hand."

"Not this morning." Trevor pointed to the bed. "Get up there and let your legs dangle off the edge. And spread em' nice and wide. I like to play with my breakfast before I eat it."

Channing blushed about ten shades of pink. But she didn't argue with him at all. Her heart-shaped butt wiggled enticingly as she crawled into the sleeper compartment.

"Like this?" she said.

Trevor noticed she had a foothold on either side of the wall. Her legs were braced far apart, as if she'd put herself on display for a man hundreds of times. But he knew better. It made her immediate surrender to him so much sweeter. "That's perfect."

He knelt on the dinette bench against the wall. His mouth was at exactly the right angle to dive deep into her pussy. He flattened his tongue and licked her from her little rosette to her clit. Up and down without stopping. Then he blew a stream of air across the wetness.

"Omigod."

"You come pretty fast like this, don't you?"

"Ah. Yes."

"Then I'll just have to make you come twice—once fast, once slow." Trevor bent his head and began to work her just with his tongue, lips and teeth. Sucking. Biting. Bestowing little teasing flicks over her clit, then he'd jam his tongue into her opening, licking her from the inside out.

Damn. Something about a woman's morning musk tasted different. Spicier. Warmer. Going down on her was a dirtier act in the daylight, rather than a lover's secret, hidden under the covers and the cover of night.

"You taste like sweet cream and honey. I could come just from eating you." His hands gripped her legs on the top near her hips. He let his thumbs lazily stroke the crease of her thighs, heightening the tactile pleasure, but never actually connecting with any part of her weeping sex.

"Well, I can definitely come like this." Channing pumped her hips into his face. "I'm already close."

"Mmm. You don't say." Trevor rolled her pussy lips around inside his mouth, sucking delicately. He focused his efforts on the button pouting for direct stimulation. First he suckled strongly and followed with quick bites from his firmed lips.

The combination set her off. Her clit throbbed beneath his tongue and he continued to use his mouth like he was devouring an ice cream cone—slurping, followed by precise short licks.

She came with a gasp, her back arched off the mattress, her ass clenched and she kept repeating, "Oh God, oh God, oh God, oh God."

He chuckled and the intimate vibration against her sensitive flesh made her cry out again.

Trevor wiped her juices from his face. His cock was twitching to get out and get some action, but he wouldn't presume Channing would be up for it, as she'd already claimed some soreness from their previous go arounds.

After Channing's legs stopped quaking, she propped herself up on her elbows and smiled at him shyly. "Get your fill?"

He licked his lips. "Breakfast of Champions, darlin'."

Her gaze dropped to the obvious bulge in his jeans. She bit her lip. "Trev, can I tell you a secret?"

"Sure. What?"

"It's sort of embarrassing."

"That's okay, Chan, we're friends, right?"

"Right."

"So tell me."

Channing blurted, "I've never done sixty-nine."

Not what he'd expected at all. "Never?"

"Nope."

"And you want to try it?"

"Yeah." She fidgeted. "So, I was wondering if you've got time..."

"Right now?"

She nodded.

"You sure you're up for it? I thought you were a little sore?"

"Not so much anymore. Besides, it'd be a pity to waste a good hard-on."

Trevor figured she wanted some sixty-nine practice before she tried it with Colby. He thought it was incredibly sweet and he doffed his clothes immediately.

Channing laughed. "You would have won the gold buckle if there was a contest for fastest clothing removal."

"My mama didn't raise no idiots, darlin', you don't have to ask me twice." He crawled up in the sleeping area. "This is gonna be fun." Trevor kissed her slowly in a drawn out seduction of mouth on mouth. He spent extra time suckling and touching her breasts, giving her time to recover from her first orgasm from him. When she started rubbing her legs together, and a soft mewl rumbled from her throat, he knew she was ready for the short go.

He smoothed her wild hair from her strangely timid face. "It's no different than givin' me a blowjob, Chan. Curl on your side, and slide my dick in deep, but don't arch your neck. And for God's sake, when you start to come, don't bite down."

She giggled and it eased some of her tension.

"Ready?"

She nodded and rolled to her left side, Trevor settled on his right. Huskily, he said, "Lift your top leg. That's it." He swooped down and took her swollen sex in his mouth again.

Channing shifted and licked the head of his cock as delicately as a cat. Gradually, she brought him deeper, her mouth made little happy humming noises and she used her hand to stroke his shaft while her fingers fondled his balls.

For being a novice, her mouth and her touch were sheer heaven. Trevor knew he wouldn't last. He focused all his attention on Channing's clit, knowing she probably wouldn't last long either.

She didn't. She came with a gasp and the intake of air around his dick made his balls tighten up.

He was so close. He rose to his knees so she could deep throat him, as he continued to tongue her softly, bringing her down from her juicy climax.

All of a sudden heat shot down his spine, a hot poker between his legs and he waited for that pulsing rush to start.

The door clicked open. Trevor looked up from between Channing's thighs into Edgard's face. In that split second, his orgasm hit, semen rocketed out the end of his cock and Channing sucked him dry while Edgard watched.

Trevor closed his eyes, threw back his head and enjoyed the hell out of it—the thundering climax and the exhibitionism.

After the blood quit rushing in his ears and his cock went half-limp, his gaze caught Edgard's again.

"I wondered if you were in here fucking off," Edgard said softly, "but I hadn't thought you were *literally* fucking off. Time to go, *amigo.* We're late." He turned and left without looking back.

Trevor fell on his side. He muttered, "Fuck."

Channing scooted around. "Trev? Is everything okay?"

She didn't need to get in the middle of this. He forced a smile. "Just great, darlin'. Just catchin' my breath."

"It's okay if you have to go."

"Unfortunately, as Edgard pointed out, I *am* runnin' late. No regrets over our sexy interlude, but can you get to the rodeo grounds all right? Or do you want me to wait for you?"

"No. You go on. I still need to shower."

Trevor kissed her thoroughly, surprised by how much he enjoyed his taste and her taste mingling on his tongue. "A sixty-nine virgin no more. You rocked my world and the horse trailer this morning, hot girl."

She blushed. "Same goes."

As he dressed he knew next time he'd remember to lock the damn door.

Chapter Ten

It didn't take long for Channing to get ready and she eagerly left the cramped motel room for fresh air and blue skies. In this higher elevation, the sun had burned away the cool morning air quickly. It was warm, but the lack of humidity made it bearable.

Her ticket was at the box office, as promised. She scanned the arena and spied the bleachers beside the chutes. Before she wandered over to her seat, she watched the action unfold in the arena.

The team penning competition was nearly over. This event fascinated her because it seemed the teams with the best times were the most experienced, unlike most of the rodeo events where youth had an edge. The two men and one woman sorting the cattle were in their late fifties. They'd separated the three calves wearing the number four into the pens faster than the next closest team by a good fifteen seconds.

So did that mean that Colby could compete in rodeo for another twenty years? Wouldn't he get tired of it? Or was this a lifelong obsession like other sports?

Channing bought a couple bottles of water. Rummaging in her bag for her notebook, her cell phone rang. She answered it absentmindedly without checking the caller ID. "Hello?"

"Channing? Is that you?"

Her stomach dropped. "Who else would it be, Mom?"

"You don't need to be snippy."

"Sorry." She inhaled slowly. "How are you?"

"I'm fine. And you?"

"Just great." *Come on. Get to it.* The only good thing about her mother's phone calls was that she didn't drag them out with inane chitchat.

"That's good. Well, the reason I called is because I've received some interesting news." Pause. "Your friend Melinda Baxter? She and her delightful fiancé Robert ran off to Aruba and were married last weekend. Isn't that marvelous?"

"Splendid," she said sweetly.

"I tell you, Melinda's mother was shocked as they'd already booked the cathedral months ago. Anyway, since Melinda and Robert skipped the formal wedding ceremony, they've rented the Gregory Art Museum and are hosting an enormous reception next weekend. Naturally, I assured Melinda you'd be in attendance."

Channing seethed. She was twenty-five years old. Her mother had no right to speak for her. But it was nothing new in her life, which was the biggest reason why she'd run away from that life. She wondered if she'd ever be able to return to it.

"You will be finished with this little...rebellion of yours by then, won't you?"

When she said *rebellion* it sounded quaint, less ominous than *run away with the rodeo.* "Maybe. We'll see."

Dead silence.

"I certainly hope even if you don't return to help your friend celebrate the beginning of her new life, that you will be back here in time to prepare for your move to—"

"I said we'll see."

Another disapproving pause. "Channing, your father went to a lot of trouble to secure the teaching position for you at Palmer. You do realize how it would look if you—"

"Yes, Mother, I'm aware of how it would look. And God knows I would never do anything to besmirch the almighty Kinkaid name."

Her mother sniffed. "Not only do I not like your tone, you are not acting at all like the responsible child I raised. I don't understand what has happened to you."

I grew up, wised up, and realized how screwed up everything is in your little world and how I don't want any part of it.

A cloud of dust heavily laced with the scent of horseshit wafted past. It amazed her how rapidly the pungent aroma had become familiar and calmed her. Not that she could share that tidbit with her mother. Jacqueline Moore Kinkaid would be appalled.

"Look, I don't want to fight with you, Mother. When you talk to Melinda give her my best."

"And?"

"And I'll talk to you soon. Bye."

Channing clicked the phone shut. Nothing had changed. She didn't fit in with her parents' social circle. Would she ever find a place where she belonged? Her gaze swept the ranch families and rodeo enthusiasts clogging the aisles and racing for the grandstand. As much as she hoped for it, she didn't really fit here, either.

Her cell phone rang again. This time she checked the caller ID. She smiled. Colby. "Hello?"

"Hey, shug, I just wanted to make sure you got the ticket and you know where you're supposed to be sittin' today."

"I'm here on the backside of the arena. I just got off the phone with my mother so I'm contemplating grabbing a beer or ten before I sit down."

He laughed and the sound warmed that cold spot within her. "Must be the day. My ma called earlier, too."

"Bet your conversation went better than mine."

"Probably. Although I doubt you got grilled on your injuries. How your horse was handlin' the travelin'. If you were eatin' right. If you were drinkin' too much. And if you were wearin' clean underwear."

She laughed.

"Are you really okay, darlin'? She didn't say nothin' to upset you?"

How had he picked up on that so fast? "I'm fine. I'm ready to rodeo. Good luck, cowboy. I'll be cheering you on."

"You have no idea how glad I am to hear that. I probably won't get much of a break, so I'll see you after that ninety-point ride."

Channing was smiling as she hung up.

ଔଊ

Colby squeaked by in the tie-down roping competition with a top-five finish. As did Trevor. Edgard got shut out.

While other events were held and Colby and Trevor and Edgard weren't competing, Channing jotted observations in her notebook. It was a good excuse not to have to talk to people. Again, she had a sudden burst of shyness.

The other wives and girlfriends looked at her a little strangely, but so far none had ventured over and introduced themselves. And she worried it'd smack of desperation if she made the first move. It wasn't like she hadn't suffered enough rejection in her life.

Colby managed to cover his bronc for a seventy-seven-point ride. The rest of the contestants didn't fare so well, which left Colby at the top of the standings and a guaranteed spot in the second round.

Likewise Trevor and Edgard had a good run and landed in the top five, also guaranteeing them a return trip the following day. Cash and Brian wound up in first place in the team roping.

The food in the concession stand was pure grease and Channing wished she'd packed a healthy lunch. Her stomach rumbled loudly.

A pigtailed girl of about four looked up from beneath the brim of her pink cowgirl hat. "Your tummy sounded like a bear growling."

"Well, maybe that's because I'm as hungry as a bear."

The girl considered her, sidled closer and then dug in her package of animal crackers, slyly passing over a circus bear. "Ya'are what you eat."

"Thank you." Channing crunched the cookie. She debated on asking the girl her name but she figured the girl would clam up, lectures of not talking to strangers dancing in her cute little head.

"That's why my daddy don't never eat chicken. 'Cause he ain't no chicken."

Interesting. She'd have to ask Colby and Trevor and Edgard if that superstition held true with all rodeo contestants all the time.

"What's your name?" the girl asked out of the blue.

"Channing."

"China? Like a doll?"

She repeated her name and the girl stared at her with enormous blue eyes.

"You shore do talk funny, lady."

"Yeah? So do you, cowgirl. What's your name?"

"Calliope Jane. 'Cept nobody calls me that unless I'm in trouble."

"What do they call you?"

"Callie. My daddy sometimes calls me Calamity Jane." She pointed at the chutes. "My daddy is bulldoggin' today." Then those blue eyes lasered into her. "What's your daddy doin'?"

Most likely his secretary, but not information she could share with anyone, let alone a sweet little girl.

"Callie!"

Both Channing and Callie whirled around to look at the harried brunette hustling toward them, her purple ropers clomping across the metal bench seats.

"Callie, hon, you need to leave this poor lady alone, can't you see she's busy?" Callie's mother gestured to the open notebook and pen perched on Channing's lap. "Sorry. She's just a chatterbox."

"Honestly, I don't mind. It's nice to have someone to talk to for a change. I don't know many people here." There. That wasn't so hard.

The brunette studied her with the same intensity as her daughter. "I'm sorry. Have we met?"

"No." Channing stuck out her hand and the woman shook it heartily. "Channing Kinkaid."

"Mary Morgan. Haven't seen you in the family bleachers before. Who're you here with?"

"She ain't gonna tell you her daddy's name, Momma, 'cause she didn't tell *me*," Callie said with a pout.

"Probably because she ain't here with her daddy, Cal."

Her rosebud lips made an "O" of understanding.

Channing hid a smile. "I'm here with Colby McKay."

Mary's eyebrows winged up clear into her straw hat. "So you're the one."

"The one what?"

"The one all them women are gossiping about."

"Yeah?" Her heart knocked against her chest. "Bad or good gossip?"

"Depends on who you're talking to." Mary snorted. "No skin off my nose, what's good for the goose is good for the gander, know what I mean? Besides, near as I can tell you're free, white and eighteen. Do what you want to and ignore all them self-righteous old biddies and cowpokes."

Channing opened her mouth but Mary wasn't close to finished.

"Like none of this stuff happened when they were rodeoin' years ago? Wrong. We've all heard the stories. And it ain't like they wouldn't jump at the chance to act young and carefree and hook themselves a hot studly cowboy if they could. I say, flip 'em the bird—"

"What bird, Momma?"

Mary smiled indulgently and tugged Callie's pigtails. "Don't you never mind, girlie."

"So Callie told me her daddy is a steer wrestler." Steer wrestling or bulldogging was another timed event where the cowboy chased down a steer. But instead of using ropes to catch the animal, the bulldogger launched himself off his horse, right at the steer as his hazer made sure the steer ran in a straight line. Once the bulldogger had a hold of the animal, he picked him up, cranked his head around and flipped him on his side. Steer wrestlers usually only competed in one event, because the money was so good—but so was the injury potential.

"Yeah. Mike Morgan. Currently ranked second. We're hopin' for a big win here and in Valentine. Then we'll go back home for about twenty minutes before we hit the *Days of 76* in Deadwood. After that we'll head to Cheyenne. Last year Mike did well in both places and we drove between Deadwood and Cheyenne five times in one week. Seems once I do get back to the ranch I'll never catch up."

"You must travel a lot, then."

"Yep. It's fun at first. Rodeo folks are the best in the world. It's like a big ol' family reunion. Then about halfway through the summer season we just wanna get back home, have a normal life, if that's possible with a kid and a ranch to run."

"Where are you from?"

"Buffalo Gap, South Dakota. What about you?"

Channing tensed up. "Outside of Boston."

"Oh." Mary frowned. "Whoa. How did you hook up with Colby?"

"Pure luck."

"I'll say." She clapped her hands over Callie's ears and said in a low voice, "He's a wily one, but man, I'd take him for a test ride any time."

Channing didn't know whether to be jealous or flattered.

"Not that he'd pick me without me twisting his arm. Despite gossip to the contrary, the real word is he's *very* choosy. He don't usually bring a woman along in his travels. Ever." She winked. "You plan on sticking around the circuit for awhile then?"

"Until Cheyenne."

"Well, good. I guess we'll be seeing you at the dances and whatever. You going to the Wild Bronc tonight? We could toss back a couple of shots."

"Maybe. Depends on how Colby does today."

Mary rolled her eyes. "Don't I know how men's attitudes depend on how they done in the arena. Pray you don't have to know how Colby reacts when he gets hurt. But at some point they always get hurt. Always." She shivered. "Come on Callie, let's get you washed up before it's Daddy's turn in the box."

"Bye-bye, China bear." She giggled and raced off.

Channing smiled. Well, at least she wasn't a total pariah.

She sat impatiently through the steer wrestling—Mike Morgan had the fastest time—and barrel racing. She was as curious to see how Colby would do in the bull riding as she was nervous.

What had possessed her to strike such a deal with him? Had she been delirious, still giddy from the amazing sex the previous night?

No, you made the deal because you want this. Even though it makes you edgy, it keys you up. And you do feel safe with him.

She snuck out and drank a beer before the last event began, convincing herself it was not liquid courage.

The family section wasn't covered with a canopy. The sun beat down on the metal and concrete making it as constricting as a sardine can. Not a breath of wind stirred. Sweat coated her skin and plastered her hair to her head beneath her hat. Most other supporters of the contestants had already left for cooler pastures.

Through a quirk of fate, Colby was the last bull rider. He'd drawn One-eyed Jack, another rank bull that'd been unridden in two dozen outs, according to Cash. But the last time he had been ridden, the rider had scored a record ninety-two.

At Colby's request Cash had ventured into the stands to share the information about what Channing might expect—although in Channing's mind it was Colby's way of gloating.

However, One-eyed Jack was also a notorious chute fighter—which posed a danger for the rider.

Channing cringed as the twenty-five contestants struggled to cover their bulls. The buck-off rate was damn near one hundred percent. Finally, Colby's name and stats were announced along with the bull's owner and rating. She moved down from the bleachers and hung over the railing, trying to get a better view of what was going on inside the chutes.

As usual Trevor was helping Colby get ready, standing behind him, holding the rope straight, parallel to Colby's body while Colby rosined up the rope in long pulls. It didn't look like the bull was putting up much of a fight. Because of the heat? Channing's hope that the two-thousand-pound animal was lethargic had nothing to do with the bet and everything with keeping Colby safe.

Colby's free arm was wrapped around the metal gate. He scooted side to side, bobbed his hat at the gate master, and man and beast rolled out.

Evidently One-eyed Jack had saved his antics for the arena, not the chutes. All four black legs were out of the dirt from the get-go, then a quick switchback and the animal was nearly vertical. Colby hung on.

Another hard spin to the right, right into Colby's riding hand, but he stuck tight, even as his hips tilted sideways. Three more vertical high jumps, another lopsided spin, followed by a fast reversal, four quick spins, one last perpendicular kick and the buzzer sounded.

He'd made it all eight seconds.

Colby did a quick release with his rope, liberating his hand, and hit the dirt ass first. The bull made a play for him, but the bull fighter distracted ol' One-eyed Jack, allowing Colby to run to safety. Even before he squinted at the screen to watch his performance, by Colby's expression, he knew he'd ridden well.

When a score of ninety-one was announced, confetti flew in the grandstand, the crowd roared approval and he tossed his hat high in the air with a loud whoop and grabbed his bullrope.

Then he made a beeline for her.

Channing's breath stalled in her lungs as Colby clambered up the fence, the metallic fringe on his chaps fluttering behind him. He hadn't even taken off his riding glove. With one hand secured on the railing, he used his free hand to jerk her close and he planted a wet kiss on her. Right in front of everyone. He did it again, with a little more flair, amidst the wolf whistles and another round of clapping.

He grinned and pressed his lips to her ear. "Time to pay up, darlin'."

Chapter Eleven

Rather than dragging Channing through the muck behind the chutes, Colby sent his saddle with Cash, grabbed his equipment bag and met her out front by the contestants' gate.

She smiled. Nervously?

He knew his answering grin was just a shade shy of wickedly smug. "You ready?"

"Umm. Yeah. How about if we have a beer first?"

"Thirsty?"

"It'd be nice to suck down something cold and wet. You look hot. I thought you might want one to celebrate. I'll even buy."

"Mighty thoughtful of you, Chan." When he placed his hand in the small of her back she jumped. He whispered, "Relax. I ain't gonna bend you over the picnic table right now."

Channing rubbed her lips along his jaw. "I didn't think you were. I just really want a beer. Don't you usually kick back after a performance?"

"Not here."

"Why not?"

"You'll see."

She sauntered up to the beer stand. The minute he was alone he was swarmed. Buckle bunnies. Kids. Rodeo enthusiasts eager to offer congrats on his ride. He dropped his equipment bag and signed programs and anything else that was shoved in his face, including a pair of tits popping out of a neon pink tube top.

It looked like Channing planned to wait for the crowd to disperse before interrupting him. Hell, the beer would be warm by the time that happened.

Colby motioned her over. The second she stood beside him, he draped his arm around her neck. A couple of disgruntled bunnies got the hint and went looking for action elsewhere. After taking a long pull off the cold brew, he sighed. "That's what I'm talkin' about. Thanks for wettin' my whistle, darlin'."

"You're welcome, sugar."

He nearly choked at the sarcasm in her tone.

One brassy-haired buckle bunny bulled her way forward and demanded, "Are you two together?"

"Yep," he said dismissively. He chatted for a few more minutes as he finished his beer. "Well, I appreciate ya'll comin' out today. I've gotta get a move on. Hopefully, I'll see ya'll tomorrow." He hefted his bag over his shoulder and kept Channing close as they exited the grounds.

"See? As much as I appreciate the fans, I'd be stuck there all damn day, which is why I usually kick back elsewhere after I'm done."

"Does that mean you're interested in going to the Wild Bronc tonight to kick back and relax with your buddies?"

Colby frowned. He didn't like it that she acted afraid to be alone with him. "Maybe. Why? Do you want to go?"

"Possibly. I met a woman in the stands today and she asked if I'd be there later."

"Who'd you meet?"

"Mary Morgan. And her daughter Callie. Do you know her?"

"A little. Her husband Mike is a nice guy. He made it in the top twelve last year at the NFR. Damn good bulldogger."

They'd reached the horse trailer. No sign of Trevor, Edgard or the horses. He unlocked the back and threw his bag in the small tack area, and motioned for Channing to precede him into the living area.

Channing immediately tensed up as she passed by him.

He seized her around the waist, spun her about and pressed her against the wall. Then he dropped his mouth over hers and kissed the living shit out of her. After he'd had his fill of her sweet lips, he pulled back and stared into her face.

"I ain't gonna start nothin' with you until I know we can finish it without gettin' interrupted. So lose the deer-in-the-headlights look. This ass is mighty fine, but I can wait a few hours yet before I make it mine."

Channing swatted him on the butt. "You sweet talker."

"Damn straight. I need to shower. After that you want to grab a bite to eat before we go honky-tonkin'?"

"Sounds good. I saw a steakhouse up the road."

"A hearty helpin' of meat and potatoes. You're a woman after my own heart."

Something liquid and sweet, like pleasure, sparked the gold in her eyes. "Should we wait to see if Trevor and Edgard want to come along?"

He almost said "Why?" but caught himself. For the briefest minute, he hated his traveling partners and he hated that he'd agreed—hell, he'd *suggested* they share this woman. But after four days, he wanted Channing all to himself.

But that wasn't what Channing had signed on for. She wanted the wild adventure of multiple partners. Even though it'd like to kill him, Colby would give her that. He suspected he'd give her damn near anything she wanted. After that, maybe he could convince her *he* was all she needed.

He smiled tightly. "Sure. As long as we don't have to wait around for them because I'm starvin'."

"I'm pretty hungry, too."

His gaze landed on the parcel centered on the mattress in the sleeping compartment. "Close your eyes, and hold out your hands—I've got a surprise for you."

For a second it seemed as if she'd argue, but she complied, although the pulse in her throat jumped. He was beginning to recognize all of her nervous quirks.

Colby reached up for the package and slid it out of the plastic bag. Feeling a little silly, he hesitated. Maybe this hadn't been the best idea.

"Colby?"

"Yeah. Here." He pressed the box against her chest until her arms wrapped around it and he stepped back, ready to make a run for it if need be.

She opened her eyes and looked down at the object she held. Her startled gaze zoomed to his. "A coffee pot? You bought me a coffee pot?"

"Ah. Yeah. There should be coffee and filters and junk in the bag on the bed, too."

"B-b-but why? You won. You scored a ninety-point ride."

"I know. But I could've just as easily lost."

"So this was just hedging your bet?"

"You might say that."

She didn't look convinced. "When did you buy it? Maybe I should ask, when did you have *time* to buy it? Weren't you behind the chutes all day getting ready to dethrone Jace Bailey as the number one All-Around Cowboy?"

"Yeah. And I didn't actually buy it. I gave Cash some cash and sent him to Wal-Mart after my ride with instructions for him to buy the nicest one they had for you." He frowned. "Is it okay? You don't hate it or nothin', do you?"

"Omigod, it's perfect!" Channing hugged it once more and then set it on the table before she threw herself into his arms, peppering his face with kisses. "Colby McKay, you are the sweetest man on the planet. I-I—I can't believe it. You bought me a coffee pot! You didn't have to."

"I know, darlin'. But I wanted to."

"Oh. Thank you, thank you, thank you." Her eyes swam with tears. "That's one of the nicest things anyone has ever done for me in my whole life." She kissed him with so much heart and sweetness, Colby felt himself getting choked up. If he weren't careful, he'd find himself falling head over heels for this precious woman.

Trying to keep it casual, he nipped the end of her pert nose and retreated. "Play with your new coffee maker, darlin'. I'll be right back to take you out for supper."

ঙ෴ঙ

They ended up eating dinner by themselves, a nice candlelight romantic dinner for two. Then they headed to the Wild Bronc. Colby didn't protest when Channing danced with Cash and Trevor—as long as she danced every slow tune with him.

Edgard had opted to catch up on his sleep in the horse trailer rather than partake in the celebration, which wasn't anything new.

Colby was having a good time drinking beer and shooting the shit with his friends. Although he was happy Channing had made new pals among the wives of the rodeo crowd regulars, he was restless.

As the night wore on he found himself getting more and more anxious. It seemed as if it'd been days since he and Channing had been alone, naked and sweaty, wrapped up together in an intimate lovers' embrace, when in reality it'd been half a day since he'd woken up beside her.

Damn. He glanced at the horseshoe-shaped clock above the bar for the fourth time in so many minutes. Channing and Mary laughed hysterically at something and knocked back another round of kamikazes.

Cash chuckled. "She's havin' a good time. But you got someplace you'd rather be, *kola*?"

"I could be a total asshole and point out that where I'd rather be tonight is an option that an old timer like you don't have with a hot young thang like her. But I'm feelin' sociable, so I'll let it slide."

"Generous of you, McKay."

Colby tipped his bottle at Cash in a mock toast. "I thought so."

A few more minutes passed and Cash sighed.

"What?"

"This ain't like you. Usually you see something you want and you take it—be it bulls, broncs, calves or women. Whatcha waitin' for?"

"A sign that my travelin' partner is gonna be occupied elsewhere so he won't see us sneakin' away and follow us, hopin' we'll entertain him until the wee hours." Colby had promised Channing he wouldn't share her with Trevor tonight, but the logistics of getting alone time with her were making him crazy.

"Shoot, that's easy enough. Leave him here. He's half-drunk anyway. He can bunk with me tonight. I got an extra bed in my room. If he acts like a jerk to me, he can sleep it off with the horses."

"Really?"

"Yep. And like you pointed out, it ain't like I'll be doin' no mattress dancin' myself tonight." He gestured with his head. "Go on, take her and get out of here before I change my mind."

He grinned and gave Cash a friendly whack on the back. "I owe you one, buddy."

"Don't think I won't collect one of these days."

Colby drained his beer and stared at Channing until she glanced up at him. Their gazes locked. Heated.

He mouthed the word "now" and her face flushed prettily.

She sucked down the rest of her drink as he ambled toward her, a man on a mission, not bothering to hide his intentions from her or anyone else in the bar.

By the time he'd reached the table, his dick was hard as concrete.

Channing scrambled to her feet and stammered as she said good night. Colby didn't hear the lewd suggestions from his friends. He didn't see the knowing looks, the winks and nudges. Everything swam out of focus but her. Channing.

He sensed her nervousness, yet surprisingly, she didn't jabber mindlessly as they walked back to the motel side by side.

Not touching. Her womanly fragrance enveloped him like a drug so invigorating he didn't trust himself to even hold her hand.

Colby unlocked the motel room door and shut it behind them, sliding the deadbolt and the chain into place. When he wheeled around to look at her and saw that her yearning matched his, he had to take a moment to regain his control, lest he tackle her to the bed and rut on her like a stag in season.

He flipped on the lamp on the table by the windows. The low wattage and the burgundy lampshade sent a soft pink glow across the room. It wasn't candlelight, but it was better than the screaming white fluorescent tubes shining down like a spotlight from the ceiling.

Finally, he found his voice, though it didn't sound like his voice at all, but a low and husky rumble. "Darlin', take off them clothes before I tear 'em off."

"Colby—"

"Now."

"Are you—"

"That was your second warnin'. There won't be a third."

Keeping her hot gaze focused on his eyes, she shimmied her orange tank top over her head and flung it in his face.

He brought the soft cotton to his nose and inhaled until her perfume filled his lungs to bursting. Then he tossed it over his shoulder. "Keep goin'."

The sassy little "fuck me" heels with yellow flowers on the pointed toes were kicked off, and kicked over, right on top of his shitkickers planted in the shag carpeting.

And still Colby didn't move.

Then the skintight, rainbow-striped capris were peeled down her slim thighs and pooled at her feet. One loud click of the front clasp and her sheer bra was gone. And as the sexy, defiant—yet strangely shy—woman stood before him in just a tiny wisp of lace panties, he lost it.

Colby scooped her up and tumbled her on the closest bed.

Her startled girlish shriek vanished in his hungry mouth as he clamped his lips to hers.

Channing was as ravenous as he was. She tugged and pulled at his clothing—vest, Western shirt, Wranglers, boxers, socks and boots—until the pieces ringed the floor around the bed and he was bare-ass naked. As he kissed her, he realized tonight she tasted different, darker, a heady sexual cocktail of tequila and a smoky hint of fear.

With one shaking hand he stripped the polyester comforter from the bed and spread her out across the plain white cotton sheets. She writhed and twisted beneath him as he glided his legs over hers, knowing the contrast of the coarse hair on his thighs rubbing against the satiny smooth flesh of hers made her crazy with want. Made her mad with lust.

Colby pinned her arms above her head. Instead of letting fast tongues and deep wet kisses escalate their mutual passion to a frenzied rush, he slowed down and nuzzled every naked, delicious, utterly bare section of skin she'd presented to him. And some areas she hadn't offered up he decided he'd take on his own.

His lips brushed the crown of her head. The desire-warmed angle of her cheekbone. Her elfin chin and her damp neck. The tasty sweep of her slender shoulders. The sinew and softness of her arms. The tempting pillow of her breasts. Her dainty ribcage that he could nearly span with his wide hands. The cute belly button, peeking out from her flat abdomen, above her line of dark pubic hair.

When he purposely ignored her pussy, already wet and fragrant and eager, she made a frustrated noise in the back of her throat.

Without missing a beat, he dragged his parted lips along the tender inside of each thigh and zigzagged a moist trail over the tops of her legs, down to her small, perfect feet. He relentlessly tongued her anklebone and she nearly shot off the bed.

"Colby!"

He growled and flipped her on her belly, keeping his palm in the small of her back as a signal for her not to move. Then he repeated his mouth-watering exploration of her oh-so-feminine dips and valleys, heedless of the quaking in her limbs and the way she tilted her ass toward him like a mare waiting to be mounted.

Since Channing couldn't see his face, he didn't hide his grin as he tasted the dimples above her butt before he licked a slow path up her spine. He nibbled on her shoulder blades, then he let his breath drift across the nape of her neck. Not kissing her, not teasing those downy soft hairs hiding beneath her tousled mane, not even touching her. He stayed still, just letting her sense his primitive need to take her, to make her his, by showing her the changes her nearness had wrought upon his breathing.

In that heightened moment, he swore he felt her heart beat faster in the air pulsing between them. His blood pounded in perfect cadence to that sensuous tempo.

No words were needed.

Colby tapped the inside of her thighs and she stretched them wider. While bestowing open-mouthed, nuzzling kisses on the back of her head and inhaling the flowery aroma of her shampoo, he speared the entrance to her pussy with two fingers. He rocked those fingers in and out of her wetness, rotating his hand to brush the callused pad of his thumb over her bottom hole. Lightly. A barely-there sweep across that extremely sensitive knot of nerves.

Channing wiggled and panted, bumping her hips, trying to wrest control from him, frantic for deeper contact.

A quick slap on her heart-shaped ass and she gasped.

He reached for the lube on the nightstand and tugged her closer to him so she was perched up high on her knees; her arms were in a "V" above her head. Her hands were fisted into the sheets. Tilting the lower half of her body to his liking, he removed his fingers from her pussy and parted her ass cheeks. Goddamn, she was gorgeous here, too. He ran his wet tongue in an extended line from her clit over her slippery slit, to circle that secret portal with the very tip of his tongue.

She whimpered a strangled sound of need.

Several times he followed that same pathway and with each thorough, more intimate pass, Channing's body softened, preparing for the invasion into that place no man's cock had ever breached.

Mine. Possession rolled through his blood. No matter what happened in the future, tonight she'd be his in a way she'd never be to any other man and she'd damn well remember it forever.

He squirted lube on his palm, working his cock in long twisting pulls. After he was sufficiently greased up, he coated his fingers and pressed them both deep inside her ass.

She moaned softy, thrusting her butt back.

He scissored his fingers in that dark recess, then pumped, stretching the untried muscles. His breathing was labored, as was hers, the desperate sounds the only noises in the concentrated silence as he prepared her. He saw no reason to give her a blow by blow on what he planned to do to her. No more sweet, coaxing kisses. Lingering touches. She was fully aware of what was happening. With the spicy scent of her arousal, he was fully aware of how badly she wanted it.

Colby inserted the end of the lube tube in her ass and squeezed. Channing shuddered. He knew the clear gel was cold, but he also knew it wouldn't stay cold for long once he started ramming his cock in and out, creating friction that would be a combination of pleasure and pain.

With one hand he pushed her shoulders down on the bed, until the side of her face rested against the mattress. Then holding her cheeks apart with his hands, he placed the thick crown of his shaft on that puckered rosette and pushed in.

Channing clenched.

He growled and probed harder, and little by little she relaxed the rigid ring of muscles.

He couldn't delay any longer and he popped the blood-engorged tip in that tight opening. Somehow he managed to stop and let her body adjust to the intrusion before he went further.

The pressure was intense enough to make her gasp.

Colby gritted his teeth. She was so fucking tight. So fucking perfect. Goddamn, he wanted to ream her. Just ram the remaining length of his dick into her impossibly tight channel until his hips were nestled between those softly rounded cheeks. Until she felt every damn inch of his hard cock impaling her virgin ass and his balls slapping her clit. Feeling every bit of his invasion so she'd never forget who'd initiated her into these dark desires she'd been begging him to satisfy.

As he imagined reaming her, he didn't envision an easy, gentle retreat as he pulled out. No. He'd plow in, deeper with every hard thrust. He'd let those supremely snug muscles grip the head of his cock before plunging past them right back in to the hilt. Over and over until that moment he exploded, shooting streams of come high and deep into her.

But he did none of that for her first time.

Colby held off on the aggressive male need to claim her, to mark her there as his alone. The yowling in his head had lessened and he eased into her rectum inch by inch, not stopping, not worrying whether his actions hurt her. Because he knew it did. He knew that it didn't matter because he couldn't stop from fucking her ass right now if the goddamn building would've caught fire.

When Colby was buried as far in as he could go, he expelled a quiet breath. He felt his blood pounding in his head, in his neck, in his arms, in his cock, all pulses like insistent sticky whispers urging him to move. Hard. Fast. Now. Prove to her who this ass and everything else belonged to.

Channing clenched and released, grinding back into him, a clear sign she was ready for more.

That was all it took. Colby slid halfway out and slammed back in. Twice. Three times. Four. This wouldn't last long. He couldn't hold out against the breath-stealing sensation of that tighter clasp milking him on every upstroke. He pumped faster, his left hand gripped her hip, holding her in place while his right hand snaked between her drenched thighs and plumped her clit.

She wailed and bucked.

The bed frame banged into the wall as he banged her with little finesse. Just raw, dirty sex. His cock tunneling in and out of that tight portal was the hottest thing he'd ever seen. His thrusts rivaled the power of a rocket booster and he was damn close to detonation.

Sweat dripped down his spine. He rubbed her swollen clit persistently. It throbbed beneath his fingers and she screamed as the orgasm burst across her wet sex in juicy ripples.

Her internal muscles clamped around his cock as her climax continued to spasm, reverberating through him. His balls drew up. He came so fast and so hard he nearly passed out as spurt after spurt of come jetted against those amazingly snug walls, until he was depleted and mindless and weak.

When Colby's eyes finally opened from near darkness behind his lids—his damn eyeballs had rolled clean back in his head, a case of vertigo tipped him sideways. He swayed and almost collapsed on top of her. When he steadied himself by running a trembling hand up her sweaty back, her whole body shuddered. Her chest heaved and masses of curly hair covered her beautiful face.

Shit. She wasn't crying, was she?

No kidding, asshole. Would you blame her?

Jesus. He'd acted like an absolute brute. Shame bloomed across his cheeks. "Chan? Shug, you okay?"

No answer.

Channing sucked in a harsh breath as he slowly removed his softened cock and her whole body flopped to the bed.

In the tiny bathroom Colby cleaned himself up and brought a warm washcloth with him to do the same for Channing. Gently, he smoothed her hair while he wiped the warmth over her tender flesh. When he finished, he tossed the washcloth away and crawled in, spooning behind her.

Luckily, she didn't squirm away from his touch.

She didn't say a single word, either.

He held her in silence for the longest time. Wanting to demand answers, needing reassurance he hadn't hurt her.

She stayed uncharacteristically quiet.

Colby pressed his lips to the back of her head. "You ever gonna talk to me again?"

"Yeah. I'm just a little stunned right now, to tell you the truth."

A long sigh escaped from him, ruffling her hair. "In a good way or a bad way?"

"Both."

His patience snapped. He rolled on top of her, pinning her hands near the headboard as he stared into her face. "What the hell does that mean, Channing?"

A beat passed. "It means I never thought I'd get to experience the passion that you've shown me. I've never had a man look at me the way you did tonight, Colby. Like I was...everything," she whispered. "I've never been utterly incapable of speech because I couldn't think beyond how you felt on me. In me. My world has never been distilled down to such an elemental need. It scares me to death."

Now *he* was absolutely stunned. And scared shitless. He'd never been more in tune with a woman—a woman who was guaranteed to leave him. And as each day with her progressed, he suspected she'd mostly likely leave him a broken man.

Instead of trying to come up with flowery love words or a sly retort, he kissed her. Pouring his heart and soul into that sweet, steady mating of mouths, hoping she understood all he couldn't say.

Exhausted, for the first time in three nights they didn't share lovers' pillow talk, or dissect how things had changed between them—even when it was obvious they had.

Chapter Twelve

Early the next morning Colby brought her new coffee pot into the motel room before he headed out to watch the morning "slack" competition. He urged her to stay in bed and rest until check-out time.

Channing didn't argue. She was wiped out. Too much tension. Too much sun. Too much booze. Too much sex.

She groaned and rolled over. Her whole body ached. Talk about sore. She'd had sex with Colby twice early yesterday morning. Oral and sixty-nine with Trevor mid-morning, and then last night...

Wowza. Hot flash. Last night had been the most erotic night of her life. Not only because she'd been initiated into the pain/pleasure of anal sex, but because she'd been initiated into the dark, possessive side of consuming lust. Hers. His. The scary beauty of it when they came together in unrestrained passion.

Maybe it'd been foolish in the aftermath of such a scintillating episode, but Channing couldn't stop from telling Colby how she'd felt last night. No. How he'd *made* her feel. Sensual. Beautiful. Desired. And he couldn't have marked her as his any more clearly than if he'd whipped out a branding iron and burned his initials into her ass.

Oh, it would be easier if she could be blasé about it. Chalk up the experience to another rocking sexual encounter and move on. Problem was, she couldn't. She didn't want to. And she didn't want to analyze why things had changed last night.

She'd rather curl up in a ball, comforted by the scent of sex lingering on the sheets as she napped. Naturally her brain wouldn't stop spinning. After fifteen minutes of tossing and turning, drifting off into blessed slumber wasn't an option.

Rather than taking a shower, Channing indulged in an hour-long bath. The heat leached out some of the soreness, but it might be a few days before her butt quit hurting. She snickered. Now she totally understood the phrase *hurt so good.*

She dressed in loose-fitting jeans and a lightweight, long-sleeved white cotton shirt, hoping it'd reflect the sun's brutal rays. Even after slathering on sunscreen yesterday, her skin had turned crimson from a day in the stands. Good thing she'd kept her hat on and saved her scalp from frying. Instead of boots she wore strappy sandals. Cool head and cool feet meant a cooler core temperature.

With her bags packed and lined up by Colby's by the door, she slurped the last of the coffee. Then she lovingly cleaned the carafe and packed it back in the box. It would probably sound silly to Colby, but she knew it would become one of her most treasured possessions.

She wasn't a stranger to gifts. Mostly big, expensive ones. Her parents had given her a BMW for her sixteenth birthday. When she'd turned twenty-one, a flawless string of pearls. But they'd never given her a gift from the heart or paid much attention to her sentimental yearning for something unique and well thought out. Like a handmade scarf. Or a pair of skates and a promise to take her to the rink for an afternoon of frolicking on the ice. They'd never really listened to her.

In a few short days Colby knew her better than either of her parents. She suspected the shrewd cowboy might know her better than she knew herself.

A sharp knock echoed in the quiet room. The maid kicking her out already? Channing lifted to her tiptoes and checked the peephole. Edgard. She opened the door. "Hey. I thought you'd be at the rodeo grounds."

"On my way. I just need to load yours and Colby's stuff in the horse trailer. Do you want to ride over there with me?"

"Sure." She touched his arm. And she thought she'd looked wiped out. She could've packed her stuff in the luggage under Edgard's eyes. "Ed, are you okay?"

"Yeah. Just worried about the events. Trev and I could sure stand to win some money today."

"I'll cheer you on, *amigo*. Although I guess I'm not bringing you as much luck as you'd believed?"

Surprisingly, Edgard grinned, leaning over to buss her cheek. "You bring me something better than luck, Channing."

"What's that?"

"Hope. Come on. Colby forgot his saddle and he's waiting, probably pacing behind the chutes."

Channing wondered. Had Colby been thinking about her and their erotic interlude from last night so much that he'd waltzed off and left his saddle behind? Maybe he was as bowled over by what was happening between them as she was because he was meticulous about his equipment.

At the rodeo grounds Edgard had parked the rig at the far end of the lot, near the back entrance. He handed her a key to the horse trailer. "Can you lock up? I gotta get this saddle over to him before he starts freaking out."

"Sure. See you. Tell him I said good luck."

"Maybe you wanna give me a kiss that I can pass along to him, too?"

"You know, that's the first time you've offered to kiss me. You feeling okay, Ed?"

"I'm feeling great. Later." He flashed her a bone-melting smile, hefted the saddle over his broad shoulder and sauntered off.

At the box office a ticket was held in her name. And it really brightened her day when several of the women from the Wild Bronc came over to chat, to tease her about her abrupt departure with Colby the previous night. The bolder ones even confided about the early days in their relationships with their cowboys and how they remembered—and missed—that urgency.

But mostly these trash-talking women wanted to tempt her into placing small stakes bets with them. A time-honored tradition, they swore. The only rule was you couldn't bet against your man.

Channing knew it was a test. And she soon discovered very few bet against Colby McKay. So she prepared to clean them out of their pocket money and she'd enjoy every minute of it.

"Let's rodeo!" the announcement boomed.

During the bareback competition Channing won twenty-five bucks. Then the saddle bronc event started.

Oh mama. The second Colby's name was announced, her whole body flushed with desire and pride.

Colby looked powerful and in command and supremely sexy as he rode his bronc to a seventy-five. He finished third overall and won a decent amount of money.

With it being the last day of the rodeo, the events were longer, because the short go was held right after the individual competitions ended.

The betting became sporadic as contestants' significant others left the stands. It'd be a long day for her. Suddenly alone, Channing regretted she'd forgotten her notebook in the horse trailer.

Two tugs on her hair. Before she could turn to see who it was, Callie hopped down in front of her. "Hey, China bear."

"Hey, Calamity Jane."

She clapped her hand over her mouth and giggled.

"Where's your mom?"

"Helpin' the hazer wrap up the back legs on his horse before Daddy goes bulldoggin'."

With her soft Midwestern accent, bordering on a twang, and big eyes, the kid was cute as bug. "Is the horse okay?"

She shrugged. "So's your stomach and your head hurt as bad as Momma's does this mornin'?"

Channing choked on her iced tea. "No."

"I'm glad, because *she* is the one who's a bear today, not you," she confided with a serious face.

Beat-up brown boots covered in dirt slid into view. "I heard that Calliope Jane Morgan." A sluggish Mary eased next to Channing. "I'd like to say she's full of it, but the truth is, my head is pounding and I feel like I could barf. Been that way since the moment I got up."

She could tell Mary was scrutinizing her from beneath oversized pink sunglasses.

"Here I was hopin' my partner in crime from last night felt just as poorly as I do. But damn, you look positively chipper today."

Channing chuckled. "Remind me why you were drinking last night?"

"Showing you how to celebrate Colby's big ride. It just didn't seem like I drank that much to feel this bad."

"Momma. You always say that."

"Pipe down, pipsqueak. You're giving Channing a bad impression of me."

Channing hid a smile as she sipped her tea. "So are you guys going to Valentine?"

"Yep. We're off to *love city* as soon as Mike's event ends. What about you?"

"We're heading that way, too."

Callie skipped across the seats to check out the vendors hawking their wares.

"Can I ask you something?" Mary said. Channing nodded. "Ain't it kinda awkward travelin' with Colby *and* Trevor *and* Edgard? I mean, Mike and me saw you and Colby take off last night. And Trev was so wasted Cash had to help him out of the bar at closing time. But this morning Cash said Trev wouldn't stay in his room and he must've slept in the horse trailer."

Channing tried to act nonchalant, dreading the remainder of the question.

"So how does that work when you and Colby want alone time? Do you guys gotta sneak off and git 'er done before Trevor or Edgard bust in on you?"

Channing blushed. No doubt her new friend would be scandalized if she admitted the sleeping arrangements. But when she really thought about it, she literally had slept only with Colby in all the nights the four of them had been together.

"Well, Trevor and Edgard make themselves pretty scarce. We switch off and take turns—" somehow she managed not to wince "—one night we're in the horse trailer, the next we're in the motel room."

"Oh." Mary seemed about to say something else but Callie interrupted.

"Momma, I'm hot."

"I know, baby. We'll be out of the sun soon."

"So can I have one of them little fans to cool off?" She pointed to the vendor wandering through the stands selling souvenirs.

"No."

"How about a necklace?"

"No."

"Then can I have a whistle? They ain't very expensive."

"No, Callie. Lord, stop beggin' me for every damn thing you see."

Callie sighed. "So can I at least have a snow cone?"

"Fine." Mary dug out a couple of bucks and slapped it in Callie's outstretched hand. "But come right back here, no fooling around."

Talk about diversionary tactics. Callie shot Channing a triumphant look that said she'd wanted a snow cone all along.

Cheeky little thing.

The steer wrestling started. Bets were placed. Channing lost ten bucks because Mike won not only the second round, but also the final go-around. Mary and Callie took off and promised they'd see her in Valentine.

Next up was team roping. Trevor and Edgard were the second competitors. The steer raced out and Trevor's rope came up short. They ended up with no time. They were out of the money except for the modest amount they'd won the previous day.

Channing squinted, but from where she sat she couldn't gauge their individual expressions. Their body language didn't lie; they were both stiff, coiling their ropes in angry, jerking motions. Ignoring the announcer's run down of their bad run of luck again. Ignoring each other. She wondered if Colby was waiting for them back in the chutes to talk to them or if he'd leave them to misery. Their moods would be sour tonight.

After another half an hour of sitting by herself, she was hungry and needed a break from the sun. She wolfed down a hot dog from the concession stand and sucked down an icy-cold beer. Ooh. That made her woozy. She glanced at the clock. It would be at least an hour before the bull riding started, plenty of time for her to grab her notebook and jot down a few observations.

The dusty parking lot was mostly empty of the usual line of horse trailers and campers. The timed events were nearly over and the contestants had already packed up and moved on to the next town. It was weird to see Trevor's trailer parked so far away. The horses weren't tied to the sides. They were probably still in the paddock waiting to be loaded until after Colby's last event.

A hot wind swirled the trash littering the grounds. Channing dug out the key from her front jeans pocket and slid it in the lock. As she stood below the pop-out metal step, she heard a loud thump inside the living area of the trailer. She waited and heard it again, but this time a grunt, another thump and loud male cursing followed it.

Crap. Were Edgard and Trevor in there beating the hell out of each other for their poor showing? She didn't have time to track down Colby; she'd have to handle this herself. Channing quickly twisted the key and quietly slunk inside, softly clicking the door shut behind her.

What she saw froze her to the spot. Edgard and Trevor weren't fighting. Rather, Trevor was naked, splayed along the back wall, beating his fists into the cheap paneling as Edgard, on his knees before Trevor's widespread legs, was noisily sucking Trevor's cock.

Holy shit. This wasn't what she'd expected at all.

Edgard raked his fingers down Trevor's rippled abs and gripped his hips. "Fuck my mouth. Hard. You want to. Do it." Then he bent his head and swallowed Trevor's cock again.

"Jesus, I can't get enough of—" Trevor's gaze caught hers. "*Channing?* What the hell are you doing here?"

Edgard scrambled back so fast he fell on his naked ass, looking up at Channing with the most horrified, embarrassed expression distorting his striking face.

Trevor stayed pressed against the wall almost as if he wanted to melt into it.

No one uttered a sound.

And suddenly, things made sense. Edgard's reluctance to have her travel along with them or to join in their sexcapade. The constant tension between Trevor and Edgard. The sniping that was clearly a lovers' spat. The truth of why Trevor disappeared every night and where he went, leaving her and Colby alone.

Oddly enough, it didn't freak her out. In fact, it was a relief. No wonder Edgard wasn't attracted to her; he was attracted to Trevor.

Trevor said, "Channing, it's not what you think."

Then another strange thought sneaked in and she blurted out, "Is Colby gay, too?"

"I'm not gay," Trevor said.

Edgard shot him a dark look.

"Okay. Bi at least. Then is Colby bisexual?"

"No."

"Does he know that you guys are...together?"

"Yes."

"And he doesn't mind?" Most straight guys she knew were extremely homophobic. *Brokeback Mountain* notwithstanding, she suspected rough and tumble cowboys, schooled in the traditional conduct of the Old West would be even more set in their ways of thinking than the male urbanites she knew.

"Colby is of the 'don't ask, don't tell' policy," Edgard said dryly. "As long as he doesn't see us—everything is fine."

"Oh." She absolutely did not know what to say.

Trevor said, "Obviously, we'd rather you didn't go blabbin' about this. It'd make life a mite difficult for us not only on the circuit, but everywhere else."

"I imagine."

Edgard scowled, stood and threaded his hand through his hair. He reached for his rumpled clothes. "I'll go get the horses."

She could've let him go. Instead, Channing stepped in front of him and placed her hand on his cheek. "No. Go ahead and finish. I interrupted your private time together. If anyone should leave it should be me, Edgard."

Her words sent shock waves through the small space.

"You're not disgusted by what you've seen?"

She laughed softly. "On the contrary."

Edgard and Trevor exchanged a look. "Meaning?"

"What I see are two of the sexiest men I've ever met, giving in to passion that I never believed existed until I experienced it myself." She felt a hot blush steal up her neck. "How can that be wrong? I'm beginning to understand it's powerfully addicting. And..."

"What?" Edgard brought her hand to his mouth. "Tell us."

"It turns me on. I've always wondered what it would be like to watch two guys going at it. I mean, face it, you're both gorgeous. You've both got incredibly beautiful, incredibly strong bodies. All those bulging muscles, rock-hard abs, broad shoulders. Big, rough hands and tight cowboy asses." Her gaze dipped to Edgard's crotch. "Not to mention those."

He grinned.

Trevor stepped forward and curled his hand on Edgard's shoulder. "What're you sayin'?"

Channing looked from one man to the next. "I'm saying, part of the reason I'm here is to experience all sorts of different sexual scenarios, right? This is one. So, I want you to finish what you started. Pretend I'm not here. I'll just be sitting over there in the corner. Watching."

Edgard didn't look convinced.

"I'm so wet thinking about seeing you guys fuck I hope you don't mind if when I can't stand it anymore, I take care of matters myself?"

Trevor leaned over to kiss her forehead. "Do what you gotta do, darlin'. Don't mind us, 'cause we probably won't mind you."

Channing picked up the chair and slid it next to the door, out of the way, and sat back to enjoy the show.

With renewed fervor, Trevor spun Edgard sideways and clamped his mouth to Edgard's. His callused hands cradled Edgard's face and he gradually slipped his fingers over Edgard's thick neck, his delineated pecs, until his thumbs brushed

Edgard's small pebbled nipples. Over and over. A softer touch than Channing expected, but without pause.

Edgard groaned.

The contrast of Trevor's light-colored hands skimming across Edgar's darker-hued skin was a stunning visual. The strength of these men, square jaws covered in razor stubble, thick tongues flashing as they kissed hungrily, their sinewy bodies swaying closer until they were pressed together. Smooth, rock-hard chest against another equally firm torso dusted with dark hair. Muscled thigh to muscled thigh, cock straining against cock, made her heart pound and her pussy dripping wet.

Edgard broke the kiss and dragged his mouth down the center of Trevor's body. Trevor widened his stance, planted his palms on Edgard's shoulders and pushed him to his knees.

But Edgard wouldn't be rushed. He licked a line from Trevor's navel to the edge of his blond pubic hair, nuzzling the skin around Trevor's twitching cock. Edgard smoothed his hands over Trevor's hips to cup his butt cheeks.

Channing squirmed as she noticed one of Edgard's hands dipped lower, tracing the crack of Trevor's ass down between his balls.

Trevor shuddered and bumped his crotch forward. "Come on. I was close before. Suck it deep."

Edgard lapped the crease between Trevor's hip and thigh, before turning to look at Channing. "He likes to come on my face, but we'll skip that today."

"Then you'll swallow every fucking drop I pump into this mouth, you cock tease." Trevor fastened his hands on Edgard's head and maneuvered Edgard's mouth to his groin. "Open up and say ah, baby."

Edgard took Trevor's cock deep in his throat on the first insistent stroke.

Trevor hissed. "Jesus, I love fucking this hot mouth." He thrust his hips harder, pulling out until Channing saw the mushroom-shaped head trail pre-come over Edgard's lips, then he'd ram back in Edgard's eager maw. Time after time.

Edgard made wet, suckling noises like a man facing a sumptuous, succulent banquet. He tipped his head slightly and permitted his jaw to go slack when Trevor's cock was buried balls deep in his mouth. Saliva dripped down his chin and neck.

"Yeah. You are all pro at sucking cock. You fucking love it that you can get me off so quickly, don't you? Baby, hold on. Here it comes."

Trevor grabbed Edgard's hair, keeping his head in position, ramming his cock in with a grunt and holding it there. "Swallow hard. Work me with your tongue and throat muscles. Oh. Shit. Yeah, like that." Apparently, Trevor was the dominant partner in this sexual relationship.

Channing's clit throbbed. Her hand snaked between her thighs and she rubbed the hard seam of her jeans, aligned perfectly over her swollen tissue, as Trevor bucked, groaned and emptied himself down the back of Edgard's throat.

She was so hot, so ready to burst, four fast strokes and a small orgasm pulsed like a flash of lightning. It wasn't nearly enough, but it'd do for now. She knew Trevor and Edgard weren't done. She squirmed in anticipation.

Gently stroking Edgard's cheek, Trevor tugged his semi-erect cock from between Edgard's rosy lips. He helped Edgard to his feet and kissed him in an erotic, open-mouthed tangling of tongues. Strong male hands smoothed rough male skin. The scent of musky male sweat and the heat of their bodies created a sultry humidity in the small space that reeked of sex and passion.

Trevor curled his fingers around Edgard's fully erect cock. Squeezing and twisting with more force than Channing had dared use on any man. But who better to know how much pressure a man could take on that rigid appendage than another man?

Again, Edgard broke the kiss. His lips journeyed over Trevor's jaw to Trevor's throat. He didn't bother to lower his voice. "You know what I want, Trev. What I always want. Now."

Trevor nodded and leaned over to snag his jeans, removing a condom from the front pocket. He ripped open the package with his teeth. Staring into Edgard's eyes, he rolled the rubber down Edgard's long shaft, slanting forward to nibble and lick Edgard's shiny smooth lips.

Edgard wrapped his own fingers around the thick girth of his cock, stroking their hands in tandem as he said to Trevor, "Bend over the table, grab onto the edge and stick that ass in the air."

Trevor moaned, angling for another heated kiss before he readily complied, holding Edgard's hand as he turned, letting his belly drape over the flat surface.

Edgard flicked his tongue down Trevor's spine as he positioned himself behind Trevor. He kicked Trevor's ankles until Trevor broadened his stance.

Trevor looked over his shoulder at his lover, his eyes bright with desire as he tilted his butt higher in invitation.

Channing watched as Edgard dropped to his knees and ran his tongue down the crack of Trevor's ass. His hands spread those cheeks wide and he rimmed Trevor's asshole with the tip of his tongue. Around and around that puckered opening, blowing on it gently and then he jammed his tongue inside.

Jesus. That was one of the hottest things she'd ever seen.

Her cunt spasmed as she remembered when Colby had done that to her last night. How the kinky, totally debauched behavior had turned her on to epic proportions.

Edgard's tickling tongue had the same effect on Trevor. Trevor whimpered and bumped his ass into Edgard's face. "Christ, baby. That feels so fucking good. You know how much I love it."

"Yes, I do." Edgard stood. "Which is why I'm not gonna let you come this way."

"You still pissed off at me?"

"Yes. Be glad I ain't tying you up and whipping the shit out of this ass before I fuck it. But then again, I know how much you love that. Brace yourself."

Trevor said, "You want some lube?"

"No lube," Edgard said and pressed the head of his cock against Trevor's asshole. "I want it to hurt." He plunged in, in one fast stroke.

"Ah, fuck," Trevor said on a long groan.

Edgard reamed Trevor hard enough the table and the horse trailer shook.

Trevor's hands were wrapped around the edge so tightly his knuckles were white. Edgard muttered in Portuguese, his hips pistoning like mad as the muscles on his ass flexed.

After one particularly intense thrust, Edgard stopped with his cock buried in Trevor's ass. He layered his sweat-covered chest over Trevor's arched back. Edgard didn't move, he appeared to be waiting for something from Trevor.

Trevor wiggled, humping the table as he moaned, "Please. Don't stop."

Edgard's silky voice inquired, "Who is fucking you, Trevor?"

"You are."

"Who am I?'

"Edgard."

"A man."

"Yes."

"Does it ever feel this good when you're fucking a woman?"

Trevor turned his face away.

Edgard withdrew completely out and rammed back in to the hilt. "Answer me, goddammit."

"No. Jesus."

"Do you ever beg a woman to fuck you in the ass? With a synthetic excuse for a cock? Or with her fingers? Or with her tongue?"

"No."

"Do you want me to pull out my big cock and stop stuffing it into this hole as hard and deep as I can?"

"No. Edgard. Please."

Edgard licked the back of Trevor's neck, trilling his lips over the sensitive bend in his shoulder until Trevor trembled. "You want what only I can give you? You don't care if she knows how much you love my cock? Shoved in your ass? Shoved in your mouth?"

Right then, Channing knew she'd been wrong. Trevor wasn't the dominant in this sexual relationship, Edgard was.

"No, I don't care if she knows."

"Beg me to finish it. Beg me to show her what I do to you. What I give to you that no one else ever has, *amigo*."

"Edgard. Please, fuck me. I'll do anything you want, just don't stop—"

Edgard growled his approval and rocked into Trevor with such force the base of the table cracked.

She'd never seen such a brutal show of censure.

"Jack off right now," Edgard hissed. "I want to see your come spewing all over your stomach."

Trevor reached between his legs, his arm pumping as his hand furiously worked his cock. He came with an extended groan that bordered on a scream.

Edgard roared, arched, his ass cheeks clenched and he pounded his meat into Trevor's up-thrust ass harder and harder until he shouted out his release. Still giving Trevor short, pulsing strokes, Edgard bowed over Trevor's back. Breathing hard. Licking. Biting. Sucking Trevor's passion-dampened skin.

Channing came in a wet gush without even touching herself, just by squeezing her thighs together. As much as she'd been unbelievably turned on by this voyeuristic episode, she knew something had happened between Trevor and Edgard in that interlude.

As they started to murmur to each other in that low lover's crooning tone, she snuck out, locking the door behind her.

Chapter Thirteen

Channing returned to the rodeo grounds in a daze. She smiled politely at the other women who were also waiting for the bull riding to begin. They were all at the point of the day—the breaking point—that they wished for the event to be over because they had miles of blacktop stretching ahead of them.

When it was Colby's turn to ride, she was surprised to see Trevor helping him prepare. Had Trevor told Colby that she knew about him and Edgard? She hoped not. Colby needed to concentrate on his riding, not whether she was weirded out by what she'd discovered an hour ago about his traveling partners.

Colby had a decent ride, an eighty-four, but his hand had gotten caught up in his bullrope. He took a couple of slow spins with the bull before the bull fighter freed him. Colby hit the ground hard and the bull had rushed him. A big gasp echoed in the arena as it appeared the bull's hooves had connected with his upper torso twice before the bull fighter chased the bull off.

Her belly muscles knotted as she observed him limping from the arena. His score was good enough to get him in the short go, but she wondered how badly he'd been hurt.

Usually, Channing loved bull riding; it was her favorite part of the rodeo. But today she could scarcely watch, as the bulls so far had been some of the nastiest she'd ever seen.

Colby didn't stay on his last bull. It jerked hard and yanked the rope right out of Colby's hand, tossing him headfirst into the gate. Colby managed to tuck and take the brunt of the impact on his right side. It took a minute before he got up again.

Even after he'd gotten ejected in the short go, Colby ended up in fifth. Good enough to finish in the money, but not enough points to move him up in the standings. He was still ranked second.

Oddly enough, Cash had won the final round of bull riding. The minute the engraved gold belt buckle had passed into Cash's hands, she made tracks to the contestants' entrance. Heedless of what his friends or others might think, when Channing caught sight of Colby, she practically ran to him.

He gave her that charming boyish grin, complete with devilish dimples, but his smile didn't quite reach his eyes. "Hey, darlin'. Didja see that ride?"

"The one where you got hurt?"

"Hell. I ain't hurt. Just got my bell rung a little, that's all."

She frowned. "But—"

"Seriously, Chan, I'm okay. I got my payout, so I'm actually a lot better than okay. I'm ready to hit the road." He gestured with his head toward the parking lot. "Trev and Edgard loaded up the horses and we're ready to go."

"You'll be able to rest in the truck?"

"Nah. I'm on tap to drive to Valentine."

Channing reached for his hand and he winced and jerked it back.

"What? You don't want to hold my hand now?"

"It ain't that."

"Then what?"

"I'm just a little sore. Forget it."

"No. Let me see."

"It ain't nothin'. Let's go."

She stepped in front of him, bumped her sandals into his boots and rose to her tiptoes to get in his face. "Let me see it or I'm dragging you back to sports medicine for them to take a look."

"I told you—"

"And I'm telling you, I'm serious, Colby McKay, so don't think you can sweet talk your way around this one. Let me see it right now."

He glared at her. Then he slowly brought up his riding hand. "Fine. See? It's a little beat up, but it's fine."

Channing glanced down and her stomach churned. His hand looked like he was wearing a baseball glove, as it was swollen to twice its normal size. Red and puffy with dark crisscrosses around the wrist. The knuckles were scuffed, rubbed raw and scabbed over. Without thinking she placed her lips on the worst scrapes. "Oh, Colby. Oh, honey, oh, baby, it's *not* fine. That has to hurt something fierce. You need—"

With his good hand Colby tipped her face to his and kissed her. Deeply. Thoroughly enough to make her feel dizzy.

"Wow." She blinked up at him. "Not that I'm complaining, but what was that for?"

"For carin' about me. It's the first time since I was about ten years old that I've had someone give me a kiss on a rodeo boo-boo to make it feel better." A wicked grin flashed. "Come to think of it, shug, when I was on that bull, on that last spin, he also gave me a real serious slam to my—"

"You are such a...*man*, using my concern for you against me for sexual favors."

"Can't blame me for tryin'."

"No. But I will tell you that no way in hell are you driving to Valentine."

He sighed. "It don't work like that. It's my turn."

"Or mine. I've haven't taken my turn churning up the pavement yet."

"You ever driven a 350 diesel pickup haulin' a horse trailer loaded down with three horses?"

"No. But that doesn't mean I can't learn."

"True. And as much as I 'preciate you wantin' to help out, I'm fine. This ain't the worst hand injury I've ever had. Hell, it's not even the worst one I've suffered through this year. I'll put ice on it when we get settled in Nebraska, okay?"

"Nice try, but you'll take care of it now. Neither Trevor nor Edgard competed in six events today, Colby. They sure as shit can drive while you rest." He opened his mouth but she made it snap back shut with a fiery look. "Don't push me on this issue."

From behind her Edgard said, "She's right. You can't drive with that hand. Besides, it ain't no big deal. I'll drive. Trevor can navigate. You might as well crawl in the horse trailer and sleep it off. You look dead beat, McKay."

Channing watched as a sense of relief crossed Colby's face. No one else probably caught it, but she did.

"Fine. I ain't gonna argue when it's two against one." He cradled his sore hand to his waist and moved to block their conversation from Edgard. In a low tone he said, "Since I'm not drivin', you gonna keep me company?"

"If you promise you'll actually rest instead of expecting me to fool around with you for the next few hours."

He bent down and whispered, "Aw, darlin', that ain't no fun at all."

She readjusted his hat so she could peer in his eyes. “I can guarantee you won’t have any fun with me *at all* for days if you don’t rest up.”

“You threatenin’ to hold out on me?”

“Damn straight.”

Colby sighed. “You ain’t a pushover, Miz Channing, but neither am I so I’ll make you a deal.”

Her heart rate increased, thinking about the last “deal” they’d struck. “Which is?”

“If I promise to get a little shuteye, will you promise to mess around with me later? After I get my strength back.” He rubbed his cheek against hers and murmured, “Damn, but I missed you today, Chan. The day seems like it’s been a week long. Seems like it’s been forever since I held you in my arms. Kissed that mouth until kisses are no longer enough and clothes start flyin’ and we’re rollin’ around between the sheets.”

Channing refused to get distracted by his sweet-talking. “I know. I missed you too, cowboy. Now get your ass up in that bed. I’ll be right there to tuck you in.”

“Bossy thing.”

“You ain’t seen nothing yet. Don’t make me break out the ropes.”

Colby lifted a dark brow. “Now that could be downright interestin’.” He ambled off, his gait more measured than usual.

Channing watched him until he disappeared inside the horse trailer and then she blew out a frustrated sigh.

“You okay?” Edgard said.

No. “I’m fine. I’m going to get him some ice and then we can take off.”

Edgard snagged her hand and turned her around. “Trev and I are concerned about what happened a while ago—”

"Don't be. My only concern right now is making sure Colby gets ice on his hand and that he gets some rest."

"You really do care about him, don't you?"

"Yes." She studied Edgard's face. He seemed just as tense around her as he had been this morning. She'd hoped maybe things would be a bit easier between them now. "Are you surprised?"

"No. I'm happy. And truth be told, I'm a little jealous." He brushed his lips over her knuckles. "You are good for him. Take care of him and we'll take care of the driving and everything else."

Channing managed to track down some gel-pack cold compresses from the first-aid tent, as well as a big bag of ice. The door was open when she returned to the trailer. With her hands full, she tripped over Colby's rigging bag, which was plopped in the middle of the floor.

Trevor caught her. "Whoa, there. Let me help you."

"Thanks." She tossed everything on the table and looked at Colby sitting rigidly in the chair by the bathroom door. His eyes were squeezed shut, his mouth was a flat line and it was obvious he was in pain. He still wore his hat, his chaps, his jeans, his boots, and his vest. Her anger surfaced. "Why aren't you undressed and in bed, Colby McKay?"

No answer.

Trevor said, "I don't think he can get undressed by himself."

She whirled on Trevor. "Then why didn't you help him?"

"Because I don't want his help," Colby snapped.

Trevor shrugged.

Take a deep breath, don't yell at him. He's hurting and he doesn't want you to know it. And he doesn't want to look weak in front of his friend.

In a breezy tone, she said, "Touched as I am that you want me to undress you personally, I'm not exactly well-versed on how to get you out of those sexy chaps." She paused and walked to him to touch the pulse throbbing in his neck, then skimmed her hand up to rest on his cheek. His face was clammy. "So, will you let Trevor help me do that much and then I'll take care of the rest of your pesky clothes all by my little lonesome?"

Heavy silence.

Finally, Colby nodded.

"Good. Boots off first."

Between them, they unhooked Colby's spurs, yanked off his boots, unbuckled Colby's chaps and peeled them down his legs. Trevor took the dirty, sweat-dampened chaps and hung them in the tack room before he said goodbye and returned to the truck cab.

Channing had noticed Colby wincing when they'd jerked on the strap between his hips. She unzipped his vest and eased him out of it, an arm at a time. Then she unbuttoned his soggy cotton shirt, keeping her eyes on his until she had to strip the material down his riding arm.

Once he stood bare-chested in front of her, she saw the bruises on his ribcage, under his ribs and everywhere across his upper torso. Purple and black splotches that looked like smears of dirt, but she knew were smudges of blood and broken tissue—a "rodeo tattoo" courtesy of rough stock.

"It ain't as bad as it looks," he said softly.

She couldn't say a word, lest she start bawling. As she rolled down his jeans, Colby sucked in another harsh breath.

She realized he had another half-moon-shaped bruise the size of a softball on his inner left thigh. And a contusion by his knee.

"Channing, darlin'—"

"I am trying very hard not to yell at you, so don't you *Channing darlin'* me."

Colby pointed to the bag on the table. "If you're determined to fix me up, there's liniment and wraps in there."

"Good." Channing rummaged around until she found the half-empty tube. "So, stubborn man, can you crawl up in bed by yourself, or do I need to get Edgard and Trevor back here to give you a boost?"

"I ain't a cripple," he grumbled. With painstaking weariness he shuffled up the ladder, his boxers hanging low off his slim hips and perfectly round little ass. Besides his underwear, he wore only his grungy gray athletic socks and his dusty cowboy hat. At any other time she might've snickered at the funny picture he made, but at that moment laughter was the furthest thing from her mind.

A loud male grunt and he stretched himself flat on his back and didn't budge again.

Channing busied herself getting an icepack ready for his hand, knowing she'd need to use the compresses for his ribs—whether he liked it or not. She rummaged in her bag until she found a bottle of Tylenol with codeine. Then she climbed up beside him. Her stomach roiled to see such a virile man so vulnerable.

Sweat coated his skin, yet he was shivering like a naked baby. His mouth was set, like that tough, determined action alone could drive away the pain.

Right. Maybe it had worked in the past, but she wasn't going to let it slide on her watch.

"Listen up, McKay. You're taking these pain pills. Then I'm icing up your poor hand and your ribs and spreading this stinky junk all over you. Once I've got you doctored up, you're going to sleep. And you'll stay up here, resting up and healing up until I say otherwise, understand?"

Surprisingly enough, he didn't argue. He merely nodded and winced when she removed his hat. Lord. If just taking off his hat hurt him, how would she get through the rest of this?

Only after she'd finished carefully tending his injuries, did she allow herself to give him the type of lover's comfort she sensed he needed from her. Her fingertips swept the damp hair from his brow. Repeatedly, she smoothed the back of her hand over the five-o'clock shadow on his rigidly set jaw. "Are you comfy enough so you can rest?"

"Yeah. Thanks."

"No problem. Is there anything else I can do?"

"Yeah. Kiss me, darlin'. When you're kissin' me I forget about everything else but how good your sweet mouth feels on mine."

"You didn't hit your head hard enough to injure that silver tongue of yours, did you, cowboy?" she murmured.

"Not hard enough to knock any sense into my fool head, either." He looked at her; his blue eyes were stark and needy. "Please."

"I'd say no if it weren't for the fact you can still charm the hell out of me while you're flat on your back and frozen in pain." She ran her thumb over the dark circle under his eye, noticing a mouse high on his cheekbone. "But I'm finding I can't deny you a damn thing, Colby McKay. So c'mere and let me lay a big, sloppy, wet kiss on you."

Channing rubbed her lips over Colby's, infusing him with all the sweetness and joy and heat he usually gave her. He melted deeper into the mattress, and let her have total control of the kiss. Of him. His surrender was as rewarding as it was arousing.

It was a long time before either one of them could speak after their mouths reluctantly parted.

“Stay with me?” he asked gruffly.

“For as long as you want,” she whispered. She pulled the flannel sleeping bag over them and rested her head beside his chest, drifting off to the solid, steady beat of his heart next to her ear.

Chapter Fourteen

A loud clank woke her from a light sleep. Channing opened her eyes and realized the trailer was bumping up and down like a logging truck, which meant they were still tooling down the highway.

She lifted her head from where it'd been resting beside Colby's bare chest. She looked up, expecting to see him sleeping, but his eyes were open and he was staring at her.

He smiled gently. "Hey."

"Hey yourself. How do you feel?"

"Like I've been run over by a buckin' bull and a wild bronc."

Channing kissed his left pec. "You *were* run over by a bull and a bronc today."

"Well, no wonder I'm feelin' it." Colby absentmindedly twisted a section of hair around his finger. "Thanks for stickin' around."

"You're welcome." She pushed up. "I probably need to get some more ice for your hand."

"My hand is fine."

"Do you need—"

He pulled her back down. "I need you to stay snuggled up to me like this. It's makin' me feel much better, shug."

"Oh."

"Of course, I'd feel even more like my old self if you took off the rest of your clothes."

Channing rolled her eyes. "One thing at a time, okay?"

"Okay. Scoot closer. I like havin' your softness and warmth wrapped around me. It's like heaven, bein' with you."

They stayed cocooned together in companionable silence. Colby dragged the fingers of his left hand up and down her spine.

Finally, he said, "I guess you found out about Trevor and Edgard, huh?"

Her stomach did a little flip. "Yeah."

"Kinda shockin' to see them like that, ain't it? That's how I found out. I walked in on them. Wanted to gouge my eyes out with a hot poker afterward."

"And it doesn't bother you? I mean, you're still traveling with them. You haven't gotten them blackballed to the 'gay' rodeo circuit or anything. Especially if people do find out, they might assume you're just like them."

He snorted. "I ain't gay. Or bi. I gotta be honest, I don't understand it, wantin' to be with another guy." A small shiver worked through him. "Trevor never once made advances toward me like that or I'da busted him in the chops—and he and I have had our share of threesomes so there's been ample opportunities. Damn. It's just plain weird. I think it must be something about Edgard alone that he's attracted to. Trev and I have been friends for our whole lives. We've been damn near as close as brothers. I always jokingly said that he'd fuck anything that walked, only I didn't know how true that actually was."

"Aren't most cowboys highly homophobic?"

"Yeah."

"Including you?"

"Yeah. If it would've been somebody else I'd seen doin' that...I might not have been so understandin'. Then I think about if someone else would've discovered them before I knew about it. How they might've started vicious rumors to get them blackballed from the circuit. Bugs me because I ain't like that.

"What they do is their business. Besides, Trev is with women just as often as I am. Or as I was before you. I don't think many people—even folks who know them well—would believe that he and Edgard are more than ropin' partners."

For the first time she thought there might be another reason why Colby had been eager to have her ride the circuit with them. "So having me traveling with you guys is good for everybody? A cover story for them, so to speak? The girl willing to do all three cowboys, when in fact, two of the cowboys are content just to do each other?"

Colby didn't say anything.

Channing raised her head and looked at him. "What?"

"I didn't ask you to come along for them, Channing. I asked you to come along for me. *I* want you here."

"Why me?"

"Because something about your fire and sweetness called out to me. From the first time I saw you, Chan, I knew you were just as lonely as I was. Stubborn about it, too." He closed his eyes. "Can we talk about this later, darlin'? I'm getting tired again."

She wanted to demand they finish the conversation now. Instead, she waited until he was dozing and untangled from his embrace. No way could she go back to sleep after that.

ઙઙ

Colby was still out by the time they reached Valentine. The motels were full, so it appeared they'd all be sleeping in the horse trailer at the rodeo grounds for at least a night.

While Trevor took care of the horses, Channing and Edgard made a run for food. They didn't talk, letting the country music on the radio fill the void in the truck.

But Channing couldn't stand it any longer. She'd keep the conversation neutral, but dammit, they were going to talk to each other and stop playing this avoidance game. She said, "Tell me how a Brazilian ended up team roping and tie-down roping on the American rodeo circuit."

Edgard turned down Reba McIntyre's "Fancy". "My mother came to America as a foreign exchange student when she was in high school. She met my father at a rodeo when she was seventeen. She ended up pregnant and they got married. About a year after I was born, my birth father died in a car accident.

"My mother was only eighteen, a widow, a foreigner with a baby and no way to support herself. So she returned to her family in Brazil. A couple of years later she married the man I consider my real father. But she kept in touch with my birth father's parents. After I graduated from high school, I came to the US for a few months to meet them. I've been coming here on and off for about ten years."

"Where do they live?"

"Outside of Laramie, which is where I met Trevor. Anyway, because I was raised on a ranch in Brazil, I realized I could make big money here on the rodeo circuit." Edgard shot her a dark look. "Here's where you could point out I'm not making big money now."

She scowled. "But I'm not like that, Edgard. I've got enough things in my own life that need fixed before I'll pass judgment on other people's problems, financial or otherwise."

"Sorry. That was a cheap shot." He sighed. "At one time I did earn money through bull riding and bulldogging, enough that I bought a ranch in Brazil about an hour away from my parents. It is so beautiful. Lush and green and secluded. I miss it."

"So how come you're not there?"

Edgard tapped his fingers on the steering wheel as he brooded out the window. "I'm beginning to wonder that, too."

"Trevor doesn't know what to do about you being in love with him, does he?"

He whipped toward her, his mouth open. "How did you know?"

"I guessed." Channing held up a hand at his immediate protest. "It's not obvious to other people. But because our circumstances—you know, the supposed free-for-all sex, and you not really being into it at all, and then seeing you guys together today..."

Edgard brooded some more. "Have you talked to Trevor?"

"No. I won't either. You can trust me. But I want to ask you something."

"What?"

"Trevor doesn't consider himself gay. So there's no way he'll let you two be together, as a real couple, 'out' in a relationship, right?"

"Right."

"So why are you still here in the US? Following him and the rodeo circuit instead of being at the ranch you love so much?"

"Because I love him more. Or at least I thought I did." Edgard parked the truck and leaned his head back into the headrest. "At the beginning of the year, Trevor hinted around he might be interested in coming to Brazil. Permanently. Living with me. Helping me raise cattle on the ranch. And he made it sound like he wouldn't keep pretending we were just roping partners. That maybe we could be partners in the truest sense of the word. No more hiding."

"But?"

"But first he wanted to spend another year trying to get to the NFR in the team roping. Trying to make his father proud. Trying to prove himself."

"I sense another 'but' coming."

"But as I'm here, spending another summer with him, chasing his dream, getting our asses beat on the circuit every damn day, I've begun to realize he is too afraid to be with me the way I need him to be. That my dreams don't matter to him, maybe they never have." He laughed bitterly. "I don't even mind the women. I've known since the first time we were together that he really is bisexual. I'm not. I never can be. I've never wanted to be." Edgard gave her an embarrassed smile. "I'm sorry."

"Don't apologize for being who you are, Edgard."

"Thank you for that. Trevor's family is very traditional. He'd be disowned if his family knew about us."

"And your family?"

"My family knows I'm gay. They've accepted it and accepted me. So when I'm there, I have a hard time understanding why Trevor can't just be what he is and not care what other people think. When I'm here, in the US, I have to pretend to be something I'm not. And Trevor can't seem to make up his mind what he wants either way."

"Is it worth it?"

"I don't know. Being with him is like a drug. When we're competing together, it's like we're really a team. When we're fucking it's like we're really in love. Every other time it sucks, like coming down off a really great high. And lately, the highs have been few and far between." His body went rigid for a second. "Shit. Sorry. Probably more than you wanted to know, eh?"

"No. Thanks for being honest with me. I've spent my whole life with people pretending to be who they're not and expecting me to be the same shallow person. That's why I ran away with the rodeo."

"Are you finding people are more real here?"

"Some more than others." Channing reached for his hand. "Like I told you the other day. I'd like for us to be friends, because the truth is, I could use one."

Edgard squeezed her hand. "Anytime, shug."

ઊઊ

By the time they unwrapped the sandwiches and set out the rest of the food, Trevor was back from exercising the horses and Colby had shambled down from the sleeping area. He looked like hell. Channing had to bite her tongue against demanding he go back to bed.

The meal was sort of strange, in that with all the sexual things the four of them had done together, it was the first time they'd eaten a meal in the same place.

Colby wasn't a good dinner companion. He complained about the onions on the sandwiches. The lack of beer. He grumbled about having to clean himself up in the tiny shower. When his cell phone rang, Channing was grateful for the chance to escape.

She wandered through the grounds. It was a lovely night, the humidity softened the air so it seemed to soothe her and caress her skin like warm velvet. Lots of folks were sitting outside enjoying the evening, drinking beer. Some kids were practicing throwing ropes. She really didn't have any idea where she was headed until she saw the glare of the arena lights and the empty bleachers.

A couple of gals were taking turns running the barrels.

Channing stayed there, hanging on the fence, on the outside looking in—again—and wondered if she'd ever find a place in her life where she fit in.

She fit with Colby. How he'd recognized her loneliness the first time he'd seen her blew her away. She thought she'd kept that secret well hidden. But she'd noticed things about him too that he'd shrugged off as no big deal.

The soft clip-clop of horse's hooves sounded behind her. She spun and saw Gemma astride a bay mare.

"Channing! Girl, what're you doin' out here all by yourself?"

"Getting some fresh air. What are you doing?"

"Letting Daisy here stretch her legs." Gemma patted the horse's neck. "She's a social butterfly. She wants to see who's hanging around the paddock. Mostly I think she's got her eye on cozying up to one of them cutting horse studs."

"She's beautiful."

"You want to ride her? She's really gentle."

Channing laughed. "Can I tell you something completely embarrassing?"

Gemma grinned. "You don't know how to ride a horse, do you?"

"Nope. Not the first thing about it."

"Well, lucky you've got me to teach you."

"The teacher being taught, that has a nice ring to it."

"You're a teacher?"

"Yep."

"Wow. That's great. What age group?"

"I'm supposed to teach high school in the fall. But my real love would be elementary kids."

"Why can't you switch and do that?"

Channing sighed. "It's a long story."

"I've got time. Come on, help me bed Daisy down for the night and we'll talk about making you into a real horsewoman."

Channing wished she would've brought her notebook. There was so much more to taking care of a horse than she'd ever dreamed. Gemma chatted as she performed the tasks she'd done a million times. When she finished she said, "Early tomorrow we'll get saddled up."

"I don't know…"

"It'll be fun, I promise." She wiped a gloved hand across her forehead, leaving a smear of dirt. "I got beer in the trailer if you want one."

Channing thought it'd be rude to point out the smudge so she didn't. "I'd love a beer."

"Good. Let's sit outside, soak in the night. I hate being cooped up all day in the damn truck."

At her campsite, Gemma pulled out two lawn chairs and a six-pack of Bud Light. She popped the tops on two cans, handed one to Channing and toasted her. "Cheers."

"Cheers."

After a long pull of beer, Gemma sighed and propped her booted feet on the cooler. "That's what I'm talkin' about. This is getting to be my favorite time of day." She grinned. "Beer o'clock."

Channing laughed.

"So, tell me, Channing Kinkaid, who you are, and why you're running with the rodeo and a buncha cowboys. You look smarter than that."

Again, Channing laughed and gave Gemma the long version of her life, the run down of her crises and conflicts and the temporary escape from it.

Gemma looked thoughtful for a minute as she finished her second beer. Then she said, "Sounds like you got out in the nick of time."

"But I do have to go back," Channing pointed out.

"You don't gotta do nothin' you don't want to. That's the beauty of being young and where you're at in your life."

"By blowing off my obligations?" she countered.

"Only person you're obligated to make happy is yourself. Is Colby McKay helpin' you blow off some steam and taking some of the starch out of your spine?"

"You might say that."

"And since I've got no life and no shame, my next question…is he any good?"

Channing sipped her beer before she let a slow smile tilt the corners of her mouth. "Oh, yeah."

"Come on, girl. Details. Vivid details."

"You've seen him on broncs?"

"Uh-huh."

"Well, rough stock ain't the only thing he can ride like a wild man. And he can ride long and ride hard, all night."

Gemma hooted. "Keep goin'."

"You know the phrase 'hung like a bull'?"

"Uh-huh."

Channing leaned forward. "Bulls ain't got nothin' on him. And believe me, when he's riding, bucking him off is the *last* thing on my mind."

"Oh. My. God. I need another goddamn beer. Better yet, give me some ice out of that cooler."

"Come on, Gemma. This isn't anything you haven't heard before, right?"

"About Colby? Or men in particular?"

"Both."

"That your way of fishin' for information on Colby?"

"Can't put anything over on you, huh, Gem?"

She snorted. "Okay. I'm gonna admit that I know Colby's folks a little better than I know him. Our ranches are only about three hours apart.

"So, here's what I know about your rough rider. He likes 'em young. He likes 'em once and then he likes 'em gone." Gemma tipped her can toward Channing. "So as I see it, from my years of wisdom, you've clean busted out of all three molds he likes to put his women in. Just maybe there's more to what's goin' on with you two than a short summer fling."

"I doubt it." Channing chalked up the increased beat of her heart to beer, not hope. "What about you? How long have you been a widow?"

"Two and a half, long, lonely years."

"And in that time..." Channing trailed off expectantly.

Gemma sank a little lower in her lawn chair. "In that time I haven't done the mattress mambo. Not once."

"Why not? You're pretty, you're fun, you're bright, you're respected, you know everything about rodeo stock—"

"But I'm old, Channing."

Channing frowned. "Old. Right. What ancient age are you? Thirty-five? Thirty-six?"

"Either you are my new best friend for saying that or Colby's gift for charm is wearing off on you." Gemma smiled briefly before she fiddled with the pop-top on her beer can. "I'm forty-seven."

Channing whistled. "Wow. You don't look it."

"I feel it. Lord. I see those young thangs—" she gestured with her can, "—like you and those eighteen-year-olds with the perky tits, and the pert asses and the pierced belly buttons...and hell, they *are* something to behold. Sleek and slick and sexy and can perform more fancy moves in public than a trick rider. No wonder no man my age looks at me twice."

Channing wondered if Gemma had noticed that Cash Big Crow always looked at her—way more than twice. Surely Gemma couldn't be that blind?

"You know how they say what goes around comes around? Well, must be karma biting me on the ass." Gemma tossed her beer can in the pile on the ground. "Believe it or not, I was one of those hot little numbers when I was eighteen. Looking at older widowed women with contempt. Thinking they were ancient. They ought to just go back home, take up knitting and leave the wild living to the good-time girls like me.

"Ironically enough, I didn't end up with one of those dreamy young cowboys my age who circled me like studs around a mare in season. I married a man old enough to be my daddy."

Crickets chirped in the immediate silence.

Channing crushed her beer can under her heel. "Oh, come on, Gemma. You can't start a story like that and then expect me to fill in the blanks or to sit here politely and not demand to know what happened. Spill it."

She smiled. "Short version: I had a terrible home life growing up. We were poor, lived in rural Wyoming, my father was abusive, my mother just took his mean mouth and his flying fists by drinkin' herself into oblivion. I wanted better. After I graduated from high school, I moved to Sheridan and worked as a waitress.

"Bright lights, big city, right? I lived in a shitty trailer with two other waitresses and worked my ass off, still going nowhere fast. And to top it off, even though I couldn't wait to get away from my family I was so damn lonely."

Channing froze. Hadn't she and Colby talked about loneliness earlier?

"About that same time, this older rancher—he was all of forty-one—would come in and sit in my section. He came in every single day, sometimes twice a day, for four months. A real gentleman cowboy. He was quiet. Polite. A great listener. Generous. Sweet." She closed her eyes. "Lord, he was so damn sweet. Totally the opposite of any man I'd ever known."

"You fell for him?"

"Not at first. I wanted me a flashy guy. I started hanging out at rodeos. Figuring a big buckle meant a big man. Hearing promises that turned out to be lies. Then one night, while I was whooping it up, not having nearly as much fun as I thought I should've been, I saw that quiet rancher from the diner. On his horse. Getting ready to compete in the bulldogging event.

"It kinda threw me for a loop because I never expected him to be the type of guy who'd take dangerous risks. He always seemed...solid. Boring. So I left my friends and snuck closer to the chutes so I could watch him compete.

"He burst out of that gate, all strength and poise and agility. Not showing an ounce of fear as he launched himself off his horse and at that steer. Flipping three-hundred pounds of animal into submission in the dirt like it was nothin'. Then he calmly stood up and checked his time. For some reason he spun my direction and saw me hanging on the railing, my jaw practically dragging on the ground from shock.

"He brushed the dirt from his jeans as he moseyed toward me. The whole time he kept coming at me, taking those slowly measured steps; his eyes never left my face. It was like I was the only one in the arena. Like I was the only one in the world. And then I knew."

"That you loved him?"

She smiled again, but it was wistful, slightly sad. "That came later, but not much later. No. I knew then that quiet power and understated grace were the true measure of a good man, not the size of his belt buckle or his intentions."

"What happened?"

"He stopped in front of me. He reached out and tucked a piece of hair behind my ear. Then he ran his rough fingers down the line of my jaw. It was the first time he'd ever touched me. So softly, yet, so...confidently. Like he knew just what I needed. He said, 'Gemma Mae, don't you think it's time you quit foolin' yourself and come on home with me where you belong?'"

Tears pricked Channing's eyes and she swallowed hard.

"I went home with him that night and never looked back."

"Omigod. I think I'm gonna cry. That is the most beautiful, romantic story I've ever heard."

"Yeah, it is. Come to think of it, you're the first person I've ever told that to."

"Now I'm really gonna start bawling."

"Well, you can understand why I've been a little reluctant to bring another man into my life and into my bed." She grinned saucily. "Especially when gentleman Steve Jansen had moves between the sheets, in the barn, on the kitchen table and anywhere else the mood struck him that'd probably give your Colby a run for his money for inventiveness. The last thing Steve ever was, in or out of bed, was boring. God, he was good. With one look he could heat me up like fire and melt me like butter."

"I'm sorry that's he's gone, Gemma."

"Me too. Not only do I miss Steve every goddamn day, I miss that daily physical connection. I miss sex. But when you've had twenty-five years of bust-the-bed-frame-scream-out-loud-raw-and-sweet-and-raunchy sex, I'm afraid anything else would be a let down. But what I wouldn't give for a second chance to have it again."

Channing wasn't the least bit embarrassed by Gemma's brutal honesty. The answering silence between them wasn't clumsy, just thoughtful.

The grass crunched behind them and Gemma craned her neck.

Cash Big Crow stepped around the heap of beer cans and leaned his shoulder into the side of the horse trailer. "Evenin', ladies."

"Cash, were you using your Indian stealth again to sneak up on us and listen to our private conversation?" Gemma demanded.

"Gemma!" Channing said, appalled.

Cash didn't smile. In fact, he had the oddest expression on his face. He didn't look at Channing either, but at Gemma, even as he addressed his comments to Channing. "Don't mind Gem. She knows I wouldn't show her my secret Indian tricks unless she asked me nice. *Real* nice."

"Keep dreaming," Gemma said.

He chuckled. "I will. Channing, I tracked you down to tell you Colby is lookin' for you. You want me to walk you back?"

"No, that's fine. I can find my way." She stood and stretched. "Thanks for the beer and the girl talk, Gemma."

"Anytime. See you bright and early, right?"

"Right. I'll be here with bells on."

"Have a good night. Ride 'em hard, girl."

Channing snickered and gave Gemma a high-five.

Cash cocked his head and looked from Channing to Gemma. "I'm afraid to ask what *that* meant."

"You should be." Gemma sailed to her feet. "Then again, it's more of a 'hands on' thing anyway."

"Yeah? Well, luckily I ain't got nowhere to be right now. You could demonstrate by puttin' your hands on me all you want."

Gemma laughed, a trifle nervously.

Cash took another step closer and frowned. He lifted his hand and rubbed his fingertips across Gemma's forehead. Gently. Three times.

"What are you doing?"

"You got a smudge of dirt right there, and a piece of grass stuck in your hair. You been rollin' around in the hay?"

"There've been no rolls in the hay for me for a long time," Gemma retorted.

"That's a damn cryin' shame," Cash said softly.

The air thickened. Channing held her breath, feeling like an interloper.

"Ah. Well, good night, Cash."

"'Night, Gem. Sweet dreams, sweetheart."

Cash turned to Channing. "Come on, I'll walk you over anyway."

After they'd reached the horse trailer, Channing said, "You know, Cash, you really should take a more direct approach with Gemma. The Indian stealth stuff isn't working. She doesn't have a clue that you're so crazy about her."

Before his face could turn any redder, Channing blew him a kiss and closed the door in his face.

Chapter Fifteen

The lights were off inside. Neither Trevor nor Edgard were stretched out on the floor. Where were they? She peered at the sleeping area. Chances were slim Colby was asleep if he'd sent Cash looking for her.

"Colby?"

"'Bout damn time you came back. Where've you been?"

"Talking to Gemma. Why? Did you miss me?"

Pause. "What do you think?"

"I think if you're gonna be a jerk to me I'll turn around and leave and go back to drinking beer with Gemma."

"Sorry. I'm just bored. A bit lonesome. And yeah, I missed you, okay?"

She smiled in the darkness. "Okay. You need anything before I come up there? Ice for your hand?"

"Nah. I'm fine."

Channing climbed up and flicked on the wall lamp at the head of the bed.

Immediately, his left bicep covered his face. "Ow. My eyes. Shut that damn thing off."

"Poor baby." *Click.* Back into shadows. "How do you feel?"

"Honestly? My hand hurts. My ribs are tender. And I'm so goddamned horny I've been layin' here, thinkin' about whackin' off for some quick relief. Except my right hand is all bandaged up and I ain't so good at goin' lefty."

She laughed and leaned over to nuzzle his neck. "How about if I offer you some relief? I ain't so good at going lefty either. Maybe it'd be better for both of us if I used my mouth."

"Uh. Yeah. Your mouth. Uh. Yeah. That'd be good."

Colby? Tongue-tied? She didn't know whether to be touched or nervous. "Since it's dark in here and I don't want to hurt you, guide me to where you want me." She placed her fingers on his lips, tracing the warm fullness.

He kissed them, briefly sucked her index and middle finger into his mouth, then he wrapped his hand around hers and shifted the covers back to set her palm on his erect penis. At some point he'd taken off his boxers so she just felt him. Long. Thick. Hard. Hot. Ready.

Channing scooted down Colby's body, avoiding bumping his upper torso. She'd rather take a shortcut and trail soft healing kisses and touches over his bruised ribs. But she knew he'd rather have a trail of hot, hungry kisses down his cock. A couple of quick hard strokes and she brought him into her wet mouth.

Colby groaned and arched, trying to shove his dick in deeper. Which lasted about a second because he winced in pain and dropped back to the mattress, letting his cock slip free from between her lips.

Channing knew Mr. Take Charge preferred to grab her hair and direct her mouth to where he wanted it. But since Colby was banged up, he didn't get to be in charge. His immobility would give her a chance to decide on the level of participation she'd allow him. For once, this was all *her* show.

Heh heh. This was going to be *so* fun.

"Channing, darlin', I can't move much, so you're gonna hafta—"

"Do whatever *I* want. My, my. Isn't this a turn of the tables?" She flicked the stiff tip of her tongue back and forth over the magic spot under the cockhead. Then she retreated to blow a stream of cool breath on the moist area.

He hissed.

She played with him. Sucking him deep into the slippery recess of her mouth until her lips brushed the base of his cock. She built a seductive, calculating rhythm with firm strokes of her hand and teasing tugs of her wet mouth that almost sent him soaring over that dark edge. Twice. But she stopped both times to nuzzle his balls. Lapping at the tight sac like a cat. She'd roll his balls in her mouth like she was sucking a lollipop.

When his whole body started to shake she knew it wasn't from a fever. Powerful stuff, being in charge. She'd have to try it more often.

Her firm lips nibbled up and down the sides of that straining length of rigid flesh until it quivered against his belly. A little lick here, a little lick there. She avoided the tip weeping for her attention.

Colby groaned and shifted his hips slightly. "Now you're just bein' mean."

"No. It'd be mean if I stopped entirely. And if you complain again, that's what I'll do."

"You wouldn't."

Channing made as if to leave.

"Okay, okay! I believe you. Jesus. Don't go, darlin'. I'll behave."

She smirked and let her hair drift up his battered body, over and over—a thousand little lashes of pleasure on his sensitized skin.

He shuddered and said, “That feels so good. Everything you do to me feels good.”

She licked his neck, much like she’d licked his cock and he moaned. After toying with his earlobe with her tongue and teeth and breath—which drove him crazy—she whispered, “Where’s the lube?”

One-handed, Colby frantically patted the area beside him and then pressed a cold metal tube against her arm.

She drew back. “You already had the KY up here? Pretty confident, aren’t you, cowboy?”

“No. Just hopeful. I’m an optimistic sort of guy; I think you forgot that about me, shug.”

Optimistic. Right. The man was just plain cocky. Channing flipped the cap open on the lube. Instead of warming the gel in her hand first, she squirted a cold line of it straight down his dick.

“Jesus Christ!” He shot up and froze at the sudden pain the movement caused before he flopped back down. “Shit. That’s cold.”

“You’ll get used to it,” she murmured and began to work him methodically with the slippery friction of her palm.

“I deserved that, didn’t I?”

“Yep. But you deserve this, too.” Channing kissed the blunt end of his cock, opened her lips wide and slid that glorious smooth male skin past her teeth, over her tongue until his shaft was buried as deep as possible in her mouth.

With one hand she feathered her fingers over his balls as her hungry mouth pumped him faster and faster, letting the lube and saliva mix together until he was sopping wet everywhere, as she knew he liked it. She liked it, too. God. She loved going down on him, as evidenced by her own thighs, sticky from arousal.

Colby began to pant and grind his hips into her face, whispering, “Please, please, yes, God, don’t stop, yes, ah, like that, more, oh, baby. I fucking love this. Goddamn you’re good at that. YES.”

The second his balls lifted, she swirled her middle finger around the wetness coating him between the legs and slid it into his anus.

“Fuck!” He sat up, grabbed her hair and held her in place as he started to come.

She kept her lips wrapped around his cock as he pulsed and exploded in her mouth. She hollowed her cheeks and sucked, swallowing every hot spurt, losing herself in his taste. In the power of making this strong man relinquish control. To her.

“Channing, my God what are you doin’…”

She lovingly lapped the tip of his semi-erect cock and wiggled and thrust that digit harder, deeper inside his tight back channel. Colby went utterly still, then he clenched his muscles, bore down hard, grinding his ass into her hand and he came again around her pumping finger.

Colby grunted but stayed upright as she pulled back completely. “You’re gonna fuckin’ kill me. That was so goddamn good that if I died tomorrow, I’d die a happy man.”

It hit her then. Colby really could die tomorrow. Something could go wrong with the broncs or the bulls or even his horse and he could be dead in a matter of less than eight seconds.

Oh God. The thought of this resilient man being a bag of broken bones. The thought of not seeing him ever again. The thought of him cold, dead and buried. She remembered the sad look in Gemma's eyes when she talked about losing the love of her life. And the fact that Channing felt exactly the same way meant...

She was in love with Colby McKay.

She scrambled back on her knees.

Of course Colby sensed her distress. "Chan? Darlin', what's wrong?"

"Um nothing. You should lie down and rest."

"Not until you tell me why the sudden change from red hot to icy cold." He paused. "You aren't ashamed of anything we've done, are you?"

"God, no. It's just...you're hurting and you should be resting not wasting time screwing around with me."

Colby snagged her by the shirt and hauled her up short until they were nose to nose. "That's about the dumbest goddamn thing I've ever heard you say. Nothin' we do when we're alone together is a waste of time."

"Let go."

"No."

Channing jerked away, and Colby winced, but he gritted his teeth and held on to her.

"See? You're hurt and you're in pain and I can't stand it. And what's worse is I can't stand the thought that this will keep happening to you. Next time maybe something even worse—" Her voice broke.

"Ssh. Take a deep breath." He brought her forehead to his lips. "That's what this is about? Me gettin' hurt today?"

She nodded, too much of a chicken to tell him the rest of her revelation. Who'd believe a person could fall in love in four days anyway? Romantic nonsense.

Yet it didn't feel like only four days. It didn't feel like nonsense. It felt…right.

"Nothin' I say will convince you that I'm fine, will it?"

"Probably not."

"Channing. Look at me."

She angled back. He kissed her with tenderness. She melted into the kiss, letting him think he'd reassured her when she wondered if anything would ever soothe her again.

Colby smoothed his hand over her scalp, intertwining his fingers in her hair. "Better?"

"Yeah."

He eased onto his back and sighed. "Now then. Why don't you strip off them britches and come up here and sit on my face?"

"What?"

"You heard me. I can't use my hands but I'm better with my tongue anyway." He grinned and his teeth shone brightly in the dimness. A little wolf-like, she thought.

"I-I don't know if that's such a good idea."

"Yes, you do. I can smell that sweet cream gathered between your thighs and I've got a mind to taste you, darlin'. Long and slow and deep. With the way I have doin' that in mind, you can't hurt me. You'll be in total control. You seemed to really like it. Hell, I'm a modern guy. I don't mind you bein' in control once in a while."

Channing felt the warmth between her legs begin to pulse with renewed interest. She stripped. "How's this gonna work?"

"Throw your leg over my chest like you were mountin' a horse. Then stay on all fours with your knees by my ears and back that pussy right into my face." He smacked his lips like she was offering him a gourmet meal.

The old Channing would've been mortified exposing so much of her less-than-perfect body to a man, her private parts especially, in such an intimate manner. But Colby wasn't just any man. He was her man, her lover. He found her sexy and hot and he wanted her as she was; flaws, fat ass and all.

"Hang on, cowboy, I'm mounting up." She kissed his belly and chest and she reversed into him, finding herself even more aroused as she dangled above him upside down.

"Oh yeah. Gimme some of this sweetness. Scoot back, shug. Just like that." Colby buried his face in her cunt.

"Omigod." At this angle the sensations were completely different. Cooler, as her hot tingly parts were riding high in the air. Wetter, as his cheeks and tongue spread the moisture from his mouth and her sex up the inside of her thighs and higher, through her muff and back to her ass. Sharper. Or it could've just been the nip of Colby's teeth. Or the constant hard flicker of his tongue.

"Like that do you?"

"Yes." The inside of her legs began to vibrate. Every bit of her skin pulsed. Channing rocked into him, whimpering as her orgasm hovered on the edges. "I'm gonna be pretty quick on the trigger this time."

"Good. Let's see if this won't spur you along." He licked and sucked and bit her clit, making little mmm-mmm noises in between slurping her juices, jamming his tongue deeply inside her pussy, fucking her with his mouth until she ground her wet sex down and came all over his face.

Afterward she fell beside him in a quivering heap, breathing hard, stunned yet again by how in tune this man was with her every unspoken need.

"Damn. I was gonna put some ice up that pretty snatch and suck it out to see how you liked that, but I plumb forgot."

"That's okay. You might've killed me."

"Come up here and give me that mouth."

"You sure wanna play kissy face with me a lot today, Colby."

"Nuh-uh. Not just today. Every day."

As Channing teasingly brushed her lips over his, the trailer door banged open. They both froze, midkiss.

Trevor laughed. "It smells like sex in here. What's a guy got to do to get an invite to the fun and games? Or am I excluded these days?"

Colby's hand stroked her face. He whispered, "Your call."

"You don't care?"

"I know part of the reason you're travelin' with us is to fulfill your fantasies of fucking two guys at the same time. We're both here. We're both willin'. You have to do whatever makes you happy, Chan."

That wasn't the answer she wanted, but maybe it was the one she needed to put things back in perspective. This was a sexual adventure. A temporary sexual adventure, nothing more. In the heat of the moment she'd just confused lust and love. She smiled and pushed back on her heels. "We're up here, Trev."

"Naked?"

"Completely."

"Hot damn. Give me a second to catch up."

Colby's face was unreadable in the dark. Was he turned on by the idea of a threesome? She knew this situation wasn't anything new for him and Trevor.

But it surprised her that even with all she'd done and seen today, the idea of being fucked by Colby and Trevor at the same time kicked her lust back into high gear.

The mattress shifted as Trevor scrambled up. "Colby, you feelin' better, buddy?"

"Yeah. My girl Channing kissed it and made it all better, didn't you, darlin'?"

"Yep." She faced Trevor and crawled to him like a slinky cat. "Since Colby is flat on his back, looks like he's a bottom. We know what I am. So guess what that makes you?"

"Very lucky." Trevor snagged her around the waist, tugged her to his naked chest and crushed his mouth to hers. His kiss was a show of aggression.

Channing gave him that aggression right back. Raking her nails over his smooth chest, digging her fingers into his slim hipbones. Wrapping her hand around his cock and jacking up and down vigorously, remembering how much he'd loved it hard and fast when Edgard had done it.

Trevor plumped her breasts and lowered his head, sucking her nipples, his teeth nipping to that point of pain and backing off when she whimpered. Using the moisture from his mouth, his middle finger drew a straight line down her belly to her clit.

The air grew heavy with the sounds of labored breathing, and the dark, heady scent of sex.

Colby said, "Channing. Come here. Now."

His voice dripped authority and...jealousy? She laid her hand on Trevor's face as he flicked his tongue over her nipple in time to his finger working her clit. She didn't want him to stop. She arched into him for more. "God. That's so good."

"You heat up in a hurry, don't you?"

"Channing." Colby's voice was sharper.

"In a minute."

"No. Now."

Trevor released her nipple with a loud pop, looked up and smiled. "Sounds like someone's ready. Are you?"

"Mmm-hmm. Do you have condoms?"

"Right here."

Channing turned and scuttled back to Colby.

He'd grabbed his cock with his left hand and was idly stroking himself. His eyes glittered challenge. "You prepared to get fucked? By both of us? My cock in your pussy and Trevor's dick rammin' into your ass?"

For a second she froze. She looked over her shoulder at Trevor. "I know it might seem a little late to ask this, but should we be chatting about STDs? Especially since..."

"Since I'm bi? Edgard is the only man I've ever been with, Channing. I don't have AIDS or anything else. Neither does Edgard, okay? We always use condoms. You're safe. We're safe. I swear. I wouldn't be doin' this otherwise."

She nodded.

Colby said, "Put the condom on me. I can't wait to see the look on your face when we're both inside you."

Her heart seemed to be pounding a mile a minute as she rolled on the condom. Excitement, fear, curiosity—all danced in her head and fired her blood. She straddled Colby's pelvis, planting her palms flat on the mattress next to his shoulders. "Are you sure this isn't going to hurt you?"

"Go ahead and hurt me. It's the kind of hurt I like." Colby kissed her with a warm deluge of passion.

Trevor traced the crack of her ass to the rosette hidden between her cheeks. A cool gel brushed over the tight spot before a thick finger worked up inside her.

Colby said, "While he's doin' that, slide my cock in that wet pussy. Take it all in one stroke."

She lifted her hips and reached back for him to guide it in. It was unbearably erotic, the way their hands touched and twined around his rigid sex together as they stared into each other's eyes and their ragged breath mingled. One downward push and all that male hardness glided right in, eased by the liquid excitement leaking from her drenched cunt.

"Bend over," Trevor urged. "I know you don't want to crush his ribs, balance on your knees. Oh yeah. Like that. Come on. Give me this ass. It's gonna feel so fucking good."

"Be careful," Colby warned Trevor. "She's new to this. Go slow and don't hurt her or I'll kick your ass."

Touched by Colby's concern, she smashed her lips to his as Trevor pressed the head of his cock into her ass and then drove straight in.

She whimpered in Colby's mouth. "Oh God. That hurts."

Colby moved his lips to her ear. "Ssh. Come on. It's okay. We've done this before. We don't have to go fast. Let your body adjust to us, darlin'. You set the pace. We can go as slowly as you want."

For a second, she wanted to stop.

"When you're ready, push down on me and Trev will pull out."

Trevor's rough fingertips scraped down her spine. "Chan? You okay?"

No. "Yeah."

A second later Trevor's cock slipped out until only the head remained inside her back channel.

Channing hadn't moved on Colby's cock at all. She was afraid to. The fullness...burned. She held her breath until she was light-headed.

"Trev. This ain't workin'. She's completely tensed up."

"You want me to stop?"

"For a second." He murmured, "Shug? What do you need?"

Someone to distract me. "Someone to touch my clit."

Colby said to Trevor, "Can you reach her?"

"Yeah. If I slide back in all the way."

"Do it."

She shuddered when Trevor's hips were once again plastered to her backside.

Trevor reached around and traced circles around her slippery clit, seeming careful not to accidentally touch Colby's cock embedded inside her. "Tell me what'll do it for you."

"Up and down. Not your thumb. Your finger. Press right *there.*" Ooh. That felt good. She relaxed a tiny bit.

Colby said, "Put your hands by my head and dangle them luscious tits closer to my mouth, darlin'."

Channing shifted and Colby's mouth latched onto her nipple. He focused on her aching breasts, switching back and forth, gently licking, then sucking forcefully, blowing across the tips, dragging open-mouthed kisses across the tops and nuzzling the ultra-sensitive bottom curves, whispering nonsensical lover's words, which calmed her.

Then between Colby's concentration on her breasts and Trevor's patient attention to her clit, she was awash in pure pleasure. Pain subsided. And before she knew it she started bumping back into Trevor's cock, hinting for a deeper thrust.

He forged forward, and then pulled back. During his slow retreat, Channing wiggled down on Colby's shaft and raised up as Trevor eased in. They built a steady rhythm and the intense burning feeling took a different, pleasurable turn. When the head of Trevor's cock brushed against Colby's through the thin tissue separating them, the pace slowed.

She arched at the response of her body, tingles chased by an intimate throbbing deep within those tissues. She groaned out loud.

Trevor said, "Does that feel good? You ready for more?"

"Yes."

"Use my cock to fuck yourself however you want," Colby said against the hollow of her throat, the tease of his urgent whisper turned her skin into a mass of goose bumps. "Show me what you like. Show me how I can fuck you next time, when it's just us."

Channing lifted her head and closed her eyes, giving herself to the moment, as Trevor picked up the pace, every forward thrust harder than the last. Colby suckled her nipples until she thought his undivided, unrelenting attention to her breasts alone would set her off.

Plunge. Retreat. A back-and-forth play of peek-a-boo of two hard cocks. The strokes became shorter. Faster. Harder.

"I'm close, Chan. Are you?" Trevor asked.

"Me too, darlin'. Grind down into me," Colby panted. "Then when I tell you, squeeze me hard."

Trevor slammed in one last time, his hands like steel bands around her hips as he came. Grunting. Holding perfectly still as her tight anal muscles milked him. She felt the pulse of his cock, but with the condom, not that hot burst of moisture.

Colby angled his hips and winced. "Faster. Hell yeah. Fucking you is a dream. Bear down."

The second she did, her orgasm blindsided her. The muscles in her anus contracted around Trevor's cock, still jammed high in her ass. As Colby's orgasm rocketed through him, she swore she felt the throbbing tip of his cock in the back of her throat. Tasted it actually. Then the rasp of his pubic hair over her clit triggered another, stronger pulsating peak and she screamed from the most overpowering, debilitating, mind-blowing orgasm of her life.

At the last minute, when she'd fallen from that hazy place of sheer bliss, she remembered not to crumple onto Colby's chest. She stayed stiff, her head hanging low, her hair pooling on the bed above Colby's head.

Trevor pulled out first. He sank his teeth into the curve where her shoulder met her neck and trailed kisses along the slope until she shivered.

"Thank you. I hope it was all you wanted it to be. It sure was all that for me. You are one sexy, fine woman." He staggered from the sleeping compartment and out of the trailer.

Channing sucked in another ragged breath, not able to think beyond the tremors still wracking her body.

"Channing? Darlin'?"

Her head snapped up at the sliver of pain in Colby's voice. "Oh crap. Sorry. I'm probably hurting you."

"No. Look at me."

She pushed her hair out of her face and angled her upper body back, keeping him fully seated inside her. The man was still hard.

Something indefinable lurked in Colby's intense gaze. "Did that fulfill your wildest fantasies, shug? Being with two guys?"

She couldn't speak, she merely nodded.

"Good. Because it ain't ever gonna happen again." His free hand knotted in her hair and he brought her face in line with his. His blue eyes flashed heat. "You're mine. And the thing you need to learn about me is that I don't share what's mine."

"Colby—"

"Your little sexual adventure is done. You understand me? Anything you need in bed you'll get from me. I'll give it to you any way you want, whenever you want it, but I'll be the *only* one fucking you, is that clear?"

She stared at him.

Colby sat up abruptly and jerked her legs around until her ankles were crossed at the small of his back. Plastered belly to belly and chest to chest wasn't enough for him. His left hand circled her nape and he brought them nose to nose, so their lips were only a breath apart. He pumped his hips, driving his cock hard and high.

"Stop. You're hurt—"

"If I'm gonna hurt, it's gonna be from fucking you until neither of us can walk. If I'm gonna pass out, it's gonna be from comin' so goddamn hard the top of my goddamn head blew off. If it takes all night, darlin', I'm gonna prove that you've moved into the number one spot of being the single thing in my life that has the power to hurt me the most."

Tears sparked her eyes and she surrendered to his need, allowing this tough but tender man to demonstrate it in the only way he knew how—with his body.

He ate at her mouth with hungry kisses. He licked her neck. Marking her skin everywhere with wet sucking kisses. Marking her with his teeth. Marking her with the scrape of his beard on her sensitive flesh. Marking her with his scent.

It was a prolonged, raw mating. Heated. Elemental. Powerful. During her first orgasm she clutched his hair and rode it out. During the second orgasm she dug her nails into his flexing ass cheeks and shuddered against his heaving chest. During the third climax she scratched his back hard enough to draw blood as she ground her pelvis to his.

Drenched in sweat, breathless, it wasn't enough. For either of them. After Colby had come again, he withdrew his still-hard cock from her swollen pussy. He pressed his mouth to her throat. "Take the condom off."

Once Channing had removed it, he used his powerful thighs to change the angle of her hips.

"I want your ass, Channing. I want to look in your eyes as I'm fucking you there. I want to suck your tits as you come. As you feel me coming and those tight muscles milking every hot burst. And if that's not enough for you, I'll do it again." He panted against her neck, sending shivers through her. "I'll fuck this sweet ass with my cock as my fingers fuck your pussy. I'll keep at it until you know I'm the only man you'll ever need."

His words, his resolve stole her reason. "Colby, please. Enough. I know—"

"No, you don't. God. You don't have a clue what I need from you. What I can give you. But I've got a mind to show you."

As she tipped his face toward hers and stared into his eyes, she saw pain. Emotional pain. Real physical pain. This...possession was taking its toll on him. Channing lifted up, and guided his cock to her rear entrance. Slowly she sank down on him, reveling in how she could change his pain and his fit of temper into bliss.

And it was bliss, an unhurried surrender as she gave him every part of her body. As he climaxed, she followed right behind him, lost in the cosseted way he made her feel. Almost like love.

Colby was wrung out and crashed with utter exhaustion. Channing studied the multitude of old white scars covering most every section of his body, wanting to heal those old wounds, touching him without restriction as she watched him sleep.

But sleep was a long time in coming for her.

Chapter Sixteen

Colby wasn't particularly surprised when he woke alone the next morning. He'd been hard on Channing. More demanding, more needy, more domineering than he'd ever been with any woman.

More of a total asshole, too.

Talk about trying to fuck her into submission.

He sighed and tried to move. He winced and groaned at the lingering body aches. From his tumble off the bulls and broncs. Oh, and his tumble straight into love with Channing Kinkaid.

Damn. He had not handled that well. He needed to clean up and come clean with her before they both did something stupid and ran away from yet another set of problems. Namely how they felt so strongly about each other in such a short time. He rolled to his side and pain shot up his arm.

"Jesus fucking Christ."

"Ah. It lives. You need help getting down?" Edgard said from the bottom of the ladder.

Colby froze. He'd thought he was alone. Actually, he'd hoped Channing was sitting at the table, enjoying her morning coffee. Waiting for him to grovel. "Nah. I wouldn't mind if you'd toss me a bottle of aspirin and a bottle of water."

"No problem."

The little fridge snicked open and shut. Edgard's head popped up and the pain pills rattled in the plastic as they landed on the sleeping bag.

"Thanks, man," Colby said as he reached for the proffered water bottle. "I feel like shit."

"You still gonna ride today?"

"Hell yes."

"I thought so. Trevor's out exercising King. You'd better get moving. It's nearly eight."

Last call for check-in time was nine. It'd probably take him at least that long to work the kinks out of his aching body, and get a fresh coat of ointment slathered on his aches and pains and wrap up his ribcage in bandages. "Is there any hot water left to shower?"

"Should be. No one else has used it this morning."

Colby flopped back down, a bad feeling churning in his gut.

Edgard sighed. "How long's it gonna take before you ask where she is, McKay?"

"Fine. Where is she?"

"She gathered her stuff early this morning and headed to Gemma's."

"What stuff?"

"Her duffel bag. Some clothes."

Fuck. Stay cool. "What'd she say before she left?"

"She said to tell you she'd see you later." Edgard poked his head over the edge of the bed again and studied him.

Colby snapped, "What?"

"What happened last night besides the threesome, *amigo*?"

"You knew about it?"

He nodded. "Trevor came looking for me after. He knew something was up with you two. He said it felt like jealousy. You wanna talk about it?"

If Colby had a problem he needed to hash out, he usually talked to Trevor, not Edgard. But as Colby had an insanely crazy jealous streak thinking about Trevor and Channing together—when Trevor was, oh, fucking *gay*—maybe it was obvious he was going off the deep end where that little spitfire was concerned.

"What happened was I was a total dickhead."

"So apologize to her."

"I don't know if that will be enough. Fuck. I'm not good at this kind of shit. I never know what the hell I'm supposed to do. Or say. No wonder I'm still single." Gritting his teeth against the pain, he sat up. Talking it out never solved a goddamned thing. He changed the subject. "Where were you last night anyway?"

"On the phone. My mother called."

"From Brazil? Something serious?"

"Yeah. Evidently, there are some problems at my ranch in the last month. The foreman wouldn't let her in when she drove up there to check on things. When he finally granted her access, she said at least fifty people are living around the main ranch house. They've butchered my cattle for food. Chopped down trees for firewood. Built some shanties…it's a big mess."

"Shit, man. I'm sorry. What are you going to do?"

"Go home. I should leave today." Edgard hopped down from the bench seat and began to pace. "Trevor has his heart set on competing in Cheyenne at Frontier Days. I can't just leave him high and dry. He needs me." He expelled a bitter laugh. "That might be a first for him."

Colby swung his legs to the ladder. "The preliminaries are in two days. There are at least four other heelers who could work with him, Ed."

"Yeah, but he's superstitious. He wants me as his heeler because we did so well in Cheyenne last year. Problem is we suck right now. So, as soon as we're out of the race for the buckle and the money, I'll be on a plane for Brazil."

Colby opened his mouth. Closed it.

"What?"

"Does Trevor know you're leaving?"

"Yep. What he doesn't know is once I'm back home, I ain't comin' back here. He's welcome to come with me. Or he can stay here. His choice." Edgard looked at Colby. "All I know is I can't do this anymore. Trevor can't have it both ways."

A heavy silence weighted the air.

Colby scratched his chin. "I wish I knew what to say."

"There's nothin' to say. Love sucks all around, *amigo*." On his way out, Edgard stopped at the door and turned back. "Piece of advice. Don't blow this thing with Channing. Don't hide how you feel about her. Because some of us don't get that choice."

Colby had nothing to say to that either. And he only had half an hour before he had to show up, pretend he wasn't beat to shit, confused as hell, and act ready to rodeo.

☙❧

"Dammit, Gemma, I'm never gonna get this!"

"Oh hush, Channing. You're doing fine."

"How long did it take you to learn to tie quick release knots?"

Gemma grinned. "I learned when I was five, so I've been doing it a long time. Come on. Let's get this tack hung up. I need to check on my stock before the rodeo starts."

Channing looped the nylon rope over her shoulder, picked up the saddle and blanket and followed Gemma into the back of the horse trailer. "Thanks for letting me shower here this morning."

"Little cramped in Trevor's rig with you and them three big cowboys, huh?"

No, it was a little uncomfortable after what'd happened last night—whatever the hell it'd been. She wasn't exactly sure. And she'd had no desire to face Colby this morning, at least until she had her wits about her. Or if she figured out what'd gone on. She sighed.

"You gonna tell me what's eating at you, girl?"

Channing didn't answer.

"Well, something's literally been eating at you. Does Colby know he left them big hickeys all over your neck? And streaks of razor burn? Did he try to bite your lips off, too? Cause your mouth is swollen." Gemma placed a hand on Channing's arm. "Oh, honey. How rough did he get on you last night?"

"Thanks for your concern, Gem, but it was entirely mutual." She sighed again. "I'll tell you later. Not right now. I need to think on it for a while longer, okay?"

"Sure thing. You know where to find me."

Channing threaded the rope over the metal holders, keeping her eyes focused on her task. "Thank you for the riding lessons and..." *Just say it.* "For hanging out with me. I guess it's obvious I don't have many friends."

"Here or at home?"

"Either."

"Why not?"

She traced the frayed end of the cotton flank strap with her fingertip. "Because I'd rather be alone and be happy with my own company than be somebody I'm not so I can fit in with people whose company I despise."

"This a realization you've come to recently?"

"Pretty much. Well, that's not true. I've felt that way from the time I was old enough to realize I never fit in any place my parents took me. Or sent me. My sister always stood out so I just stayed in the background. I tried to blend so no one noticed how out of place I was."

"Then like me, you're better off alone. If them kinda folks you were living around can't see you're the genuine article, then screw 'em. The way I see it, at least horses and cows appreciate all you do for them everyday. And they sure as shit don't talk about you behind your back."

Channing laughed.

"I'm a quart low on girlfriends myself, Channing. Steve's friends' wives were way older than me. He and I weren't blessed with kids. I basically disowned my family. Frankly, since Steve was my best friend practically all my life I didn't need anyone else."

The clank of D-rings against the metal barrier filled the silence.

Gemma grunted and slapped her hands on her jeans. A cloud of dust rose up. "Well, that was downright sappy. And we ain't even drinkin'." She looked at Channing, lifted her brows and smirked. "Yet."

They parted ways. Gemma went to check on her small group of steers and her stock foreman behind the chutes and Channing headed to the main entrance to pick up her ticket at the box office.

In the family area, Callie stood and waved her over. It made her feel ridiculously happy they'd saved her a seat.

Channing hefted her bag and slid across the wooden bench, already feeling her muscles getting sore from the horse ride. And from Colby's hard riding last night. "Morning. How are you guys?"

"I'm fine." Callie smiled brightly. "But momma ain't feelin' so good this morning."

Mary scowled at her can of 7-Up. "Thanks for sharing that with the world, Cal."

"You whooping it up again last night, Mary?"

"No. I was tucked in bed and sound asleep by nine."

"Hmm. That's too bad. Maybe you've got the flu or something."

"Or something." Mary dug out five bucks from the front pocket of her Rockies and passed it to Callie. "See that lady selling drinks?" Mary pointed to the vendor loitering at the top of the staircase. "Please get me another soda, and some juice for yourself. But don't buy nothin' else, Callie. And come right back here when you're done. I mean it."

"Sure, Momma."

The second Callie disappeared Mary leaned closer. "It's not the flu. I'm pregnant."

"Wow." Channing didn't know what else to say. Was Mary thrilled about the pregnancy?

"Me and Mike have been trying to have another baby for a while. A couple of years actually. It just didn't seem like it ever was gonna happen. Looks like it did."

"Congratulations. Does Mike know?"

Mary smiled. "I told him right after I barfed up breakfast again and decided to pee on the stick. That man's got a shit-eatin' grin on his face a mile wide. We haven't told Callie yet. The girl can't keep a secret to save her life."

"She *is* only four, Mary."

"True."

The saddle bronc competition started. Channing held her breath when Colby's name was called. He bucked off within three seconds. She scrutinized him as he sauntered off the dirt, putting on a macho show for everyone, acting like he was just fine.

Damn foolish man.

An hour later Cash and Edgard posted good times in the calf roping. Colby didn't fare so well. He ended up with no time. He hadn't even made it off his horse.

A sick feeling settled in the pit of Channing's stomach. Colby wasn't fine. She had no choice but to sit in the stands for a few more hours, fretting. Luckily, Callie's constant chatter distracted her.

The steer wrestling competition began. Mike Morgan was scheduled second. Mary and Callie yelled advice from the stands as the steer raced out.

It happened so fast Channing nearly missed it. Mike threw himself at the steer as the animal reversed direction and came right at him. Man and beast ended up in a dusty pile in the middle of the arena with Mike on the bottom. Dazed, the steer wobbled to its hooves and bounced toward the gate. The bulldogger didn't move.

Mary stood up. "Omigod. What happened?"

"Momma? Why's Daddy layin' on the ground?"

"Ssh, baby. I don't know."

Two officials trotted out and crouched down beside Mike. After a discussion, one of the guys gestured for another official. Another discussion. He in turn signaled for the sports medicine team.

"What in the hell is taking so long?" Mary said.

They all watched in horror as a stretcher was hauled out.

Mary swayed forward over the railing and Channing caught her. "Hey. Take a deep breath, Mary. Don't pass out on me."

She nodded and breathed deeply, squeezing Channing's hand until Channing lost all feeling in it.

They carried Mike away to a smattering of applause and the announcer's assurance that updates on Mike Morgan's condition would be made available as soon as possible.

"I have to go," Mary said. "I have to see if he's okay. Oh God. What if he's not?"

"Momma?"

Mary looked at her daughter, torn in two directions. "Maybe it'd be best if she didn't come with until I know more—"

"You go on, Mary. Callie and I will stay right here. Hanging out. Eating junk food. Checking out all the vendors to see what new trinkets they're selling today, won't we, Cal? You go."

"You're sure?"

"Go."

Mary sprinted up the stairs two at a time.

The minute her mother was gone stoic Callie started to cry.

Channing pulled the little girl on her lap and let her bawl. Several of the other wives and girlfriends came over to offer help, but Callie wanted nothing to do with any of them.

Not once during the hour that passed did Callie beg for cheap toys. Or sugar-laden snacks. Nor did she demand to know where her mother was. Or if her father was all right. Or why they couldn't leave. She just curled into Channing and clung to her like a scared monkey.

"Channing!"

She spun around to see Colby limping down the bleacher stairs.

"Colby? What are you doing here?"

"Mary Morgan sent me."

Channing couldn't read in his eyes whether it was good or bad news.

"She wants you to bring Callie to her."

"Okay." She looked down in Callie's frightened eyes and tried to gently pry her arms from around her neck. "Hey, Calamity Jane. Gather up your stuff. Let's go see your mom."

But Callie wouldn't let go. Finally, Channing just carried her out.

Colby led them through a cordoned-off area to a small, airless room underneath the main grandstand. Inside, Mary hovered next to Mike, who was awake but on a stretcher with his knee heavily bandaged and his wrist in a sling.

Callie squirmed out of Channing's arms and launched herself at Mary, sobbing, "Momma you didn't come back and didn't come back and I thought my daddy was *dead*!"

Channing felt like she'd been kicked in the solar plexus. That poor little girl. Acting so brave when she'd been torn up inside. How many other rodeo kids went through this on a regular basis? How many wives and girlfriends and mothers and fathers? How did they deal with it, day in, day out? Year after year?

"Oh, baby. It's okay. See? He's not dead. Just banged up."

Groggily, Mike Morgan said, "Hiya, punkin. Didja see me wreck? I think we oughta buy that steer and grind him into hamburger, huh?"

Mary stepped around the end of the stretcher. "Channing. Thank you so much for watching Callie."

"No problem. Is everything okay?"

"We'll know more tomorrow. As it sits now, Mike has a torn ACL that's gonna require surgery. We're heading off to Omaha in a little bit for X-rays and tests. And probably a trip to the operating room."

It sounded so serious. So permanent. Everyone knew—but nobody said out loud, that this could be a career-ending injury for Mike Morgan. "Is there anything I can do?"

Mary bit her lip. "I haven't really thought it through until now, but it's occurred to me we can't take the horse and the horse trailer along with us to Omaha."

Colby moved in behind Channing. "Don't worry about it, Mary. Take care of your family. We'll get your horse and trailer back to your ranch somehow."

Relief crossed her face and she hugged Colby. "Oh thank you. You guys are our family, too. I'll get the truck unhitched and get the trailer keys. I'll be right back." She leaned over to whisper to Mike before she and Callie hustled out.

Channing whirled around right into Colby, hovering behind her. She frowned. "Why are you still here? Aren't you going to help Mary?"

"Nah. I'd just get in the way. Besides, Mary has hitched up that trailer more times than any guy on the circuit."

She rocked to her tiptoes and got right in his face. "Yeah, but unlike most guys, she is pregnant. And I don't think hefting that hitch in her condition is the best idea, do you?"

"Shit." He vanished.

Outside the contestants' gate she heard the announcement for the start of the barrel racing and saw Gemma and Cash arguing.

"—and I'm tellin' you, it ain't your fault."

"How so? That was my bum steer, Cash. And I'll be goddamned if I'll sit here and do nothin' when I could be helping them."

"Hey, guys," Channing interrupted. "What's the problem?"

Cash's handsome face was distorted into a full scowl. "The problem is that Wonder Woman here feels guilty and thinks she needs to take the Morgan's horse and trailer back to South Dakota. By herself."

A heated pause sparked the air like fireworks.

"If you're just worried about her going alone, I could go with her," Channing offered.

Gemma awarded Cash a smug smile. "See? Problem solved."

"Except for one tiny detail. You don't have your big horse haulin' truck here, Gem. Your foreman needs the big diesel to pull the trailer for the stock. There's no way you can pull that monster rig of Morgan's with your small block Ford."

"But *you* have a big enough one?"

Cash grinned slowly.

"I'll knock that grin clean off your face, Cash Big Crow, if you don't get rid of it right now."

His smile didn't dim one iota.

"Fine. Yours is bigger. I doubt you'll let me touch it. So are you volunteering to drive your big, bad machine to Buffalo Gap? That mean you're just gonna abandon your horse and trailer here? For at least a day?"

"No. I hadn't thought it through that far."

Trevor sauntered over. "What's the commotion?"

While Cash and Gemma stared at each other, Channing gave Trevor a brief rundown.

"Okay. Here's what we'll do. Hook up Cash's truck to the Morgan's trailer and take Mike's horses to their ranch. Then you two will turn around, come back here and pick up Cash's empty horse trailer on your way to Cheyenne. Because I will have driven Gemma's rig, loaded with both of your horses to Cheyenne."

They looked at each other. Cash shrugged. "Works for me."

Gemma snapped off, "Fine. But if you wreck my truck, Trevor Glanzer—"

"I'll ride along with him and make sure he obeys all traffic laws," Channing said. "Then I'll watch your trailer until you get there."

"Good. Let's get everything loaded up."

Trevor caught Channing's arm. "Why are you doin' this? Wouldn't you rather ride with Colby in my truck?"

"Between you and me? No. I need some time to clear my head." When Trevor balked, she added, "Your part in last night's festivities had nothing to do with it, okay?"

He nodded. "I sure understand needin' some time to clear away the cobwebs. I'll pass the information on the change in plans to Edgard. He can help Colby with our horses. Unless you'd rather tell Colby yourself?"

"No. I know he still has the bull-riding event to get through. But I'd like to get out of here as soon as possible because he's liable to make a big scene."

Or worse, Colby might not care at all that she was gone.

Chapter Seventeen

Cheyenne, Wyoming, was all abuzz for Frontier Days, for the "Daddy of 'em All", one of the oldest rodeos in the country. During the ten-day run, four hundred thousand people visited the town, which had a population of fifty thousand on a good day.

For the first time on this journey, Channing had time to gaze out the window and take in the scenery. As she and Trevor drove across the Sandhills of Nebraska, she marveled at the endless space of the Wild West. Big, blue sky. Sagebrush and groves of squat, twisted trees. The rocky buttes and the clean, dry air. Wyoming was just as rugged as she'd imagined. She wondered if Colby's ranch looked anything like this slice of heaven.

Trevor checked them into Gemma's assigned spot and began the feeding and exercising process for the horses. He didn't turn down Channing's offer of help. She was pleased about how much she'd remembered from following Gemma around while she'd done chores. Even Trevor didn't tease her too much about being a greenhorn.

Gemma's campsite was on the other end of town from where Trevor and Colby had reservations. Channing was beginning to think she should crash with Gemma. Motel rooms were booked solid around Cheyenne for fifty miles. All four of them bunking in the horse trailer would be just a little too close for comfort on more levels than she could name.

Plus, she liked Gemma. Not only did they have fun together, Channing knew she could talk to Gemma about anything and Gemma wouldn't pass judgment. It was heartening because she'd never connected with anyone so quickly.

Except for Colby.

Damn. Why did everything always come back around to that man?

Because you're crazy in love him.

No. That wasn't it. What she felt for Colby was lust, plain and simple. Maybe a little trust. So he made her feel safe. He made her laugh. He made her twist and writhe with pleasure. He also made her mad enough to spit nails. Still, he had a silly, sweet side as well as a domineering side that was hot as hell.

Before Channing began checking off his fabulous physical attributes, she had to face facts: she'd fallen for the cowboy.

So the question was, what did she do about it? They'd started this...*thing* with a clear end in sight. She'd known from day one it'd never work out and they'd part company—not only because of the clichéd differences between a country boy and a city girl.

Besides, she'd never fantasized that Colby was going to slip a ring on her finger and promise his everlasting devotion. The only thing he was devoted to, near as she could tell, was the rodeo.

Which brought up another issue. After seeing Colby's injuries, and then Mike's arena crash, she didn't know if she could stomach Colby getting beat to crap on a regular basis. Year in, year out. He might not keep aiming for the upper tier in the NFR, but she suspected he'd never give up rodeo for good.

A soft rap sounded on the door. Her stupid heart skipped. Too soon for Colby to have made it to Cheyenne. "Come in."

Trevor stepped inside.

"I just wanted to let you know I got the all clear from Gemma to take her truck tonight. So you'll be without wheels."

"Where are you going?"

"To meet my family. They've taken some time off from the ranch and they're in town for a couple of days to watch me compete."

"Cool. That sounds like fun."

His thoughtful gaze caught hers. "Do you want to come along? You could pretend to be my girlfriend."

"Why would I want to do that?" Other than the fact Trevor wouldn't want his family to know about his boyfriend.

"If it comes up, it'd explain why you're traveling with us. Rodeo is a small world, Chan." He looked away, a bit sheepishly.

"What aren't you telling me?"

"You know Colby's family is gonna be around, too?"

She nodded, not entirely sure she wanted to hear what he was about to tell her.

"Well, I'll warn you not to get your hopes up that he's gonna introduce you to them."

"Why not?" slipped out before she could bite it back.

He rubbed the furrow between his eyebrows. "Honestly? Because you ain't the type of girl that Carson McKay wants his son to get involved with. He's already havin' to deal with Colby's older brother, Cord, and that mess. He'd hit the barn roof if he found out Colby was doin' the same thing."

Why hadn't Colby mentioned his family problems to her? They'd only talked in generalities. Now that she thought about it, she'd mostly talked about her life. "What mess?"

"Cord married a gal from Seattle. Marla, his ex-wife now, thought she wanted to be married to a real rancher. Live out West. When she found out bein' a rancher's wife was lots of hard work and not horse rides at sunset like in them romance novels, she kept threatening to return to the big city. She lasted two years. About six months ago she followed through with the threats and left Cord with their son, Ky. Cord's been pretty messed up by the whole situation, which is why this is Colby's last chance on the circuit.

"So, we all know this gig with Colby is temporary, Chan. Colby ain't gonna risk upsettin' his dad by introducin' you, when not only are you a city girl, you won't be around much longer anyway."

Trevor knocked any hope right out of her. "Well, that puts things in perspective. I appreciate you telling me the truth. But I'll still pass on acting the part of your girlfriend."

"I didn't mean—"

"Never mind. I'll hold down the fort until Gemma shows up. And if I get bored with my own company, I'll wander around. You don't have to baby-sit me."

He smiled sadly and chucked her under the chin. "You make it sound like bein' with you is a chore, Channing."

They looked at each other for the longest time before Trevor slanted his mouth over hers and kissed her. Sweetly. It was probably meant to be a friendly peck. A show of comfort. Immediately, it morphed into heat and need.

Amidst twisting tongues and relaxed touches, the greedy part of her brain reminded her that *this* is what she signed on for—mindless, down and dirty sex, not love. Or the illusion of love.

Unlike Colby, Trevor hadn't alluded to the idea there was more between them than a hot, uninhibited coupling whenever the mood struck them.

While Channing kissed Trevor, she unbuckled his belt, then loosened his Wranglers. Sliding her hand inside that tight denim she found him firm and ready.

"Hang on." Trevor edged back and toed off his boots. He shucked his jeans and the rest of his clothes.

Channing marveled at his nude body. Ripped muscles. Smooth skin punctuated in spots by white and pink scars, large and small. She trailed her fingers over his defined pecs then to the little strip of hair arrowing the center of his torso, watching his cock jump when she lightly drew her fingertips from hipbone to hipbone. "You are a beautiful man, Trevor."

"Thank you, darlin', but as I'm standin' here buck-ass naked except for my hat, we gotta do something about all them clothes you're wearin'."

Trevor unbuttoned Channing's shirt, leaving kisses along every inch of skin he exposed an inch at a time. Her blouse fluttered to the floor.

He cupped both big breasts in his hands and suckled her nipples through her sheer bra. The combination of his wet, hot mouth on the silky material and his razor-stubbled cheek rubbing on the upper swell of her breast dampened her thighs with want.

And made her feel unbelievably guilty. She arched away from him. "Trevor. Stop. I-I can't... We can't. I'm sorry."

Neither of them said anything as they dressed in awkward silence. She knew she'd never be with Trevor again, and the relief she felt surprised her.

"You okay?" he murmured finally.

"No. Why do I feel like I was about to cheat on Colby?"

Trevor sighed. "I suspect for the same reason Edgard makes me feel like that after he knows I've been with a woman. Guilt is something new to me. It ain't like I haven't ever hid from him I still like women. Nor did I promise that I'd quit fucking them."

They hadn't talked about Edgard at all on the trip from Valentine. "How did you end up with Edgard?"

"Funny thing is, I heard that phrase *turned gay* and never understood what it meant. My whole life I never looked at another man that way. Touched a man that way. Wanted a man to do the same to me. Doing things to me I'd thought were wrong." His hand stopped. "Lord. Then I met Edgard and shit. Something about him turned me upside down. Turned me loose and turned me on.

"At first he was reluctant to be with me because I wasn't gay. I'd never been with a man. But after we were together a couple of times, I couldn't stay away from him. I couldn't get enough. It's like he's a goddamn drug. I ain't been with no other guys. It wasn't like he flipped a switch in me or anything. It's just him."

"Do you love him?"

"Don't matter if I do or not. Kinda like you and Colby. Things you can't control will keep you from bein' together. Makes me sick to my stomach. I guess that's why they call it lovesick, huh?"

She knew what it felt like to be a lovesick fool, too.

He tipped her chin up, cradling her face in his hands. "Thank you, Channing. Not only for...everything we've done, but for bein' a friend. It means a lot to me."

"Me, too."

"If you need anything call my cell." Trevor peered at her. "You do realize that Colby and Edgard will roll into Cheyenne late tonight."

"Which is why it'll be better for me to stay here."

"Okay. See you tomorrow."

Her fake cheer disappeared the second the door closed.

Channing's sexual fling was over. Time to quit running from her problems. If she'd learned nothing else on this trip, she'd discovered she did have a backbone. From now on she'd live her life on her own terms and woe to anyone who tried to stop her.

She flipped open her cell phone. Scrolled down until she found the number she wanted and hit dial. Seven rings later the answering machine kicked on.

"Hi, Mom. Hi, Dad. I just wanted to let you know to go ahead and RSVP *yes* to Melinda's wedding reception invitation. I'll be back in town soon. I'll call when I have more details as to when. Good-bye."

Channing slept surprisingly well for being in another strange town and at a strange new place in her life.

ঙ৪ঙ৪

When Gemma returned the next afternoon, after she checked on Daisy, she stalked into the living quarters in the horse trailer and went straight for the booze. She flopped in the small easy chair, knocked back a can of beer and sighed. She seemed to notice Channing for the first time. "Oh. Hey."

Channing said, "Hey yourself. Bad day?"

"You might say that."

"Everything went okay getting the Morgans' horses back?"

Gemma scowled. "Unloading the horses and the trailer was the easiest part. It was the drive that was the worst. I'm tired and strung as tight as a new barbwire fence."

"Why? Didn't you and Cash trade off driving duties?"

"Yes. But that ain't what I'm talking about." She pointed a finger at Channing. "Don't get me started on that man."

"What happened?"

Gemma took a big swig of beer and blurted out, "He made a pass at me! He waited until I had my hands full of blankets and tack and then he pushed me against the trailer and kissed me like a crazy man."

"Oh." Channing hid a smile. "So it was that bad, huh?"

"God, no. That man surely knows how to kiss. His mouth is like—" Her embarrassed gaze connected with Channing's. "It just shocked the hell out of me. And instead of chalking it up to a fluke or a mistake, he kept jabbering his whole life story to me because I 'needed to know about him' if he and I were gonna get involved."

"Did you tell him yours?"

She shook her head and snagged two more brews, tossing one to Channing. "No. It gets worse. Because I told him there was no way he and I would *ever* get involved. When I pretended I wasn't listening to him? Then Mr. Smooth started describing all the sexy things he planned to do to me once he got me naked. In detail. In glorious, Technicolor detail."

"Oh wow."

"Damn man." Gemma slurped the beer. "Made me so twitchy when he ran his finger up the outside seam of my jeans, I jerked the steering wheel and we skidded to the shoulder.

Before I could catch my breath and chew his ass, he hauled me across his lap, and..." She gazed off into space.

Channing kicked Gemma's shin lightly. "Oh, no, you don't. Details, now, Gemma. Vivid details."

"Lord. I'm forty-seven years old. This is so embarrassing."

"Huh-uh. Spill it."

Gemma's eyes were unfocused. "He pulled me into his lap and kissed me until I couldn't breathe. Then we started messing around, touching, more like frantic groping, and things turned really hot and we both got off...with all our clothes on. That hasn't happened to me since I was seventeen."

"So you're saying he makes you feel young?"

"I'm saying he makes me feel like an old fool, Channing. He also makes me feel guilty as hell." She rolled the beer can over her forehead. "It felt like I was cheating on my husband."

Channing let Gemma regain her composure before she said, "You can only do what you feel is right, Gem. But you're neither a fool nor are you old. Didn't you tell me if you were offered a second chance, you'd take it?" She hesitated. Screw politeness, Gemma would just ask her the question outright. "Are you resisting Cash because he's Indian?"

"God, no. That don't matter a lick to me."

"Then what?"

"Besides the fact I'm a good ten years older than him?"

"Wasn't Steve older than you? Why does age matter?"

"It doesn't. Damn. It's just...scary, okay? I'm set in my ways and I don't know if I can change. What man wants to deal with that kinda stubborn woman?"

"Cash does, apparently."

"So it would appear." Gemma kicked Channing's foot. "When'd you get so smart, girl?"

"I'm not feeling so smart. And let me tell you, I can totally relate to the guilt thing." Before she chickened out, she blurted out everything that had gone on with her, Colby, Trevor and Edgard, only leaving out Trevor and Edgard's secret, since it wasn't hers to tell. She also puzzled out loud on why she felt like she'd been cheating on Colby with Trevor when she'd just kissed Trevor.

Gemma wasn't as shocked as Channing thought she would be. "You know, I kinda wondered if that wasn't the case with them suddenly picking you up as a new traveling partner. Those boys have a wild reputation." She waggled her eyebrows. "So, two men at once, eh? I've always wanted to try that."

Channing choked and barely stopped beer from coming out her nose.

"Of course, I never could share that little secret fantasy with Steve. To be the focus of the attention of two men? Yeah, sign me up."

"Hello?" Cash said through the screen door. "I hear voices, you guys in here?"

Gemma froze. Her panicked gaze flew to Channing's. Had he been eavesdropping on their conversation?

"Yeah. Come on in, Cash," Channing said.

He sidled in, pausing just inside the door, practically wringing his black Stetson in his rough-skinned hands.

"What's up?"

"Just wonderin' if you gals were thinkin' about goin' to the opening dance tonight?"

Gemma opened her mouth to object but Channing shot her an arch look. "Yes, we are. Why?"

"Colby had two tickets and he sent me over here to give 'em to you."

Channing bit back the urge to ask if Colby had given Cash the two tickets because he didn't plan on attending tonight with her. "Thanks. Are you going?"

"I reckon I'll pop in for a bit." Cash stared hard at Gemma. "You *will* be dancin' with me, Gem. Don't try to hide because I'll track you down." And he disappeared.

Gemma said, "Shit," and drained her beer.

"Well, looks like our night just got a whole lot more exciting."

Chapter Eighteen

Live country music twanged through the speakers. Hundreds of people were talking at once. Four fights had already broken out and he'd spent the last thirty minutes fending off the most persistent buckle bunnies he'd ever met.

It was only eight o'clock and Colby considered getting really drunk. Especially when he looked over at the table where his family held court and the "surprise" his father had brought along.

A surprise by the name of Amy Jo Foster. The young woman whose family had been neighbors of the McKays for forty years. The young girl his father had stupidly decided might be a good candidate as Colby's future wife.

Lord. And Amy Jo was just a *girl* of nineteen. She'd actually blushed when they'd been talking and his arm had accidentally brushed her breast.

His little sister Keely didn't seem too thrilled Amy Jo had been invited to Frontier Days either. Even though Keely and Amy Jo were the same age and lived five miles apart, they'd never been best friends. Keely claimed Amy Jo was a goody-goody—the worst kind of insult hell-on-wheels Keely McKay could level on another person.

Colby studied his mother's face from beneath his hat brim. Had Carolyn McKay been in on this *surprise*, too? Probably not.

His dad had been browbeating him, claiming Colby needed a good woman to settle him down. His mother had assured Colby he'd want to settle down when he met the right woman.

His gaze strayed to Amy Jo. It wasn't like she was ugly as a mud fence. She was pretty in a coltish way. Reed thin, all long arms and legs. Long white-blonde hair and a pink complexion, near as he could figure because she blushed all the damn time. Enormous eyes the vivid color of the Wyoming sky. When she wore her hair in a pair of pigtail braids, she reminded him of the Swiss Miss Instant Cocoa girl. Or more accurately, her younger sister. *Much* younger sister.

Colby sighed and glanced at the clock again. He missed Channing. They hadn't had a chance to talk about his stellar asshole performance from the other night. He'd been too much of a chickenshit to call her cell phone as he'd driven Trevor's rig to Cheyenne last night. Some things had to be done in person. Especially apologies. Then last night after they'd pulled into the campground at the opposite end of town from Frontier Park, they had to set up, take care of the horses and, by the time he and Edgard finished, it'd been damn near two in the morning. Too late to call her. This morning he had to register for his events, pay his fees and he'd spent the afternoon with his family, leaving no time for him to wander over to Gemma's campsite.

So...maybe if he played his cards right tonight, they could sneak outside and kiss and make up. Then he could get up the gumption to tell her all the things that'd been weighing on him before she left him for good.

"Hey, cowboy. Buy me a drink?"

Colby turned slightly. Yep. Another buckle bunny trying her luck. He shrugged and didn't respond, hoping she'd get the hint.

She didn't. Long scarlet nails inched up his shirt. She crowded in so he was enveloped in silicone, rhinestones and a cloud of perfume. "Maybe you'd rather dance?"

"Maybe you'd like to get your paw offa him or I'll bust it off, starting with those ugly fake claws," a striking brunette said as she wrapped her arm around Colby's waist.

"Run along, little girl," the bunny hissed.

"Darlin'," she cooed sweetly to Colby, "you want this washed up old hag, or would you rather have a young hottie like me rockin' your horse trailer?"

Colby tried not to laugh as he dropped a kiss on her temple. "I'll take you, sweetheart."

The buckle bunny spun on her ugly high-heeled boots the color of raspberry Kool-Aid and disappeared into the crowd.

Colby looked down at his sister and grinned. "Thanks, Keely."

"You're welcome. Although it totally creeps me out to have to ask you this. Are they *always* all over you like flies on shit?"

"Nice visual," he said dryly. "But yeah, pretty much."

"Dude. That sucks." Her face brightened. "Hey, maybe there's a way you could keep them away tonight. Pretend you're madly in love with Amy Jo. Dance with her. Sit with her. Hold her hand and stare into her eyes. Normal *nice*, boring courtin' shit that'd make me gag. But I know she'd totally go for it."

Keely's steely blue eyes were a bit too gleeful. "And this would be solely for my benefit?"

"Absolutely." She ducked out of his embrace. "Ooh. I'm bailing before that hot bull fighter I'm chasing thinks I really *am* with you." Keely shuddered. "Later, bro."

Colby watched his sister saunter off and the trail of young bucks hot on her heels. Keely McKay was smart as a whip, as beautiful and unrefined as a wild horse, and held a razor sharp tongue that'd stripped the skin off of more than one unlucky cowboy. With an independent streak as wide as her stubborn streak, she considered raisin' hell her God-given right. Woe to the man who wound up trying to tame her and win her heart.

What would Channing's family say about their daughter? Did they even know her heart? Her wild streak? Her secret desire to be tamed and inflamed?

As Colby made his way back to his family table, he ran into Trevor, who appeared eager to get away from his own family. "Where you goin'?"

"To the bar. And if I don't come back, don't tell them where I went, okay?"

"Okay. Have you seen Channing?"

"Ah. No."

Panicked, he grabbed Trevor's arm. "Something happened to her?"

"Nope." Trevor dropped his gaze. "I just haven't seen her since last night."

Colby recognized his guilty expression. Jealousy roared through him like a raging forest fire. "You son of a bitch."

"What?"

"Did you fuck her when you saw her last night?"

Trevor's stubborn chin rose a notch. "So?"

Somehow he'd expected Trevor to deny it. Or Colby had hoped that Channing knew he'd been serious about his threat that no other man touched her besides him. "That's all you've got to say to me is *so*?"

"What's the big deal? Isn't that why she's travelin' with us? For a little variety?"

Colby loomed over his friend and growled, "I am gonna kick your sorry faggot ass right fucking now."

Trevor didn't back down. In fact, he stepped up. "Back off, McKay. I'm warnin' you. I'm in a piss-poor mood, half-drunk and rarin' to beat on someone. Since you're in my face it can just as easily be you."

"You prepared to bleed for her?"

"Probably more than you are."

"What the fuck does that mean?"

"Aren't you the one who told me you wouldn't be jealous if Channing and I spent time alone together? And now you are? Since when do *you* think you have the right to freak out about anything concernin' her? Especially when we both know the minute Channing shows up here tonight you're gonna pretend you don't even know her."

"Low blow, Trev."

"Yeah? Well, nothin' happened between me and Channing last night anyway. Not that it matters. You and I are both good at lyin' to ourselves and neither of us is in a position to be makin' promises to no one. Our families have pretty much seen to that, ain't they?" He angled his hat toward the McKay table. "Is Amy Jo the one your dad picked for you?"

Colby was livid and snapped off the first thing that came to his mind. "It ain't none of your business." He turned and walked it off.

He hated this whole situation, mostly because he hated that Trevor was exactly right.

Or were he and Trevor both wrong? If they couldn't make changes in their own lives, who could?

When Colby reached the table, he granted Amy Jo a big smile and offered his hand to her. "How about if you and me dance? There's a couple of things I'd like to talk to you about."

ഋഌ

Channing and Gemma had fortified themselves with a little liquid courage before they headed to the big dancehall blowout. Luckily, their campsite was within walking distance of the building, so if they knocked back too much beer, they'd have no problem stumbling back to the horse trailer.

Seemed everyone in Cheyenne had shown up. The place was loud and crowded. The tables were all full. Boots stomped. Shiny shirts and belts sparkled. Laughter rang out. Booze flowed.

Gemma knew tons of people and introduced her to everyone. Channing felt herself retreating. Becoming quietly observant as she faded into the background.

They'd found a tall table to stand beside and a round of fresh beers had miraculously appeared. Gemma talked loudly over the music and conversations. "Opening night of 'The Daddy of 'em All'. What do you think?"

Two cowboys went skidding past on the sawdust floor, fists and hats flying until some brave soul stepped in and broke it up and made them take it outside.

Before Channing could answer, a brunette placed her hands over Gemma's eyes from behind and growled, "Guess who?"

"Justin McBride?" Pause. "Keith Urban?" Another pause. "Is it...Keely McKay?" Keely squealed and Gemma whirled around to squeeze the girl a big hug.

Even if Channing hadn't heard the familiar last name, the family resemblance would've tipped her off. This dazzling, dark-haired woman with eyes the color of sapphires and big dimples was the spitting image of Colby—in petite, feminine form.

"Channing? This is Keely McKay, Colby's baby sister."

Keely shook Channing's hand. "Baby sister. Everyone treats me like I'm twelve. I'm almost twenty-one."

"You'll be twenty-one in another two years," Gemma corrected, and knocked Keely's hand away from her beer. "Anyway, what're you up to besides no good?"

"I came down with Mom and Dad to watch Colby compete." She grinned saucily. "And to find a bad cowboy who wants to lead me astray. Can you introduce me to one or ten to save me some time?"

"Right. Doesn't Daddy keep an eagle eye on you, since you've been known to get into a fair amount of trouble?"

"Yes." Keely's smile vanished. "An eagle eye in the form of Amy Jo Foster. We're sharing a room, which means I have to be very quiet if I want to sneak out at night."

"What's Amy Jo doing here?"

"Daddy's attempt at matchmaking."

Gemma glanced at Channing and then away quickly. Channing knew something was up. She didn't dare ask, because she was more than a little afraid of the answer.

"Plus, she's keeping the buckle bunnies away from him." Her blue eyes widened. "Shit, here comes Daddy. You didn't see me," she said and squatted down, before she scooted away, ducking through the throng of people until she vanished in the crowd.

A tall, sturdy man sauntered over. He looked to be around sixty, ruggedly handsome with a square jaw, high cheekbones, those familiar compelling blue eyes. Dark hair beneath his cream-colored cowboy hat. He flicked a quick glance at Channing and focused his attention on Gemma. "Where'd the wild child go?"

"Why, whoever do you mean?" Gemma asked innocently.

He rolled his eyes. "If you see Keely again, tell her I'm lookin' for her. I've survived raisin' five rough and rowdy sons. That one little girl is gonna give me heart failure yet."

"They say what goes around, comes around."

"Her mama and me weren't ever that wild."

Gemma lifted a brow. "If you say so. Carson, this is my friend Channing Kinkaid."

Carson tipped his hat. "Nice to meetcha, Miz Kinkaid."

"Same here."

"Where're you from?"

"Massachusetts." Right then, Channing knew she couldn't be more ostracized than if she'd answered *Mars*.

"Ah," Carson said.

A moment of forced silence.

"Channing is also friends with Colby," Gemma added.

Carson's gaze narrowed. "You don't say."

Sweat dripped down her spine in the wake of Carson McKay's accusing stare. She waited for him to quiz her.

But he decided to ignore her. He and Gemma started dishing dirt on other rough stock contractors. Channing's feet itched to make tracks for the door. They'd only been here an hour and she was ready to leave.

A minute later firm male hands landed on her hips. "Dance with me." She turned and Trevor tugged her away from the table to the dance floor.

There wasn't much chance to talk as Trevor whirled and twirled her through three fast songs. When the power ballad "You Look So Good In Love" began, she fully expected they'd exit the dance floor. But Trevor pulled her into his arms, keeping her at a respectable distance as they swayed to the beat.

"Are you havin' fun?" Trevor asked.

"No. Are you?"

"No. Bein' here around my family makes me realize how much I love bein' on the road."

Channing laughed.

"It ain't funny. Times like today I *am* tempted to pack up and move to Brazil."

Trevor danced her backward. She looked behind her to make sure she wasn't about to plow over someone, when across the way she saw Colby, his hands clamped on the ass of a young, willowy blonde whose mannerisms and carriage screamed "real cowgirl". They did the old bump and grind, oblivious to anything but each other.

Her breath caught and something inside her broke. Any secret stupid hope that she had about a future with Colby McKay evaporated like smoke.

Trevor noticed she'd gone rigid. He peered over her shoulder to the couple dirty dancing and froze. He whispered, "Ah hell. I'm so sorry, Chan."

Breathe. She remembered Keely's matchmaking comment. "Is she the one his dad brought here?"

No answer.

"Trevor?"

"Yeah, Carson brought her. Her family's ranch borders the McKays' and—"

"Don't tell me any more."

"All right."

Channing couldn't stay on the dance floor, pretending her world hadn't just crashed around her. When it felt like her heart was being stomped on by dozens of pairs of spiked cowboy boots. She stepped back away from Trevor so fast she stumbled into the couple behind her. Her clumsiness set off a chain reaction, which reached Colby and his new paramour.

Their eyes met. His registered surprise, then guilt. Hers, she knew, held nothing but desolation.

Channing fled. She thought she heard someone shout her name but she didn't stop. She skirted the area where Gemma was fending off Cash and ran straight out the door. She didn't quit running until she'd arrived at the horse trailer.

She madly packed the few personal items she'd brought with her. She dialed a cab company to pick her up and take her to the airport. She didn't care where she escaped to as long as it was far away from here.

While Channing scrawled a quick note to Gemma, she sucked down a beer. She was totally unprepared for the vicious hammering on the metal trailer door.

"I know you're in there, Channing. Open up," Colby said.

She didn't budge. She mouthed *go away* to him.

Several more ferocious knocks rattled the whole trailer. "Goddammit. Open this fucking door right now or I swear to God I'll bust it down. And you know I don't make idle threats."

Chapter Nineteen

Seething on the inside, but maintaining an outward calm, she opened the door.

Colby burst in like an angry bull out of the chute, nostrils flaring, eyes red, his bulky body shaking with rage. He latched on to her upper arms, jerked her against him and smashed his mouth to hers.

Channing fought him. Kicking, biting, digging her nails into his shirt, trying to claw his heart so she could rip it into shreds like he'd done to hers.

After she nearly bit his bottom lip, Colby swore, spun her around and braceleted her wrists in his hands behind her back. "Knock it off, you little hellcat."

"No. Let me go and get out. I don't want you here."

"Tough shit."

"I'm not kidding. Stop manhandling me. Maybe your girlfriend likes it, but I don't."

Instead of releasing her, he tightened his grip and put his mouth right next to her ear, laughing softly with a hint of malice. "She is not my girlfriend. If you'd give me a goddamn minute to explain—"

"I don't care about your stupid excuses."

Colby hissed, "Sure you don't, shug. That's why you're actin' all jealous like this."

Channing twisted her wrists in his rough hands. "I'm acting like this because I've got a cab coming any minute. I'm leaving. So let me go."

"That sounds good. We'll take the cab to my motel so we can hash this out in private."

"We have nothing to hash out."

"Wrong."

He wheeled her around and cupped her face between his hands. He settled his mouth over hers, foregoing the earlier brutal kiss and giving her sweetness and tenderness that brought her tears to the surface.

Damn him. Channing realized she was starved for this man's touch. The way he alternately inflamed and cherished her. The way he instinctively knew which one she needed.

Yet, her breath hitched in her chest, reminding her of the pain that'd been circling her heart for the last day. She broke the kiss. "Colby—"

"Don't leave me." He tracked soft kisses up her jawline. "Please. I missed you, darlin', something fierce. Stay with me tonight." Over and over his lips brushed the hair covering her ear as he seemed to breathe her in. "Promise me you'll stick around so we can talk this through, okay?"

Say no.

A thick pause hung in the air.

Finally, she swallowed her pride and whispered, "Okay."

"Thank you." He hefted her satchel over his left shoulder, grabbed her right hand and they sprinted to the waiting cab.

Channing paced as she waited for him to unlock the door to the motel room. "How'd you get a room?" she asked, when she meant "*Why* did you get a room I didn't know about?"

"My folks had an extra reservation because my brother Cord and his son were supposed to come. They gave it to me instead."

"Oh."

The room wasn't anything different than the other cheap rooms they'd crashed in for the last week. In the darkness her senses were attuned to sound. The thump of her bag on the carpet. The rattling wheeze of the air conditioner kicking on. The click of the chain as he secured the door. The blood rushing in her ears. The *shush shush* of his bootsteps on the carpet as he moved in behind her.

"We'll talk later. Right now I need to be inside you before I lose my ever-lovin' mind. Let me show you how much I missed you."

No. She would not relinquish control to him this soon. She turned and sank to her knees. She had him unbuckled, unzipped and in her mouth before he knew what hit him.

"Goddammit, Channing, that's not what I wanted... Oh fuck that feels good. Oh, darlin', just like that. Baby, don't stop."

Channing sucked him off, taking her own sweet time to build him to madness. Dangling him over the edge of reason again and again before she relented to his begging whimpers and finished him in her mouth.

Colby staggered backward and sagged on the bed.

She escaped to the bathroom. Maybe if she cowered in there long enough he'd fall asleep and she could sneak out because being here was a bad, bad idea.

Two seconds later, two raps sounded on the door. "Channing? You okay?"

Crap. "I'm fine."

"You gonna hide in there all night?"

"Maybe."

Colby laughed. "Well, as long as I've got your undivided attention, let me set you straight on a few things."

"I can turn the water on so I don't have to hear you," she said with false syrupiness.

"And I can break down this cheap-ass door so you've got no choice but to listen. You really want that, darlin'?"

"No." Before he could sweet-talk his way around her, Channing blurted, "Did you ask Amy Jo to come to Cheyenne?"

"No! Why would you ask—"

"Because Trevor hinted *you* told your dad to bring her here for you."

"Trevor was drunk. My dad's been tryin' to fix me up with her for the last year. Poor thing is shy and unsure of herself and she needs a little—"

"Little Amy Jo didn't look so shy and unsure of herself when you two were dirty dancing," Channing retorted.

He chuckled again. "Amy Jo asked me to teach her to dance like that because she don't know how. And it appears she's already set her cap for some cowboy back home. So she's tryin' to shed her wholesome image. I showed her some pointers. Plus, she wanted to rub it in Keely's face. And my cheeky little sister deserves it after taunting Amy Jo all these years."

"Oh." What else could she say that didn't make her sound like a jealous idiot?

Silence. Colby sighed. "Shug, please come out here."

Channing cracked the door an inch and peered at him. "You left your ropes in the horse trailer, right?"

"Yep. Just me, just you." He held out his empty hands. "See?"

"Okay." The second she scooted out, he blocked her attempt to dodge him and hugged her spine to his chest.

She tried to squirm away.

"What's this? I thought you liked me? Now you're treatin' me like a leper?"

"I still like you. I just don't know why I'm here."

Colby kissed her crown. "Because I missed you. Talkin' to you. Touchin' you. Getting to know you. We've had fun learnin' about each other, haven't we?"

"Do you mean in the biblical sense?"

He tapped her ass. "No. I meant in every sense. I want to be with you, Channing. And not just with my dick in your mouth."

She leaned back, allowing his solid warmth to seep into her. "You didn't like it?"

"I loved it. But I don't know why you felt you needed to distract me. I wanted to touch you, too. Lord, I'm achin' to put my hands on you. But I can wait until you're ready. And. Ah. It don't have to be tonight."

That shocked her. Wasn't this thing between them supposed to be about sex?

Colby whirled her to face him. A hint of hesitation darkened his eyes. "Are you comin' to the afternoon rodeo tomorrow to watch me compete?"

"I'd like to but I don't have a ticket. I've heard they're pretty hard to come by."

"I bought one for you today." He sifted her hair through his hands. "Your hair is so soft. You smell so good. Everything about you is soft and warm and sweet."

Channing was melting. Giving in.

"And after the rodeo I've planned something special for us."

"Do we get naked for it?"

Colby scowled. "Maybe I'd like to spend time with you with our clothes on, Chan."

"That'd be a first."

"You're pushin' your luck, darlin'. I'm tryin' to be civilized. Givin' us a chance to talk this out."

Channing stood on her tiptoes and licked his neck. "I like you uncivilized and wild. Talk is overrated. I'd rather fuck it out."

Another weighty pause. "Your choice. But now that you've made it you don't get to change your mind."

Then he was on her. Kissing her, tearing at her clothes. In the blink of an eye she was naked and at his mercy.

They crashed to the bed in a tangle of arms and legs. Colby crushed her to his chest and rolled with her so she was writhing beneath him.

He scissored his legs on the outside of hers, immobilizing her lower half. He encircled both her wrists together in his large hand and pinned them above her head.

Colby's free hand slid between them. He plunged two fingers inside her wetness. He coated his shaft with her juices, guided his cock to her entrance and drove in.

Channing groaned. Yes. This is what she wanted, what she understood about this man. The primal need.

Body to body, forehead to forehead, he thrust into her. Long, hard deep strokes. Not fast, not slow. Just strong and steady and true.

"Why haven't you ever let me love you like this? Face to face? Heart to heart? So I can look in your eyes while I'm makin' love to you?"

Because it's not lovemaking, it's just sex.

"What are you afraid of?"

That you'll see my feelings for you and cut and run.

"Look at me, Channing Kinkaid."

She angled her chin up an inch.

"What I said the other night? I meant it. Maybe it was crudely put instead of poetic, but I meant every damn word."

Play it cool, play it dumb. Breezily, she said, "Oh. Remind me again what you said. I don't remember."

A calculating look came into his eyes. "Oh I'll remind you all right."

Channing realized she'd made a huge mistake baiting him.

"I told you that you are mine. You belong to me. Remember now?" He rocked his hips with short, precise thrusts.

Her body softened for his, yet her mouth remained clamped shut as a rusty well cover.

"Maybe I should repeat it. Then you can say it back to me so I know you understand. And remember."

God. He was relentless.

"Say it. Say you're mine."

Channing blinked as he thrust. In. Out. In. Out. In a compelling rhythm as exotic as it was arousingly familiar.

"Say it."

She couldn't believe he was doing this. Pushing her emotions as he pushed her body to the limit.

"You're mine. Say it."

She stared at him, pretending a detachment she didn't feel.

No change in his expression. No change in the solid motions of his thrusts. No change or concession in the words he demanded from her.

"Say you're mine."

Channing turned her head away.

With his chin he forced her face back level to his and peered in her eyes. "Goddammit, Channing. Say it."

She watched him warily. Physically, she wasn't scared of him, but at some point in the last hour, on an emotional level, he'd set out to conquer her. Completely. He wouldn't be satisfied until he had her total surrender. And she was teetering on the brink of submission.

"Say it."

Channing shook her head, wanting to distract him with her hands. Her mouth. Anything. But she was totally under his control.

"Say it. Say you're mine."

She found her voice. "Why?"

"Because you *are* mine and you'll damn well admit it. Say it."

"I can't."

"You can. You will. Say you belong only to me."

"Damn you, Colby. Why are you doing this?"

"You needed a reminder, remember? Say it."

The repetition of his words *say it say it* was stuck in her head. The repetition of his body plunging in and out of hers stuck her pleasure center like a thousand needles.

"Say it. Say you're mine."

"No."

"Say it. I won't stop fucking you. We'll be here in this bed, locked together until you admit to me out loud what I see in your eyes, Channing Kinkaid. What I feel in your body whenever I touch you. So say the words to me so I can say them back to you."

Was she prepared to give in to him? Especially when he hadn't clarified if he meant that she belonged to him only for the rest of the night? Or did he mean forever?

Maybe she should take a chance and find out.

Channing locked her gaze to his. "I'm yours."

Fire danced in his eyes. He set his jaw and rocked into her harder. "Again."

"I'm yours."

"Again."

"Yours." That tingling pressure for release began to build low in her belly.

"Whose? Say my name."

"Colby."

Sweat dripped down his temple. "Who do you belong to?"

"You. Colby McKay."

"Goddamn right you belong to me."

She arched her hips, wordlessly begging for more.

Colby fucked her with a ferocity that left her breathless. Helpless. Like nothing else that had ever happened to her before that moment mattered. Staring into his heated blue eyes, she saw his determination. His need. His discipline of possession. His utter obsession with her. But she didn't see love.

"Colby—"

"Mine." He thrust hard. "Mine." Another pounding thrust that knocked the bed frame into the wall. "Only mine, Channing. I'll kill the next man who so much lays a hand on what's *mine.*"

The orgasm caught her off guard like a summer storm and burst through her with the elemental power of lightning and thunder.

Colby didn't yell out his release or miss a stroke as he came silently. She felt the hot bursts of semen inside her pussy and then warm liquid seeped out from where they were still joined.

He simply said, "Again. Another reminder so you don't forget."

Colby had taken her at her word; they'd fucked it out. He fucked her until the pleasure was too much, until her body shuddered and quaked, until her brain overloaded on bliss and she passed out in his arms.

Chapter Twenty

Channing woke up. Naked. She rolled over and groaned.

Colby's side of the bed was rumpled and empty, except for the ticket on the pillow and a note, which read:

Today, we talk it out. C U after the perf. Love, CWM

She glanced down her nude body, expecting another set of his marks of passion. She saw none. They were all internal. Mental. But definitely permanent.

After a quick shower she gathered her stuff and headed for Gemma's campsite. She opened the door and a swell of heat blasted her. It'd be blistering hot in Cheyenne today.

As she turned around, Channing bumped into Carson McKay, who wasn't exactly thrilled to see her sneaking out of Colby's room.

"Umm. Morning, Mr. McKay."

His eyes narrowed to pinpoints. "Hey. I know you. You're that friend of Gemma Jansen. A *friend* of Colby's, too." Carson gave her a once-over. "You mind tellin' me what you're doin' slinkin' out of my son's room?"

Her first thought was to lie.

Carson stared her down. Letting his gaze wander to the love bites on her neck Colby had given her that hadn't faded yet.

Judging her. Appearing to find her lacking. Just like her own father. Just like everyone else in her old life.

Her back snapped straight. "Your son invited me into his room. You can ask him what we were doing, but since he's a gentleman, I doubt he'll kiss and tell."

No response from Colby's father. Just another cold hard stare.

"You're wastin' your time with him. I know my son. He ain't—"

"Maybe you don't know your son as well as you think. And if he chooses to waste his time with me, then I don't see how it is any of your business. Now, if you'll excuse me." Somehow she managed to walk away instead of running like a scared rabbit.

Gemma's trailer was empty. Channing had a few hours to kill before the rodeo started so she wandered through the vendor stands and the midway. She cruised through the gift shop. Studied the bronze statue of the late Lane Frost for a long time. A reminder that even the best athletes in the world succumbed to forces beyond their control.

Frontier Park was huge, the biggest outdoor rodeo arena in the world. After the Air Force paratroopers sailed in, and the state rodeo queens in attendance were announced, and a barbershop quartet from Riverton belted out "The Star Spangled Banner", it was time to rodeo.

With so many competitors at Frontier Days Rodeo, the individual events were spread out, instead of all the events running one after the other like at other venues. Rough stock riding was interspersed with timed events. Colby ate dirt on his saddle bronc ride. He posted a decent score of 4.5 in tie-down roping. Unlike other rodeos where bull riding was always last, here they were sprinkled throughout the afternoon.

As she waited, she began to wonder just what his plans were for later. Anticipation made her heart race and she almost missed his name being called.

The bull, Nobody's Business, hadn't been ridden in twelve outs. Channing perched on the edge of her seat, expecting a good match up.

The chute opened to the roar of the crowd. Colby looked spectacular as he rode, synchronized to the bull's movements like he'd ridden him every day. The buzzer sounded. He'd made it the full eight seconds.

For some reason instead of watching the first instant replay on the big screens, she kept her gaze on Colby. He'd gotten hung up. Not his hand in his bullrope, but his spur was twisted around the flank strap.

The bull fighters were trying to get him loose, but the bull hopped and jumped. The next scene seemed to happen in slow motion, Colby's body sliding under the bull when the bull lunged sideways. Both the bull's back legs came down on Colby's left thigh. Then the bull hooked Colby's vest and tossed him in the air.

The crowd gasped.

Channing leapt to her feet.

Even in the upper tier of the grandstands she could hear one bull fighter screaming for the sports medicine team, while the others chased the bull away. Colby's leg was bent at an odd angle and he was prone on the dirt.

A dozen people milled around on the arena floor. It wasn't long before the far gate opened and an ambulance zoomed in, kicking up dust. Colby was loaded on a stretcher, shuttled in the back end of the ambulance and whisked out amidst wailing sirens and nearly complete silence in the arena.

Stunned, she just stared at the churned up patches of dirt where Colby had fallen. How long she stayed motionless, she didn't know.

Finally, people behind her yelled, "Sit down!"

She made her deadened body move and she exited the stands in a daze.

Channing had no idea where they'd taken him. She knew if she tried to sneak back in the contestants' area without a pass, she'd get escorted out by security. She wandered along the fence—for how long, she didn't know. Someone shouted her name.

She whirled around and saw Cash barreling toward her. He grabbed her in a bear hug. "Have you heard anything about what happened to him?"

Channing shook her head.

"You saw it, right?"

She nodded.

"Okay. The bull landed on his leg and broke the femur in his left thigh. A bone fragment caused a rupture in his femoral artery. Very serious stuff. I ain't gonna lie, Channing; it is life threatenin', so they rushed him to emergency surgery. They also were talkin' about a collapsed lung where the bull hooked him."

"Omigod." She was glad Cash held her upright because her knees gave out.

"His family is already gone. I'll drive you to the hospital."

The truth hit her and she began to shake harder. "Cash, his family isn't going to want me there. They don't even know about me."

Cash placed a gentle hand on her cheek. "It don't matter if they want you there, Channing. *Colby* will want you there."

She nodded and ducked her head to hide her tears.

"Cash!"

Gemma ran up, out of breath. "What are you doing out here? You're up in about five minutes. They're looking for you behind the chutes."

"I'm gonna have to forfeit this go. I'm driving Channing to the hospital."

"I'll take her." Gemma's arm circled Channing's shoulders. "Colby would be pissed if you didn't ride on account of him. So get back there and cover that bull. Meet us there later."

Cash nodded and reluctantly trotted off.

Channing was absolutely numb. She let Gemma lead her into the parking area. The heat from the blacktop nearly scorched her lungs. She didn't remember anything about the ride to the hospital, as she was too busy praying that Colby would still be alive when she got there.

ઉઇઉ

Eight excruciating hours later the surgeons gave the news to the family. The doctors had stopped the hemorrhaging, which was their first concern. Then they'd fixed his collapsed lung. After that, they began surgery on his leg and inserted an intramedullary rod down the center of Colby's thighbone.

Colby was in intensive care in stable condition. With physical therapy he'd walk again. Even ride a horse. But the doctor's prognosis for Colby continuing his rodeo career even part-time wasn't good. Colby had a long road of therapy ahead of him. Months.

Channing heard all of this information secondhand from Trevor and Edgard. And Gemma. And Cash. She'd hidden herself away in a tiny lounge off the main family waiting area. Not wanting to intrude on the McKays. For her own self-preservation she would not insert herself in a situation already rife with trauma.

For all those hours Colby was in surgery, she'd paced. Worrying. Wondering. When she'd received the news he'd pulled through, she'd curled into a ball and wept. Colby was alive. That was all that mattered.

"Channing?"

She looked up when Gemma plopped beside her on the dilapidated loveseat but she couldn't muster a smile. "Yeah?"

"It's been hours. You want something to eat?"

"No. I'd just throw it up. Thanks, though."

"Okay. That's fine. How long do you want to stay here?"

"Until I can see him. Let me rephrase that. Until I can see him in private. Without me having to explain who I am to his family." Not that *she* knew who she was to Colby.

His words *mine mine mine* echoed in her head.

But what did that mean?

"You realize that might not be for a day or two. The McKays have all but circled the wagons 'round him. Cord, Colton and Carter will all be here tomorrow."

Crap.

Gemma frowned. "Why do you say that?"

Channing wasn't aware she'd muttered the word aloud. "Because me sticking around wasn't part of our arrangement. Colby and I had always planned to part ways after Cheyenne. Now is just as good a time as any for me to leave."

Gemma's eyes froze into chips of ice. "You're just gonna take off like nothing's happened? Like it don't matter he's laying unconscious and beat up and practically dead in a hospital bed?"

Channing winced at Gemma's hard slap of words. "No. But maybe you'd like to give me a chance to explain myself before you go jumping to conclusions."

"Fine. I'm listening. But even you gotta admit things are different now."

"Yeah, they're probably worse, Gem." Channing leaned against the concrete wall and resisted beating her head into it. She closed her eyes. "How long is Colby going to be in the hospital? A week? Two? When he's well enough to leave, he'll have to return home to the ranch because he won't be able to take care of himself. His family will expect to do that, as they should. You really think they'll want me—a strange woman from the East Coast—around?

"Do you think *Colby* will want me underfoot? God. When he was injured in Greeley he'd get all pissy whenever I fussed around him. The man is stubborn. And proud. He didn't want me to see him as weak so he took chances he shouldn't have. That injury wasn't nearly as serious as this one is. He'll have *months* of physical therapy, *months* of being dependent on others. So if I drop everything in my life and move to Wyoming to help take care of him, he'll resent me. I know he will. I couldn't stand that, Gemma. He's too important to me." Her voice broke.

Gemma pressed Channing's head to her shoulder and let her cry. When the worst of the jag was over, Gemma smoothed the hair from Channing's damp cheek. "You know, I'd like to argue with you and say you're wrong, but I have a sneaking suspicion you're exactly right."

"I wish I wasn't."

"Me too." Gemma handed her another Kleenex. "I'm sorry I was hard on you."

"That's what friends do, Gem."

They stayed locked in silence for a while. Gemma sighed and scooted away. "So what are *you* gonna do, girlie?"

"Same thing I've been doing, I guess. Hide out until Colby's family leaves and then I'll sneak in to see him. After that, I have some things to deal with at home that I've been putting off."

"You gonna stay there? Back on the coast where your folks live?"

Probably not. "I don't know."

"Remember, my door is always open. If things don't work out for you with your family or your job, look me up. I can always use another set of hands to muck out horse stalls. The company would be nice too, Chan. I'm gonna miss you."

Channing actually smiled for the first time in hours. "Thanks."

"No problem. This whole situation sucks all the way around." Gemma stood. "Call my cell when you're done here and I'll come get you and take you to the airport."

Channing nodded.

Hours passed. Trevor, Cash, Edgard and several other cowboys on the circuit came and went. She watched from the shadows at end of the corridor. No one paid any attention to her. She'd spent her whole life blending into the background and she was damn good at it.

Around five a.m. Channing was jostled awake. She blinked up into Keely McKay's curious blue eyes.

"Channing, right? Gemma told me to keep an eye on you. My folks are gone. Colby isn't awake, but he is alone if you want to see him."

"Thank you," she whispered.

The room was small and filled with a medicinal stench. A ghostly sound of Colby's breathing apparatus echoed, as well as the constant *beep beep* of the machines keeping him alive.

Channing bit her tongue hard to stop a gasp from escaping.

His leg was in a cast. Most of the rest of his body was covered up with blankets. He had tubes in both arms. He didn't look frail; he looked…like a wounded warrior.

She approached the side of Colby's bed, curling her fingers around the metal railing. Her tears fell. "Oh, cowboy. Ain't you a sight for sore eyes."

No response.

She brushed her fingertips across the scraped-up knuckles on his hand and studied his unconscious face for the longest time, hoping for a sign of some kind.

Increased activity in the hallway signaled it was time for her to go.

Channing kissed his forehead and moved her lips to his ear. "Get better soon. When you're back on your feet, cowboy, come looking for me because I'll be waiting. No matter where I am or what I'm doing I'll be waiting for you. For as long as it takes. And I'll say the words you were so hell bent on hearing from me last night. I love you, Colby McKay. Don't you ever forget it. I'll say it again. I love you."

Walking away from him was the hardest thing she'd ever done, even when she knew it was for the best. For now.

Chapter Twenty-One

One week later...

Trevor sipped his fourth beer and watched Edgard loading the last of his tack in his luggage. "You sure you don't wanna take that saddle? It's awful damn nice. Nicer than mine."

"No. You can have it. Or you can sell it. I don't care either way."

Pause. "Maybe I'll keep it around for when you come back."

Edgard sighed, but he didn't look up from zipping his soft-sided suitcase. "I already told you, Trev. I'm not coming back."

Trevor ignored the stab of pain near his heart. He drained the lukewarm brew and reached for another.

Thud. Edgard's last bag hit the floor.

The silence between them was deafening.

Edgard said, "When are you going to Cody?"

"Tomorrow. Early."

"Who're you going with?"

"Cash and Brian. Colby's cousin Dag."

"Good luck. Dag's a great heeler."

"Thanks." He fiddled with the metal tab on the beer can. "You sure you don't want me to take you to the train station?"

Edgard laughed softly. "That wouldn't be wise, *amigo*."

"It ain't like I'm gonna make a big scene, Ed," Trevor scoffed.

"I know. Maybe I would." Edgard briefly shut his eyes. "Shit. I'm not gonna do this. I can't do this anymore."

Edgard ran his hand through his hair. A gesture of frustration Trevor had come to recognize in the last two years he and Edgard had been together. Off and on. In secret. He knew it wasn't fair to either of them.

Trevor wanted to get up, walk over and smooth Edgard's dark hair back in place. He ached to soothe him and tell him everything would be all right. But mostly he wanted to wrap his arms around Edgard and beg him not to leave.

But Trevor did none of that. He just steadily drank his beer, waiting for the numbness to settle in and ease his sorrow.

Edgard opened the door and tossed out his luggage. Then he closed the door again and braced his shoulders against the wall.

Automatically Trevor stiffened.

"Don't worry. I'm not going to make you uncomfortable by telling you how I feel. You already know. I just wish things could be different."

Trevor swallowed a drink and the lump in his throat. "Me too."

"Take care of yourself, *meu amor.*"

"You too."

A truck horn honked outside.

Without another word Edgard turned and walked out of his life.

Trevor stayed seated until he heard Gemma's rig drive away. Then he slowly stood, shuffled to the door and locked it.

He shoved the rest of the case of beer up in the sleeping compartment and crawled across the mattress. He cracked open a fresh can, lay flat on his back and let the tears come.

Chapter Twenty-Two

Eight weeks later...

Colby McKay sat on the front porch of his parents' house with his leg propped on a folding chair and scowled at the darkening sky. Fucking clouds. If it was gonna be cloudy, at least the damn things should be rain clouds. They needed the moisture in a bad way.

A dry autumn breeze drifted through the eaves, rattling the wind chimes. He'd been home for two months. A doctor ordered bed rest after his leg had been busted up like a cheap 2X4, and his lung had seeped air like a leaky balloon.

As glad as he was not to be pissing in a colostomy bag or wheeling himself around in a chair for the rest of his life, it stung his pride that his family was forced to take care of him at the family homestead for the time being. For six long goddamn months.

Oh, they didn't seem to mind. His mom was happy to have him home in any capacity, happier yet he was done with life on the road. He was still shuffling around on crutches with a brace on his leg like a gimped-up old man, but at least he wasn't flat on his back.

Still, there was something mortifying about his mom or his sister doing his physical therapy exercises with him every damn day. That little sadist Keely liked inflicting pain on him. He'd warned her paybacks were a bitch and he'd invited Amy Jo over to keep him company on occasion. But he suspected the only reason Amy Jo showed up was on the hope she'd run into his brother Cord.

Colby felt useless. He couldn't stay by himself in his beloved log cabin on the other side of the canyon. His mother claimed she didn't trust him not to do too much, too soon. Helping Colton with chores was out, too. His dad had told him there'd be plenty of chores waiting for him when he'd healed up properly. Next spring. Even Cord gave him pitying looks, and Cord's life was even more fucked up than his.

But mostly Colby sat around wondering what the hell he was gonna do now that his rodeo career was history. Sure, he'd known at the end of this season he'd have to scale back and compete locally only on weekends. So it'd come as a complete shock when the surgeons warned him if he started riding bulls or broncs again, he could end up in a wheelchair permanently.

Not a chance he was willing to take.

For the millionth time Colby's thoughts turned to Channing. He knew that wasn't why she'd bailed—because he was no longer a rodeo cowboy, now that injury had forced him into being just an ordinary Wyoming rancher. He doubted she'd skipped back to her old life after she'd had her sexual adventure of traveling the rodeo circuit with a trio of cowboys. Or that she'd forgotten about him as she was on the Eastern seaboard teaching readin', writin' and 'rithmetic.

Probably they called it something else at that fancy-pants school where she was hiding away.

No doubt Channing was hiding. From him. From herself. From what she'd said to him in the hospital when she didn't know he could hear her. Colby didn't have any idea what to do about fixing things. Hell, he *couldn't* do anything about it until he was a whole man again.

Lord. He missed her. After one glorious week Channing meant everything to him. During the last night he'd spent making love to her, showing her how he felt, he knew she'd never just waltz away.

I'll be waiting.

But where? It seemed as if Channing Kinkaid had dropped off the face of the earth.

A couple of weeks back after he'd gotten through the worst of the pain, he'd taken a chance and called her cell phone only to discover it'd been disconnected. That left him adrift because he didn't know her parents' names. He didn't know where she lived.

But he did know he loved her.

The wind blew the scent of sage and dirt. For a second, he thought he caught a whiff of Channing's perfume. Wishful thinking. There weren't a lot of wildflowers in Wyoming in the autumn.

He sighed. Maybe he'd nap. At least when he was asleep he didn't think about this shit. And he could dream about her wrapped up in his arms in the middle of his king-sized bed back at his place. Just the two of them alone for a change. No traveling partners. No interruptions.

The front door opened and his mother hustled out with his nephew Ky cocked on her hip. She pitched Colby the portable phone. "We're out of milk and diapers. I'm running to the store. Do you need anything while I'm in town?"

Colby shook his head. He'd drifted into that dreamy state right before sleep when the phone rang. He snapped, "Hello?"

"Colby McKay, you sound like a bear with a sore paw. How you doing?"

He relaxed. "Getting better every day, Gemma. And you?"

"I can't complain. Hey, is your dad around?"

"No. He and Cord and Colt are sortin' cows with the cattle broker. Why? What'd you need?"

"Hang on." A rustling sound crackled on the line as she moved the receiver on her end. "No, Channing, those don't go there. Put 'em in the sun porch."

Colby froze. Then his heart raced. "Gemma? What the devil is goin' on?"

"Sorry 'bout that. What did you say?"

"Did you say Channing is there? At your ranch?"

"Well—"

"*My* Channing is at your ranch?"

"Yeah."

"Since when?"

"Awhile."

Colby practically growled. "How long has she been there?"

"She's been here almost six weeks. Where've *you* been?"

"Right here! Why in the hell didn't she tell me? Why didn't *you* tell me, Gemma?"

"Not my place."

"Goddammit. I don't know whether to take a horsewhip after you or her."

"I don't like the direction this conversation has taken, Colby McKay."

He breathed deep, trying to calm himself. "Sorry. It's just...I've spent the last month tryin' to find out where she is!"

"So now you know. My question is: What are you gonna do about it?" Gemma hung up.

A shaft of sunshine spilled across the porch railing. Colby glanced at the sky. The gray clouds had cleared out, revealing a radiant blue horizon.

A sign that he'd finally get a chance to clear up some of the issues that'd been clouding his mind?

He grabbed his crutches and his keys and he was gone.

Chapter Twenty-Three

Meanwhile, back at Gemma Jansen's ranch...

"You always make me do the shitty jobs," Channing half-complained.

"That's part of learning the ropes and working on the ranch. Somebody has to do them."

"Yeah? I wish you would've told me this before I packed up and moved here."

Gemma leaned on the pitchfork, her face serious. "Do you have some regrets about shucking life in the city for shucking corn?"

Even covered in horse shit and hay dust Channing couldn't hold back a big grin. "Not a single one."

"Good." She pointed to a mound of golden hay. "Spread that around. I've got to make a call. I'll be right back."

While Channing shoveled hay, she considered the idea that she might have some regrets.

After she'd left Colby in the hospital, she'd flown home. It'd taken less than a week for her to realize she couldn't fathom spending her life living up to someone else's expectations. Contrary to her parents' accusations, *she* hadn't changed. She was finally ready to accept that who she was on the inside was who she wanted to be on the outside. All the time. Not just for a week during rodeo season.

So Channing had quit her job before she'd even started it. She'd sold the few things she'd owned—including her BMW—bought an old Dodge truck, packed up and had driven across the country to the wilds of Wyoming.

It'd been the best decision she'd ever made, besides hooking up with a sweet rodeo cowboy who made her laugh, made her mad and made her scream. The last time she'd seen him, lying in that hospital bed, he'd made her cry.

So far her only regret was that she hadn't found the guts to personally visit that cowboy. The couple of times she'd called his folks' place, his father had said Colby was resting. She figured she'd give him another week of recovery time before she took a road trip and tried her hand at wooing him face to face, Western style.

Gemma kicked a stall door shut on her way back into the barn.

"Who'd you call that put you in such a bad mood? Cash?"

"Why in the world would I call Cash Big Crow when I haven't seen or heard from him in over two months?" Gemma's face turned bright red whenever Cash's name was mentioned.

Channing shrugged. Not her business. They'd either figure it out, or they wouldn't. It made her sad to think that Trevor was too much of a chicken to buck his family's expectations and had let Edgard go back to Brazil alone. "Hey, you want to shoot some pool tonight at the Lantern?"

"Nah. We've got too much to do. Let's stick around here."

"Great." Channing quit leaning on her pitchfork and got back to work.

Two and a half hours later, Gemma disappeared again while Channing finished in the barn. She heard a vehicle zooming up the driveway and gravel crunching as it came to an abrupt halt. A metal door slammed.

"Channing Kinkaid, get your butt out here right now."

Colby? Was here? She tossed her leather work gloves on the wooden tool bench.

"That was your first warnin', shug," he yelled.

Channing sucked in a deep breath and stepped into the sunshine. She shaded her eyes with her hand and caught a glimpse of Colby hunched over a pair of crutches beside a dirty black pickup.

Her heart absolutely soared with joy. He was a little battered, a little thinner, but he was there.

And mad as the dickens.

"What in the hell is wrong with you? You're livin' in Wyoming now? Less than three goddamn hours away from me and you can't be bothered to let me know?"

Channing swallowed the lump in her throat. "I did let you know. I called out to your parents' place a couple of times and talked to your dad." She froze about twenty feet from him when the truth hit her. "He didn't tell you I called, did he?"

A muscle in Colby's jaw flexed. "No. He didn't. I'll deal with him later. Right now I wanna paddle your behind for thinking I'd ever—"

She held up her hand. "Stop right there. I thought when we saw each other again you'd at least sweet-talk me a little, cowboy. Seeings you're so good with that silver tongue. But instead—"

"Instead I'm standin' here like a dumbass because I can't run to you and scoop you up in my arms where you belong."

She paused and stared at him, her heart in her eyes. "How about if I run to you?" she said softly.

"Oh God, darlin', please. I'm dyin' over here."

Channing ran.

He caught her on his right side and hauled her against him. Colby kissed her, not like he wanted to devour her, but with pureness. Gentleness. With his heart and soul wide open. Like he was giving them a memory to reflect on for the next sixty years when they looked back on this moment. She drank him in and filled him back up, sharing, drowning in everything they freely gave to each other.

She buried her face in his shirt, inhaling the warm intimate scent of him. "I missed you, Colby. God. I was so worried about you."

"You were?"

"Yeah. I wanted to die when you got hurt. And in the hospital I realized I would wither and die if I didn't have you in my life."

"So that's why you left me?"

Channing butted her head against his stubborn chin. "Temporarily. I had things to get straight in my own life first. And you had other things to worry about than me. We both know you wouldn't have wanted me around those first few weeks while you were recovering."

"True. I've been grumpier than an old bear. Been in a lot of pain. Been kind of an ass to everyone, if you wanna know the truth. But a big part of that was because I didn't know where you were, shug."

"I've been here. Waiting for you."

Colby's big, gentle hand shook as he wiped away her tears. "You know I would've been here sooner, had I known? Nothin' would've kept me from you, Channing."

Channing kissed his palm.

"So whatcha been doin' here the last six weeks?"

"Learning how to ride a horse. Learning how to take care of livestock. Learning how to cook. Learning everything I can about life on a ranch."

"Why?"

Her eyes twinkled. "See, I've got my eye on this hot ranching cowboy..."

Colby grinned. Dimple and all.

She melted.

"Yeah? Well, there are a couple of things expected of a proper ranch wife that Gemma can't teach you." He frowned. "At least, I hope to hell she ain't been tryin'."

"You're the only man for the job."

"Always. Forever and ever amen. I don't share what's mine."

"You made that crystal clear a couple of times." Channing looked him dead in the eye. "I love you, Colby McKay."

"I know."

Her jaw dropped.

Colby closed it with his finger and kissed her. "You told me once, and it was enough to stick in my head forever. Although, it kinda seemed like a dream, but I remember you comin' to see me in the hospital. I heard what you said. It's what got me through, the idea that a sweet, sexy, sophisticated woman like you loved a roughneck like me. Loved me enough to tell me you'd be waitin' for me. No matter what." He brought the back of her hand to his mouth. "I'd get on one knee, but I'm still pretty beat up. So I'm just gonna ask you outright. Will you marry me, Channing Kinkaid?"

Without hesitation she blurted, "Yes!"

"Hot damn." He readied his crutches. "Get in the truck. You're drivin'. We're goin' to the preacher right now before you change your mind. Then I'm takin' you home where you belong."

She almost forgot her list of demands after Colby said *home where you belong*. But this was too important. "Ah-ah. Hold it right there. If I take you on, there'll be conditions."

His eyes narrowed. "Should I be afraid of these conditions?"

"Maybe." Channing grinned. "One: You'll be in my bed. Every night. No boring, once a week missionary-style vanilla sex. I expect you and I will both work to keep our sex life as hot and titillating as it has been."

"Titillatin', huh?" He grinned. "I'm down with that."

"Two: I wanna have kids. Lots of kids. But not right away. I want you all to myself for awhile."

"Same goes, shug."

"Three: Between you still recovering from your injury and me being a novice at living on a ranch, we'll have to be patient with each other. Your family will have to be patient with me. I've been an outsider in my own family for my whole life, Colby. I don't want to be an outsider in yours, too."

Colby leaned on his crutches and stared directly into her eyes. "You are my family now. Besides, Mama already loves you because I told her all about you."

Channing didn't have to feign surprise. "You did?"

"Yep. And she's gonna kick my dad's butt when she finds about him not tellin' me that you called, 'cause she knows how I've been pinin' by the phone waitin' to hear from you." He smiled evilly. "So I think I'll let her handle him. She can punish him way worse than I ever could."

"Good. Because I'm in for the long haul. I don't want little picky stuff to tear us apart when the big picture is so promising." She smoothed her fingers along the dogged set of his jaw. "Any questions?"

Colby kissed the inside of her wrist. "One."

"Shoot."

"Is this where I tell you I love you?"

Channing's eyes filled with tears and she nodded.

"I love you, Channing Kinkaid. You make me the luckiest, happiest man in the world. Life on the ranch ain't always gonna be rainbows and butterflies and the heart-poundin' excitement of rodeo, but dammit, it will be *our* life. I'll spend every wakin' hour makin' sure our life together fulfills your every fantasy."

Deliriously happy, she snagged his hat and plopped it on her head. "Is this where we ride off into the sunset, cowboy?"

"Yep." Colby kissed her. Long. And hard. "I'd much rather ride you, but hey, I can adapt to anything you throw my way."

About the Author

To learn more about Lorelei James, please visit www.loreleijames.com. Send an email to lorelei@loreleijames.com or join her Yahoo! group to join in the fun with other readers as well as Lorelei. http://groups.yahoo.com/group/LoreleiJamesGang

Look for these titles by
Lorelei James

Now Available

Rode Hard, Put Up Wet
Dirty Deeds
Running with the Devil
Beginnings Anthology: Babe in the Woods

Coming Soon:

Cowgirl Up and Ride
Running on Empty

There's nowhere to run and no place to hide from old wounds and demons for the vulnerable woman behind the bawdy attitude.

Tamara's Spirit

© 2007 Nicole Austin

How ironic to be captured by an Indian when not one of the Shooting Star Ranch cowboys is available to race to her rescue.

City girl Tamara Dobbs lives on the ranch to be close to her friends and even closer to her gorgeous cowboys, but still she feels discontent, fragmented. From the minute she runs into the new guy—sexy, unflappable equestrian, Dakota Blackhawk—she runs from the intense emotions he evokes.

On first sight, Dakota knows nothing will stop him from claiming the brazen little princess as his own—heart, body, and spirit. He'll accept nothing less. While he would gladly take on the fight for her, she must face her own battle to become whole. Taking her out of her element is the only way he can help the sexy, stubborn woman.

Tamara may survive the emotional roller coaster ride, but she still must conquer the ultimate challenge…forgetting what others want her to be and becoming true to herself.

Available now in ebook and print from Samhain Publishing.

Enjoy the following excerpt from Tamara's Spirit ...

With a deep sigh he moved behind her, boxing her between the fence and the steel bands of his arms as his hands held a firm grasp on the top rung. The warmth of his big body enveloped her. Tamara felt a heated flush rise from her breasts and over her neck to settle high on her cheeks. It took every ounce of willpower she possessed to keep from leaning back against him, luxuriating in his presence surrounding her.

His breath created a hot caress against her ear as he leaned forward and began speaking. The sexy, raspy baritone slid over her skin like heated molasses, slow and sensual. "Watch them, princess."

The firm caress of his lips brushing against the shell of her ear made her breasts feel heavy, achy, her cunt warm and wet. The whisper of his breath over her neck made her body shudder.

Fucking need to get laid. And soon!

"You can tell the female is ready to be mounted. Her cunt is swollen. See how her hot juices slide from her vagina in anticipation of taking the stallion's big shaft. She wants him. Every muscle is tensed as she waits for him to come to her, to fill her up."

Oh shit! How about filling me up, stud? She had no problem imagining how the horse felt. Tamara was reacting the same way as Honey—flesh quivering, pussy lips swollen and dripping—wet and ready. If only she were able to have an enjoyable experience with one man, but she knew better. For her, orgasm required more stimulation than one cock was capable of delivering. All of her attempts at one-on-one sex in the recent past had left her frustrated. She was not able to get off anymore without at least three big cocks fucking all her orifices at once.

Her body readied itself anyway, betraying Tamara and confusing her jumbled thoughts. Her breasts were so full, needy. It took all her self-control to keep her hands on the fence rail and not rub the small globes or tweak her peaked nipples. Dakota's heady, masculine scent enveloping her made her clit pulse. The silky material of her panties flooded with her cream, the scent of arousal rising on the heated air between them.

"She wants this, weeps for it." Dakota whispered the words against her ear.

Tamara watched as Brock walked the big stallion into the corral at a measured pace, keeping the horse under his rigid command. She tried to keep the animals at the center of her attention instead of the big man behind her. She made a concerted effort to keep her breathing steady so he wouldn't know how much his words and actions affected her, but a knot of sexual need twisted her stomach as she watched the horse pace close behind the mare.

She felt Dakota moving, the heat of his body warming her back, intense sexual energy crowding her closer to the fence. Tamara was certain his actions would mirror those of the stallion's cautious yet eager approach to the filly.

"You can feel the stallion's anticipation of shafting the mare—see it in the trembling of his body. He can smell the scent of her need as her body prepares itself for him. He knows she is wet and all he has to do is mount her from behind, sliding his huge cock into her slick, ready passage."

Hell fucking yeah, she screamed within her head.

Tamara stifled an inward groan as Dakota's thick erection pressed against the crevice of her ass, hot and insistent. He was so wonderfully hard and long. Her legs became weak as he rocked against her. She couldn't resist pushing back into the harder-than-steel length of his questing shaft or take her eyes off the scene taking place in the corral before them.

Brock led the stallion toward the mare at an angle, not allowing the horse to mount right away. He kept the stallion far enough away from the mare so all the horse managed to do was extend his neck over and nuzzle her genitals.

Fuck! That had to feel good.

Dakota continued to speak against her ear, sending tingling currents of electricity through her entire body. Right then she would have risked everything to feel his mouth teasing her wet folds, his tongue lapping at her inflamed clit.

"First he will taste her desire, let it roll around on his tongue and fill him with her essence. He'll lap up as much of that sweet cream as he can, teasing the mare. Make her long for what only he can give her."

The wet swipe of the stallion's big tongue over Honey's sensitive folds had the horse screaming out in need. Tamara felt an echo of the same need ooze from her sensitive skin as Dakota continued to rock his erection into the crease of her ass.

He felt better than good. He felt like something she needed with a desperation bordering on obsession. She wanted nothing more than to drop her jeans, spread her legs and impale herself on his thick length. Have every hard inch filling her all the way to her empty heart.

"See the way Honey's muscles ripple beneath her skin as she anticipates Rowdy's long cock ramming into her? She wants to feel him pounding into her hot cunt, stroking her sensitive walls."

Hell yes she saw it. She shared Honey's eagerness to experience such a glorious impalement. Dakota created a longing in her well beyond anything in her experience. It burned through her body with an incomprehensible molten desire.

They watched as Zeke braced the mare, providing a bit of physical support as the stallion mounted her, his forelegs and chest resting over her back. The stud looked downright primal, single-minded in his desire to mate. He rutted around until he was properly aligned with the mare then slid forward, driving his shaft into her body, his teeth nipping at her neck. Animal grunts and cries of passion rose in the air.

At the same time, Dakota thrust his cock against her ass, his teeth capturing the tender flesh where neck and shoulder meet. Tamara's eyes clamped shut as carnal wants flooded her system. The words he spoke between swipes of his tongue over the pulse point in her neck were lost in her lust-fogged mind. She dissolved into a mass of quivering, hypersensitive nerve endings.

Time lost all meaning for Tamara. She had no idea how long she stood there with the big stud rocking against her ass. All she knew was she desired him more than she ever had any other man. Yet desire wasn't quite right. This reaction was much more, reaching toward becoming an all consuming requirement. She needed his cock filling her, making her complete.

She was astonished to find watching two horses fuck, combined with Dakota's words, was turning her on so much. More than any porno flick ever had. As the stallion groaned out his satisfaction, Dakota's moan filled her ear.

"I want you so much, princess."

Hell yes!

LaVergne, TN USA
06 March 2011
218998LV00001B/114/A